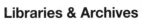

ACCOUNT RENDERED
AND OTHER STORIES

ACCOUNT RENDERED AND OTHER STORIES

Marjorie Eccles

CHIVERS

British Library Cataloguing in Publication Data available

This Large Print edition published by AudioGO Ltd, Bath, 2012.
Published by arrangement with the Author

U.K. Hardcover   ISBN   978 1 4713 1363 9
U.K. Softcover   ISBN   978 1 4713 1364 6

Printed and bound in Great Britain by
MPG Books Group Limited

CONTENTS

CONTENTS

FOREWORD

by Peter Lovesey

One of the joys of writing short stories is that you can be bold and explore settings and themes outside the limits of your novels. *With one bound she was free!*

Marjorie Eccles is known for her intricately plotted police procedural novels featuring Superintendent Gil Mayo and Inspector Abigail Moon, set in the fictional Black Country town of Lavenstock. But in her short stories she ventures further afield, into Egypt, France, Armenia, Austria and South Africa. As always, she writes from a secure knowledge of each location; we can tell at once that these are places she knows well, and not merely as a tourist. The intensity of *The Egyptian Garden* speaks of an intimate knowledge not only of gardening, but also of the daunting challenge of making a garden in Cairo

You will find much in these pages that is familiar territory in Marjorie's writing. Her fascination with family loyalties put under strain by the prospect of inheritance is central to *Peril at Melford House* and *Portrait of Sophie*. In case that is too confining, she gives us stories set in the walking-country of the Pennines and the Scottish Highlands.

1

Yet a word of warning is necessary: you may well find yourself ambushed by something you haven't ever encountered in a Marjorie Eccles novel. You will time-travel to the Siege of Mafeking. Or to the Second World War. You'll get the strange thrill of the supernatural. Just when you think you know how a story will come out, you'll be hit by a double whammy—surprise on surprise.

The one thing I can safely predict is that you will get the sense of completion, of justice done, that is the hallmark of every Marjorie Eccles story. She can bring the most tangled plot to a satisfying conclusion.

Now, why don't you enter her world? With one bound you are free!

REMEMBERING KAZARIAN

Murder is never an end in itself. It is, on the contrary, only the beginning of things.

At any rate, that was what Kazarian said, and he should have known. He was Armenian by birth, and if anyone knows about murder, it is the Armenian nation—or what is left of it, after the genocide of 1915: that mass slaughter, when nine-tenths of the nation were driven into exile, scattered to the corners of the earth, or driven by the Turkish janissaries into the desert and left there to rot, unburied, so that their bones whitened and are said to give off a phosphorescence in the dark, even yet.

Blood has watered the sparse soil of Armenia. Murder is written on its stones. Murder can never be forgotten, or forgiven. That was what Kazarian said.

Murder is what has brought Paul Enderby, a London lawyer in his mid-forties, here to the capital of Armenia. It is why he is sitting on a wooden bench under a fig tree in a shadowed courtyard in Yerevan, too hot to do anything more than swat flies, drink strong wine and watch the old men playing *nardy,* while he waits for Zarouhi. It is supposed to be the cool of the evening, but the stones of Yerevan hold the heat of the day. The city is a dust bowl between the bare hills, a city older than Babylon. Now magnificently resurrected from the ashes and ruins of its former self, it has wide main thoroughfares lined with grandiose buildings and monuments to Soviet power, constructed in Armenian tufa, basalt and marble—blue, black and rose-coloured, some of them splendid. Away from the main streets, concrete tower blocks of apartments dwarf the old, traditional, flat-roofed houses, which theoretically should have been swept away long ago on the tide of modernization and reconstruction. But, as always in communist-dominated cultures, reality overcame the intention. The long proboscises of countless building cranes still pierce the skyline, the endless mess of construction work goes on as it did ten years ago, and much of the city remains an unfinished building site. I shall be sorry, thinks Paul Enderby, if ever the old Yerevan disappears entirely, but I shall believe it when I see it.

Zarouhi works as a translator. She is attractive, almost as beautiful as was Paul's wife Arus, with that slender, dark-eyed grace which characterizes the young women of Armenia. But she is of a different generation, and where Arus was gentle and compliant, Zarouhi is vigorous and liberated. She has been to the State University, and will not waste her time learning to cook and knit and bring up a family. Paul met her the first time he came to Yerevan, after Kazarian, who was distantly related to her, died. She was fourteen, and at the peak of her sexuality, for Armenian women mature early. She knows that he was charmed by her then, that he is now free and unencumbered by a wife, and hopes she is the reason he has been drawn back again, after ten years. But everyone speculates as to why he is here—not least, Paul himself.

The first time he came, he had done what his friend Kazarian had asked of him in the event of his death: he had taken the pouch containing dry, gritty soil from the homeland, cherished by Kazarian's family for seventy years and kept inside the polished copper urn in the niche beneath the sacred icon; he had scattered a handful over the coffin so that Kazarian, like his father, and his grandfather before him, was symbolically laid to rest in the native soil of his ancestors. Then, to those of his family who had miraculously survived the holocaust, or who had returned from exile after union with Russia made life possible again, Paul had transferred what their kinsman had left them what was to most of them a fortune, but was in truth shamefully less than might have been expected, Kazarian's affairs being as they were at the time of his death. Finally, he had brought back to Yerevan the rusty key with which Kazarian's grandfather had locked the door of his house before being driven into exile.

It was the least he could do.

The counters click faintly as the old men move them across the board. The little fountain—there is always a fountain, that symbol of life, somewhere in Yerevan—tinkles coolness into the air. A fan of white doves clatters across the sky. From inside one of the houses, a caged bird sings its heart out against a background of raucous pop music. The Tataryan brothers, Stepanos and Ezras, heat the grill in the corner of the courtyard and prepare meat to thread on long, sword-like skewers for the shashlik. An aroma of spices and burning charcoal fills the air. Children shriek and play the same sort of games children play everywhere. The women sit under the trees, knitting and gossiping.

Zarouhi is late, as she often is. She will arrive in a great rush of apologies, smart as a whip in her silk shirt and jeans, and toss her head at the disapproving looks of her mother. Her mother does not feel that her daughter's education has done her much good. Be that as it may, Zarouhi is naturally quick and intuitive, and if nothing else, has learnt persistence. She knows what she wants and she is determined she will get it, one way or another. She will not leave Paul alone for instance, probing and questioning and making assumptions that are sometimes uncannily accurate.

He feels uneasy at the thought, and wonders

once again at the compulsion that has made him return to this small, rocky country.

The first time he came was in springtime, when the air was mild and benign, and wild flowers bloomed on the mountains—pale yellow and mauve everlasting flowers, stiff and dry and wiry, conditioned by the lack of moisture in the thin soil. In the city, the apricot trees blossomed against rosy-domed churches; dark-robed, tall-hatted priests flapped past the fountains playing in Lenin Square. Now it is summer, the city is dust-clogged, and everything vibrates and shimmers in the dry, burning heat. On the mountainsides, little grows in the parched earth except bitter wormwood, the wild aromatic absinth. The very rocks are scorched almost to vitrification.

Only Mount Ararat is eternally the same: cool, blue and remote, glimpsed at every vantage point, a perfectly symmetrical, snow-capped peak suspended against the pinkish sky, where the Ark is said to have come to rest after the Flood and from whence Noah sent the dove across the waters, to return with a sprig of olive in its beak. Once part of Armenia, but now on the other side of the redrawn borders, Ararat belongs to Turkey, the old and not forgiven enemy, a potent symbol of all that was lost. Symbols and historical associations are part of the very fabric of Armenian life and culture. The sight of Yerevan's eternal flame, burning high above the city for the million lost souls who perished in the massacre, never fails to bring tears to Armenian eyes. Simply the thought of it made Kazarian weep, though admittedly he wept easily.

He was a big, ebullient man, with a deep bass voice, a huge rumbling laugh, and liquid brown eyes, which Paul's secretary said reminded her of Omar Sharif's. He had the same ability to turn women's heads; they went down helpless before his smile, willing to be seduced, although knowing he had no intention of marrying them. He was always larger than life, even when he and Paul were at school together, in the East End of London. A handsome lad, not clever, but sharp in the ways where money was to be made. He was as wily as a monkey, but his charm, or an adroit lie, invariably got him out of trouble.

His father had worked as a porter in one of London's leading hotels, and was killed when a luggage trolley, overburdened with some VIP's expensive leather suitcases, toppled over on top of him, rupturing his spleen. His mother quickly remarried and departed elsewhere, leaving Kazarian to be brought up almost entirely by his grandparents within the refugee, immigrant community which had formed a small enclave in the district where Paul lived. From the day they were placed at adjoining desks at school, there was an immediate rapport between the two boys, despite—or

8

perhaps because of—the differences in each one's temperament and upbringing. They spent most of their spare time together as they grew into their teens, at discos and football matches, experimenting with smoking, lager-drinking and girls. Later, their paths began to diverge: Kazarian grew streetwise and successful, while Paul found it necessary to opt for the more boring, but safer, path of serious study. Even then, he was a conformable young man.

He never completely lost touch with Kazarian, however. As his friend, Paul had always been welcome to join in any gathering or celebration in the community of exiles, to drink with them the inevitable thick, sweet coffee and imported Armenian brandy, and he continued to see them, having none of Kazarian's impatience with the old men's reminiscences and yearnings for the homeland, none of his scorn for songs and poetry mingled with tears. On these occasions he was transported to another world from the drab, high-rise flat where he lived with his parents and sister. He fell in love with the idea of Armenia and its fiery history before he ever saw it.

'Tell me about London,' says Zarouhi now.

'Again?'

'Again and again!' Her eyes are hungry.

They have driven out to this restaurant in the coolness of the mountains, out of

9

the traffic-jammed streets, away from the smothering dust and the heat and noise of the city, whose lights wink far below in the darkness. They have eaten spotted trout, char-grilled meat and red caviar, and Paul has, after the first mouthful, avoided something spongy and pale pink, some unspecified, processed part of an animal, said to be a delicacy. They have brought their glasses of brandy and tiny cups of coffee out on to the terrace. Zarouhi perches nonchalantly on the narrow parapet built above the vertiginously plunging ravine, its sides clothed with stunted oaks whose stubborn roots have somehow managed to find nourishment between the rocks.

Kazarian used to perch in just the same insouciant manner on the rail of his flashy cabin cruiser, glass in hand, careless of his safety though he could swim only a few strokes. But then, he always thought he had a charmed life.

Zarouhi puts a red-nailed hand on Paul's arm and repeats her request.

It is her one desire to leave Yerevan and go to London, which she imagines to be the acme of Western civilization. *Yeraz* means dreams, and her head is too full of them, as her mother constantly tells her, to no effect. But it would not be so easy, even in these post-glasnost days, to find the means, or to cut through the red tape of bureaucracy and uproot herself. In any case, where would she,

10

a foreigner, find work in London, Paul has several times asked her, among the thousands already unemployed? He reminds her about Kazarian's grandparents, arriving there during the Depression, via New York and France, after failing to make a new life in either place, and being forced to take the most menial jobs in order to survive . . . for what else was there for a wine-grower and a carpet-weaver, however skilled?

'Pooh!' she says, waving aside objections. He knows that she thinks he could help her, that he is rich—as, by her standards, he is. And there are other, unspoken thoughts hovering on the air. That her slim, olive-skinned body is his for the taking, in exchange for the promise of what he can do for her. Not, he is certain, a virginal sacrifice. All the same, he is sorry for her, caught in a situation she can't change, but she is not, and never can be, Arus, and he says nothing.

After a waiting silence, she sighs and then returns to the attack, pointing out persuasively that, after all, Levron Kazarian, too, had once been poor, before he became wealthy beyond the imaginings of his kinsmen. Paul wishes she would change the subject.

He finds it impossible to explain Kazarian to any of them here, especially to Zarouhi, to convince her that his money was made as wildly and extravagantly as it was spent, that he came by it dishonestly, or at least by suspect

11

wheeler dealing, sailing always on the windy side of the law, and that if he had not died when he did, he would most likely have ended up in prison. She would not believe what she didn't want to believe. And she would wonder why Paul, as his friend and semi-official legal adviser, had done nothing to prevent it—and perhaps with some justification.

Loyalty to an old friendship had in fact made him try, only Kazarian wouldn't listen. He was on a tide of success, everything he touched was turning to money, he simply turned his back on the idea of inevitable retribution. And that was when they had to part company, in a business sense. Paul had pulled himself up by his bootstraps, he was one of the few from their comprehensive school who'd obtained a university place, and he was now a respectable and moderately successful lawyer. He intended it to remain that way. He couldn't afford to involve himself in dubious dealings that meant keeping his mouth shut, however generous the rewards. He had not only himself to think of—by then, he also had Arus.

As with most of the important things in Paul's life, it was through Kazarian that he met Arus. Kazarian had, in fact, taken her out himself once or twice before they met, but when Paul made a beeline for her and Arus, flattered by his persistence, began to respond, Kazarian gave in gracefully enough. There were, after all, always plenty other fish in the sea as far as he was concerned, though Paul noticed that whenever they met, Kazarian couldn't keep his eyes off Arus for long.

Whilst her parents would have preferred her to marry one of their own countrymen, they loved their only daughter too much to deny her anything, and as soon as Paul was able to provide her with a reasonable home, they were allowed to marry. They had an Armenian-style wedding, with a great deal of drinking and feasting after a solemn ceremony according to the rites of the Orthodox Church. The guests threw sweetmeats for good luck and pushed paper money between Arus's fingers, pinning more on to her wedding dress as she danced with Paul, at once graceful and sensuous, to the haunting, evocative music of the Motherland. Kazarian gave them a handsome wedding present and wished them luck.

Their marriage, it seemed to Paul, was perfect, but it never does to be too complacent. Life has a habit of turning round on you when you least expect it, as he found when Arus died giving birth to the child she had wanted so passionately, for so long, and the child with her. It is something he cannot contemplate, even now, without pain, overwhelming guilt, and despair.

Zarouhi drains her brandy and asks for another. She has drunk too much, so Paul pretends not to hear her request. Equality is

13

still an ambivalent concept in this traditionally male-dominated society: to see a man drunk on wine, brandy or vodka, or a combination of all three, is scarcely uncommon and is regarded with amused tolerance, but women are a different matter, and she has already attracted the unspoken but very evident disapproval of the waiters and too much attention from the other diners. Her mouth becomes sulky at his refusal, so he sits beside her and smiles at her. He is a little unsteady himself.

The Armenians are a tenacious people, as witnessed by their struggles over the centuries against their innumerable enemies, from Assyrians and Turks, to Tsarist Russians and Azerbaijanis, and Zarouhi is nothing if not true-born Armenian. But this tenacity is becoming somewhat tiresome as, once again, she harks back to Kazarian, citing him as the shining example of success, with his lavish lifestyle, his Mercedes, his Thames-side apartment, his glamorous women. News of all this reached even here, and his name became a byword for munificence: on the rare occasions he visited his relatives, he would arrive laden with gifts and spend money like water. The fact that he never invited any of them back to London to share his good fortune never seemed to have occurred to them. But to Paul he remarked scornfully that he found them backward and naïve: the truth was at once harsher and more subtle, and Paul was angry at his contempt and lack of understanding. He recalls this as Zarouhi begins yet again to ask about Kazarian's boat, and that last trip they took together, a topic which endlessly fascinates her and arouses her curiosity, and because this is something he doesn't want to talk about, he makes the mistake of saying shortly that Levron Kazarian had not been the plaster saint everyone thought him. And before he can stop himself, he adds bitterly that some people might have thought he had it corning to him when he fell off the rail of that floating gin palace he called a cabin cruiser.

They have machines here to split the stones, cracking and crushing them smaller and ever smaller in order to achieve something approaching a soil that can be tilled. Paul's thoughts would have been better left unexpressed, he realizes too late as, like the coiling nests of snakes revealed when those stones are lifted, Zarouhi's suspicion rears up, to be followed quickly by triumph. She does not need to say anything. He knows what she is thinking. He experiences a moment of panic.

He supposes she has reached the truth in the same way that he knew who the father of Arus's child, was, by a combination of intuitive knowledge and deduction.

When Arus failed to conceive, he had refused to consider either of them undergoing the necessary tests, since he had no doubt of the cause of their childlessness. He had picked up a severe viral infection when he was at college, rumoured to leave one sterile, which at the time he'd dismissed as typical undergraduate humour, an unwarranted and feeble joke, but one which now redounded sickeningly. So much so that he couldn't bring himself to speak about it.

Although Arus was basically gentle and feminine, she had been born and educated in London and, like her contemporaries, had been taught to think independently. Above all, there was a core of something adamant in her, common to all Armenian women, who are proud and strong, their natures forged in the fires of adversity. That was something Paul should have remembered, when an issue as important to her as that was at stake. He should have known that she would go ahead with her own tests, regardless. And afterwards . . .

She must have been told that the chances were that the fault lay within him, counted on the fact that for his part he would never consent to suffer those humiliating investigations, and would therefore never know for certain.

But if only she had turned to anyone else but Kazarian!

Paul is only too conscious of how Zarouhi's mind is working. He is beginning to have some inkling of what is in store for him, to see that he has given her the lever she has been looking for. She cannot possibly know how Kazarian died, or why, but she has instinctively homed in on his guilt, she senses that here is something he will do anything to avoid discussing, though there is no proof of what happened, and there never will be. She moves closer to him, with such an expression of cold calculation on her face that he recoils, with a dangerous backward movement that almost overbalances him. He wobbles, arms flailing. A moment passes while someone manoeuvres past Zarouhi with a drink in his hand, then, just as Kazarian did, that day on his boat, Paul loses his struggle. He goes over the edge with a scarcely perceptible sound, that is magnified by Zarouhi's scream of horror, and by others as they join her to gaze down into that stony abyss where no human body can have survived. In the same way that Paul gazed down into the sea at Kazarian struggling to keep afloat, before he raised the alarm, having waited just long enough for it to be too late.

But Zarouhi would swear that as Paul's body teetered on the parapet, he could have saved himself, had he so wished.

In that split second before he made his choice, did Paul Enderby have doubts? Did it come to him that he may simply have imagined Zarouhi as his Nemesis, his goddess of retribution and vengeance? Did he wonder whether he might have been wrong about

17

Kazarian, and Arus? Or did he feel relief in surrendering at last to his punishment?

It hardly matters in the scheme of things. It is no more than another scratch on the scarred landscape, a tiny speck in Armenia's history of murder and bloodshed, begun thirty centuries ago, and not yet ended.

MURDER IN A TIME OF SIEGE

They would soon be reduced to eating the horses. The idea was nathema to any Britisher—they would do it, of course, if it was a question of survival, but thank God it hadn't come to that, not yet.

The small township in the middle of nowhere lay sweltering on the unending, sun-scorched expanse of the African veld. A hitherto pleasant, orderly and uneventful place, now seething with fifteen hundred defending troops, surrounded by the enemy, Mafeking had suddenly found itself turned into a garrison by virtue of its strategic position on the borderland railway.

The first actions of the Boers had been to cut through the telephone wires, tear up two miles of railway line and seize the waterworks outside the redoubts—though as to this last, they might have saved themselves the trouble: there remained an ample supply of water within the town from tanks, and from wells drilled through the rock. Three months of siege had followed, yet morale stayed resolutely high. Though the bombardment had been heavy, loss of life and the numbers of wounded had been comparatively light so far, mostly confined to the military in their storming parties against the enemy. Relief was expected daily, but was not yet forthcoming. Belts were tightened further, while the overall commander, Colonel Baden-Powell, the idol and hero of the hour, continued to keep General Cronje and his Afrikaaners busy, driving them back with his cavalry sorties and causing them considerable losses. His indefatigable, cheery confidence was immensely heartening to the townsfolk. Better than a pint of dry champagne any day, good old B-P!

Undeterred, the Boers celebrated the first day of the new century by shelling the women's laager. Fortunately, only one person was slightly injured.

Then, on the ninety-ninth day of the siege, Edward Carradine was arrested for murder.

* * *

Mafeking upon the hundredth day of siege sends loyal devotion to your Majesty, and assurances of continued resolve to maintain your Majesty's supremacy in this town.

Having despatched this doughty telegram to his Queen, via a trooper valiant enough to risk breaking through the enemy lines and riding with it to Pretoria, Mr Frank Whiteley, the mayor of Mafeking, forsook his bicycle for once and made his way down the main street. The town lay baking under the dry wind; red, gritty dust puffed out from under his boots at every step. An upright man with a clear and steady gaze, he was deeply tanned by his many years under the suns of Africa, thinner than he had been by reason of the privations to which they had all been subjected in recent months, here in Mafeking. Ever since he was seventeen, he had followed the business of an interior trader and hunter, in partnership with a brother-in-law in Bulawayo, and no one was better acquainted with, the territories and people of Bechuanaland and the country north of the Limpopo than he. He loved and understood Africa and the African people almost as much as he honoured England and the English. His hard years in this land had made him a man of foresight and courage. But at the moment, he was also a man beset by worries: namely, the great loss to him of his company stores, recently reduced to rubble by heavy shelling, his business already in decline because of the war, the longing for his absent wife and children, the continuing need to eke out food supplies. The responsibility—entirely his—of looking after five hundred women, children and nuns in the women's laager. And not least, the troubling business of Edward Carradine, an all-consuming anxiety which almost eclipsed everything else.

Carradine! That unfortunate young man who had arrived in Mafeking with such high hopes and was even now languishing in a makeshift gaol until he could be moved to prison in Pretoria.

Although he was of good family, his people English immigrants who had interests in the diamond industry in Kimberley, and it was understood that he would, in time, come in to a not inconsiderable inheritance, Edward Carradine was of that new breed which needed to prove that they could make their own way in the world, a young man of independence who had chosen railway engineering as his special field. Due to this, he had been called to Mafeking to work on the Bechuanaland Railway. On the outbreak of hostilities he had immediately leaped, with characteristic enthusiasm and impetuosity, in to the foray as a volunteer fighter in the amateur army, four hundred of its number being native Africans, who augmented the forces drawn from the ranks of the British South Africa Police and the five hundred strong of Colonel Hoare's irregular cavalry. Since the township was bursting at the seams with police, the mayor should have felt able to leave Edward Carradine to them, despite their somewhat backward methods of detection, but he could not. It was a damnable business, but he could not simply wash his hands of this rash young man, a friend, a fellow Britisher, tiresome and foolhardy though he had turned out to be.

Nor could he push the problem aside in his homeward progress. At every step he was greeted by friends and acquaintances wanting to discuss Carradine and the whys and wherefores of his incarceration. And when eventually he thought he had spoken to the very last of them, coming towards him was that prince of good fellows, Baden-Powell himself, but having other things on his mind, thank God, than Carradine. 'Never fear, Frank,' he greeted the mayor. 'We shall win through, come what may, and no small thanks to you and your calmness in the face of adversity. We are fortunate indeed in having such a stout fellow to maintain and support us in our efforts!'

Frank was uneasy with such compliments. A man of action, he preferred deeds to words. He was a notable game-shot and had had desperate adventures, had escaped being trampled by a rogue elephant and had saved a companion from a rhinoceros by great personal daring, and still his only comment on being congratulated on his bravery had been: 'It was to be done, and I did it.'

He waved the flies away and sought an answer now as B-P clasped his shoulder and made further congratulatory remarks on his capable administration. 'I said at the beginning I would sit tight and keep my hair on, and that's all I have done,' he replied at last with a smile, taking off his hat and wiping his face with a bandanna.

The mayor's noble brow, compensated for by his luxuriant, drooping moustache, attested to the fact that this was not to be taken literally, and the twinkle in B-P's eye showed he appreciated the joke. 'That's the ticket! It'll take more than brother Boer to prevent we Britishers from holding aloft the flag, eh? *Nil desperandum,* Frank, *nil desperandum* has always been my motto!' And with the parting shot that Lord Roberts had promised relief within a few weeks and he had therefore placed the garrison on full rations again, the intrepid commander went on his way down the street, whistling and cheerful as though he had not a care in the world.

Frank accepted most of these comments with reservations, having more knowledge of the stubbornness of the Boer character than most of the British commanders. He was not alone in having the greatest admiration for Baden-Powell's leadership qualities, but it was with growing alarm that he thought of the colonel's last rash statement, relative to his own rapidly dwindling stores of provisions, hitherto so carefully husbanded. When the events of war began moving to a crisis, he had foreseen the strong possibility that Mafeking might fall under siege, and its people be forced to capitulate, not to the Boers, but to starvation. Planning for survival was second nature to him, and, prepared for the worst, he had collected enormous stores of staple foods and medical supplies. The resulting diet was monotonous, to be sure, with no fresh meat other than that obtained through forages by the soldiery into the local African villages—something which the mayor strongly deplored—but it was a diet which kept hunger at bay. It was in no small part due to his native Yorkshire prudence that the story of the resistance of the gallant little garrison, which had not been expected to last out a month, had already become the stuff of legend back home in England.

If he had been vouchsafed the knowledge that Mafeking's ordeal had but reached the halfway mark, he would have been even less sanguine.

Leaving behind the cricket ground and the racecourse, a now ruined hotel and several private houses turned into hospitals, he approached his own residence, about a mile distant. This was a smart bungalow with a pitched gabled roof, surrounded by trees, a low wall and iron railings, with a striped awning to keep out the sun, and draped lace curtains at the windows. The most English home, the most hospitable rendezvous for British friends in Mafeking. At the corner of the garden, the flagpole defiantly flew the Union Jack. It was in this house, at one of Sarah's 'at homes' that Edward Carradine had first met Kitty Rampling.

With this sombre reminder of happier times in his mind, he entered his now cheerless house, empty of all but servants, for his wife

25

Sarah, and his little boy and girl, were six thousand miles away, at home in England. But safe from the perils of war and starvation, thank God.

Sarah had not wanted to return home. She had stayed with him throughout the anxious period, when peace hung in the balance, while the gathering clouds of war began to darken the sky, and other women fled. 'My place, as your wife, is here, by your side!' she declared, willing to enrol herself in the band of women who, rather than seek the safety of Cape Town, had elected to stay, and nurse the sick and wounded. Duties at which she would have excelled, as she did in most things. During the eight years they had been married, Sarah had proved herself to be everything a man could want in a wife: handsome, smiling and good-humoured, a woman of cultivated tastes and true Yorkshire grit. He counted himself a lucky man.

'Do you not think, my dearest,' he had answered in a low voice, 'that you would not be the greatest support and comfort to me, the best friend a man might have at his side at such a time? But I should be a lesser man had I so little regard for your safety—or the safety of our children.'

It was only this last persuasion which had induced her to travel with the children the nine hundred miles to Cape Town, on the last train before the line was blown up, and thence to take ship for the long journey to England. Now, her piano stayed as a silent reminder of her presence, the inexorable dry, dust of the plains which insinuated itself everywhere collecting upon its keys, her books gathered more dust as they stood unopened on the shelves, her sketchbook and watercolours put away, her sewing laid aside. Only her precious garden remained as she would have wished it. Frank tended it himself and would not leave it to the African boys. He missed her as a man might miss his right arm, but he had no regrets as to his decision.

How was he to answer her, when he wrote to her about Edward Carradine?

Carradine had been a favourite of Sarah's, a popular adjunct to Mafeking society, agreeable, amusing and clever, if too outspoken in his extraordinary opinions, which he was wont to state with no little vehemence and even less tact, and with no expectation in the world of being disbelieved. He had lately aired his view, for instance, after one glass of wine too many at Frank's table, that it was a barbarity to hunt the ostrich and the elephant, not pausing to reflect that this happened to be the basis of Frank's livelihood. Ostrich feathers for fans, boas and hats, for debutantes to wear in their hair. Elephant ivory for piano keys, billiard balls, oriental carvings and jewellery, for every decorative use that could be imagined. His was a luxury trade which had made him, if not rich, then comfortably off.

'With respect, sir,' Carradine had continued heatedly, 'you do not realize the significance of what you are doing! Mark my words, these magnificent animals will one day be hunted to extinction and disappear from the face of the earth! You hunters resemble the ostrich you hunt—you run away and hide your heads in the sand!'

Frank had managed to conceal his anger and lighten the embarrassment at this rash and ill-considered statement—for Africa was vast, the bounty of her wildlife inexhaustible, was it not? Culling was necessary to keep the elephant population down, to preserve the trees and vegetation they destroyed. He made some humorous remark about the ugly, bald and manifestly unmagnificent ostrich, which occasioned smiles all round and passed the moment off. He would not take issue with one who was a guest in his house and moreover, despite his brashness, was, for the most part, a very likeable fellow. His greatest fault lay in his youth, which time would overcome. His heart was in the right place. And to do him justice, Carradine had later apologized.

It was Sarah who had warned Frank of what was happening between Carradine and Mrs Rampling, and the gossip it was causing. A certain coolness had always been evinced towards this lady by the female population, if not by their husbands, but it was impossible for someone of Sarah's warm-hearted and generous nature to follow suit, and she had been at special pains to be agreeable to her.

Kitty Rampling was pretty, lively, engaging, and thirty-five if she was a day. She had made an unfortunate and apparently disappointing marriage. Her husband, George, was considerably older than she was, a brute of a man, a sullen individual with a great propensity for quarrelling, a man with whom Carradine, for one, had recently had a violent argument. He was said to owe money all around the town—as he certainly did to the mayor. Too busy, it was rumoured in the racecourse bar, drinking and losing on the horses what money remained to him to be any more suspicious of his wife's affair with the handsome young railway engineer than he had been of countless others. She held him in the hollow of her cool little hand—or under her thumb, depending on which way you regarded Kitty Rampling. She was small and feminine, wore pretty frocks rather than the fashionable, mannish coats and skirts, the shirtwaists and the ties which the other ladies favoured at the moment, and had huge, innocent brown eyes.

Foolish and infatuated as Edward Carradine might be, however, Frank could not believe that he was the sort of man to shoot another, and in the back, too.

There was no getting away from the circumstances, unfortunately. He had been

29

discovered one evening outside the Rampling bungalow, kneeling over the man's body, blood on his hands. It was popularly supposed that Rampling had come home unexpectedly, and discovered his wife and Carradine *in flagrante delicto,* and a furtherance of their quarrel had ensued, though why the shooting had occurred in the street remained a mystery. Nor had the gun ever been found.

Carradine denied he had been with Mrs Rampling. His story, not necessarily believed, was that he had been walking homewards along the street when a shot had rung out and the man walking in front of him had collapsed. He had run forward, discovered the injured man to be Rampling and had supported him in his arms, only to find him already dead. It was thus that the next man on the scene, the mayor, who had been working late and was bumping homewards on his bicycle, awkwardly carrying a Gladstone bag full of papers, came round the corner and found. him.

His arrival was followed in but a few moments by others, including the ever-present police. Everyone was shocked; no one had liked Rampling and no one wanted to believe in young Carradine's guilt, and it was at once suggested that Rampling had been killed by some sniper's bullet, regardless of the fact that the shooting had occurred almost in the centre of the town. Other equally baseless suggestions followed: that one of Rampling's creditors had come after him, or, with more support, that due to the inadvisability of arming the natives, one of them had run amok. Or that maybe drunken soldiers had been involved: the troops were not all disciplined regulars, and unruly incidents were not uncommon. However, Carradine's presence outside the Rampling bungalow, the gossip about his association with Kitty Rampling, together with that recent angry clash in the racecourse bar between himself and her husband, witnessed by many, made him a prime suspect.

The mayor, sitting in his empty house, could find no answer to his own pressing problem of what was to be done about the matter.

*   *   *

The siege continued, Mafeking still miraculously holding out after more than six months. But the fortified trenches encircling the town were not proof against Cronje's onslaughts, and casualties grew, despite the warning horn blown from the lookout whenever the Boer's twelve-pounders were being loaded. Small acts of courage and heroism were reported daily among the loyalist civilians, the women and children, the native servants. The townspeople buried their dead and began to eat the horses.

However, with the letters and dispatches which still got through came news to stiffen the sinews—that Ladysmith, another beleaguered town, an important railway junction in Natal, had been relieved after a hundred and twenty days. It was reported that the Boers were losing heart. It was also reported, once again, that relief troops were within five miles of Mafeking, and B-P promptly earmarked several more horses for a celebration dinner for the whole town, cheerfully urging everyone to bolster their courage, reminding them that their sacrifices for Queen and country would not be in vain. The relief forces were, unfortunately, driven back with heavy losses.

Mrs Rampling, recovered from her prostration at the death of her husband, had refused to move out of her house and into the women's laager, and stayed where she was, retrimming her pretty hats and entertaining off-duty officers at afternoon soirees. She had grown noticeably thinner, her skin was transparent, but it only enhanced her looks and increased the lustre of her big brown eyes.

Carradine was still imprisoned, half-forgotten in the troubles of the moment, and allowed no visitors, and the mayor was looking, and feeling, ever more anxious. Problems, other than the exigencies of the moment, weighed heavily on his mind. Carradine had once accused him of burying his head in the sand, but he knew he could not do so for ever.

He thought of his last letter from Sarah, and felt worse. 'If Colonel Baden-Powell is the most popular man in England—as there is no doubt he is,' she had written, 'then the most popular man in all Yorkshire is the mayor of Mafeking. News of his courage and the tireless work he is doing there has travelled across the continents, and has made his wife and children very proud.'

What would she think of him now, if she knew?

The Bechuanaland dusks were short, the nights cold, and, after cycling briskly home one evening, shaken by what he had heard that morning, the mayor was promising himself a tot of carefully hoarded brandy before the scanty meal—dried biltong again, no doubt, which was all his servant would be able to provide—as he walked into his sitting-room.

There he found Edward Carradine, sitting in his own favourite chair in an attitude of great melancholy, twisting round and round in his hands an object which had previously been standing on one of the small tables in the room—an ostrich egg, mounted upon ebony, and painted with a charming, delicate depiction of flowers of the veld. He was regarding it intently. Perhaps his time in prison had taught him to abandon his scruples with regard to ostriches.

Frank's greeting could not have been more heartfelt. 'Carradine, how extremely glad I am to see you!'

Carradine was very pale from his

incarceration, his ruddy good looks diminished, with lines drawn about his mouth. Frank looked at him with pity and saw that he had lost his youth. 'They have let me go, Frank,' he said. 'I had become nothing more than an embarrassment to them; they had to release me.'

'I have never doubted they would do so, my dear fellow—in fact, I have expected it daily! I have spared nothing in arguing with the officer in charge for your release, given him every assurance that a man of your character could have done no such thing!'

Carradine maintained silence at this, until finally he said, 'There is still no trace of the weapon, and they inform me they have better things to do at the moment than to search for it. So there is nothing to prove my guilt, and she—Mrs Rampling—supports my story that I was not with her that night.' An inscrutable expression crossed his face. 'She even submitted to her house being searched, but of course no gun was found there. No doubt some unknown native with a grudge against Rampling will be the convenient scapegoat,' he finished bitterly.

'The scapegoat?'

Carradine did not answer the question, looking down at the ostrich egg once more. 'She painted this, did she not?' he remarked at last.

Frank regarded him gravely 'Mrs Rampling

did indeed, and gave it to my wife on the occasion of her birthday. She is not untalented in that direction.'

'In other directions, too.'

The pretty trifle in Carradine's hands trembled. Frank reached out and removed it from him.

Suddenly, the young man sprang up, almost knocking over the lamp on the table beside him. 'We must talk—but outside! I have for some reason developed a strange aversion to being inside four walls!' He laughed harshly and strode to the door.

Frank followed him into the cold dusk. The light was fading fast and the sky was the colour of the brandy Frank had been denied, shot with rose and gold, the garden smelling of the jasmine Sarah had planted around the door. He sank on to a seat that still held the warmth of the day, under the jacaranda tree, while Carradine paced about. Suddenly, he turned and faced the mayor.

'I did not fire that shot, Frank.'

Frank moved the toe of his boot about in the red earth, deflecting a column of ants. He moved his toe away and the ants regrouped themselves and went on. He busied himself with his pipe. In the light of the match, a column of fireflies whirled. The rich aroma of tobacco overpowered the scent of the jasmine.

'I know that for an indisputable fact, Edward.'

Carradine stood very still and upright, his hands clasped behind his back, looking down at the mayor. 'Do you, Frank?' he said at last. 'Do you, indeed?'

Frank saw the young man struggling to come to terms with something which he now recognized, and perhaps had subconsciously known all along. 'It was not I who shot him either, my young friend.'

'Then who?'

The sound of the lookout horn suddenly rang out from the redoubts, echoing through the town, signalling that the Boers were mustering for another bombardment, a warning to take cover while there was still time. A distant noise and confusion broke out as the townspeople ran for shelter, obeying the edict that civilians were to stay indoors as far as possible during an attack so as not to hamper the trained volunteers, competent to deal with such a situation. Hoofs clattered down the street, wagon wheels rumbled, a few shouts were heard, but presently came the ominous waiting silence to which they had all become accustomed, the lull before the shelling, and retaliatory mortar fire, began. The interruption might have been a mere rumble of thunder for all the attention the two men paid to it.

'If I did not shoot him, and you did not, then who did?' Carradine repeated tensely. 'If—' He could not go on.

Frank decided to help him. 'It was the blue diamond that started it, was it not?'

Carradine started. 'How in the world did you know of that?'

'My wife had the story of it from Mrs Rampling herself. I fear,' he said carefully, looking directly at the young man, 'that the lady is of some—acquisitiveness. Sarah told me how you had procured the diamond for her.'

'How I did so in hopes that it would buy her love, though I knew I could never marry her?' Carradine was suddenly in a passion. 'How I beggared myself to procure it? No, I wager she would not have told Mrs Whiteley that! I was—infatuated, there is no other word for it. I have had time to come to my senses and see that, at least. Infatuation that I thought was love. Through my brother's good offices, I was able to obtain the diamond at a fair price, though its value was still staggering and it cost me all I possessed in the world, and though my expectations for the future are not nearly as high as many suppose.' Carradine came to a wretched halt, and then said, 'I see I must tell you everything . . . Between us, we may arrive at the truth.'

Frank, who already knew the truth, said nothing, looking at the brilliant stars pricking the darkening sky. Every sound was exaggerated in the expectant stillness, the shrill of the cicadas, the croo-crooing of sleepy

37

doves, a shouted command from the defences.

Carradine sank on to the seat beside Frank. 'She knew I had bought the diamond. I had had it set into a ring for her, but it took me some months to pluck up enough courage to put it on her finger, with all that such an extravagant gesture implied. Though there could have been no marriage between us, our friendship had not yet reached . . .' He faltered, a deep and painful flush mantling his pale cheek. 'However, she had given me to understand that, on that very evening, she would accept the ring from me, and thereafter our relations would be somewhat different. She allowed me to put it on her finger before we dined. Rampling came home unexpectedly, just as we had finished our meal. He was drunk, but not so drunk that he did not immediately see how it was between us. He burst into a vile stream of abuse and Kitty became very—excited, I think, is the only word that will serve.' Carradine passed a hand across his brow. 'How can I explain this? Her husband's abuse did not appear to distress her—indeed, those big eyes of hers softened and sparkled, colour came to her cheeks when he actually raised his hand to her—it was almost as though she was enjoying it! As if there was some strange complicity between them . . . Maybe, even, a kind of love. I think I began to see my folly, how I had been deceived, even then.'

The desperate young man buried his face in his hands. When he raised his head, his face was wet with tears. 'Nevertheless, I squared up to Rampling. I could scarcely tell him to get out of his own house, but I warned him that he must not lay a finger on his wife. Whereupon, he laughed insolently and swaggered outside. 'Are you going to leave it at that, Edward?' she asked. 'No, by God, I am not,' said I, and rushed out after him, intending to knock the fellow down. But, stumbling in the darkness, I had not reached him before . . . before the shot rang out and he fell down dead. And that, I swear, is the truth of what happened.'

Into the silence erupted the loud crump of the first mortar shell, followed by another. A horse whickered in fright, and the night became hideous with noise and flames. Within the little garden, Edward Carradine sat as though turned to stone.

'How could I have been such a fool? Seen with hindsight, it is so obvious—Rampling coming home, apparently unexpectedly, finding me in intimate circumstances with his wife, strutting out like that . . . Either she had arranged matters so, or she seized her chance. In any case, she had estimated my nature well. She knew I would go after him, prompted by her.' He said, his voice hard and dry as pebbles, 'She would have shot me, like a dog.'

'Had you not stumbled. By the merest chance, or divine intervention, just as the fatal

39

shot was being fired. So that the wrong man received the bullet.'

'She would have shot me,' Carradine repeated bleakly. 'In God's name, why?'

'For love of money, Edward, for this.' From his pocket, Frank pulled forth a small, soft leather pouch and from that withdrew the costly blue diamond ring, its radiance undimmed in the starlit darkness. 'For greed, the life of one young man less important than the glitter of a diamond she could not resist.' He had no need to add that, having obtained the diamond, she had no more use for Carradine. 'An ugly thought, is it not?'

'Supposing I had indeed been the victim? Rampling would have been the first to have been suspected.'

'I believe he had prudently bought himself an alibi'.

'And what of the revolver—what did she do with it?'

'There is a well, not six yards away.'

'But beyond where Rampling fell. She did not pass me, Frank.'

Frank saw again the moonlit street as he had come upon it—Carradine kneeling over the dead man, the revolver lying between the young man and the Ramplings' door, heard again the sound of running feet which heralded the arrival of others on the scene in moments. What else could he have done, but conceal the weapon in his Gladstone bag? A pity he could not have swallowed it, he had thought afterwards, as the ostrich swallows large stones, bricks or even chunks of metal to aid the process of digestion in its gizzard. It had lain on his conscience just as heavily ever since.

'She threw the gun towards me, purposely to incriminate me. And you picked it up, did you not? Frank, I owe you my life.'

Frank did not say that it was Sarah to whom Carradine owed his life, prompting him as if she had been beside him, telling him that this man could not be capable of murder. 'I could not let an innocent man hang,' he said, and added words he had used once before: 'It was to be done, and I did it.'

Yet he had paid for his action with the sleepless nights that had followed. For the first time in his life, he had trifled with the law, and the burden of it had been heavy.

Until he had remembered the story Sarah had told him, of the blue diamond.

He held the sparkling jewel out once more to Carradine, but Carradine shrank from it as though it had been a snake. 'She may keep it, for all I care!'

'Don't be a fool, Edward. It is yours by right.'

'How did you come by it?'

'She asked me to return it to you.'

Carradine laughed bitterly. 'Once I might have believed that!'

41

'It is true. When I saw that gun lying there on the ground, I picked it up with scarcely a thought, but when I took it out of the bag, at home, I recognized it as one I myself had sold to Rampling twelve months ago. It was one of several I wished to dispose of and he insisted on taking it on trial. If he was satisfied with its performance, he would pay me—which, I might add, he never did! When I recognized what was once mine, I took it to Mrs Rampling and confronted her with it. Our conversation was—interesting. She subsequently asked me to return the diamond to you.'

'In exchange for your silence? Am I expected to believe that?'

Frank said gravely, 'There was no need to ask for it.'

'I don't understand. Why did you not take the gun to the police when you knew to whom it belonged? I would have been released immediately—instead a guilty woman has gone free! You call that justice?'

Justice was a slippery notion, as Frank had discovered since coming to this land, not as clear-cut and unequivocal as it seemed in Britain. Sometimes, the Africans did it better. 'Free? I think not.'

He had known native tribesmen who had decided to die, and did so. Through shame or dishonour, loss of face. Had the knowledge that she had accidentally shot the husband she had, in some curious way, loved, worked upon

42

Kitty Rampling so that she had lost the will to live? Maybe that was too fanciful, but he could not forget his meeting with her three months ago—that hectic flush on her cheekbones, the cough, the feverish brightness of her eyes. The loss of spirit, the fun of playing dangerous games at last over for her. 'She was ill, very ill, Edward. She knew that she had not long to live.'

'What? Kitty?' Carradine sat in stunned disbelief. his complexion becoming, if possible, even paler than before. Then he leaped up, all that he had suffered on her account instantly forgiven. 'I must go to her!'

Frank placed a hand on his arm. 'Too late, my friend, too late. She died this morning.'

With a groan, Carradine sank back, covering his eyes with his hand.

Frank had obtained her written confession, on his promise that he would wait until after her death before handing it over. He had immediately done so that morning, after hearing the news that she had died. His action in retaining the gun had not been viewed very gravely by the Chief of Police—who had, after all, himself known and been entranced by Mrs Rampling—it had been humanely prompted, he thought, and in any case, without her admission, her guilt or otherwise would have been difficult to establish. The authorities would have been bound to release Carradine after a time, and it was his opinion that the

43

spell in gaol cooling his heels had done the hotheaded young fellow no harm at all, rubbed a few corners off, in fact.

The shelling had stopped. There would be no more that night. People were emerging from shelter, and a growing noise and confusion travelled across the night, from perhaps a mile away. Carradine raised himself, and the two men walked out of the garden and stood looking out across the darkness, lit by flames soaring skywards. Not a house remained standing in the street where Kitty Rampling had lived. A pall of smoke rose like a funeral pyre over the area of flattened buildings. A Red Cross ambulance could be distinguished standing by.

Mafeking's siege was nearing its end. Victory or capitulation, one of them must come soon. Its story was played out.

'Come,' said Carradine, beginning to walk rapidly down the road, 'let us see what we can do to help.'

THE SEARCH FOR OTTO WAGNER

'Wagner?' she said. 'I thought he was a composer.'

'Otto, not Richard, my ignorant little love. Architect, not composer. Austrian, not German.'

'Oh, well, go if you must. But count me out. I shall go to Tenerife.' A pause. 'With Angela.' There was a world of meaning in that pause.

So, here he was, six weeks later, no Sylvie, and himself halfway through the first day of his first visit to Vienna. Distinctly underwhelmed by it at the moment, if we're being honest. A beautiful, cultured city, which for some reason had less to say to him than almost any other major city he'd ever visited, a circumstance that had put him out more than a little. Orlando expected the reality to come up to the expectation, and was always annoyed when it didn't.

As a tourist, which he was for this morning only, he was in the sort of mood which made the city seem overcrowded and schmaltzy: he hadn't cared to visit the Spanish Riding School, and disdained to view the sights vulgarly from a horse-drawn landau. St Stephen's Cathedral seemed to him like the monkey house at the zoo, its glories obscured by too many people milling around. Tacky

Mozart souvenirs met his eyes everywhere he turned—and the *sachertorte* with which he was now indulging himself was not wickedly rich, gooey and intensely chocolatey as he'd been told it would be by everyone who knew he was coming here, but a tired, dry and crumbly affair, edible only by reason of the excellent coffee that washed it down. His interest in the Prater and its Ferris wheel was minimal, he was already fed up with references to Harry Lime. And the smell of horse was overpowering.

As a professional . . . well. He'd known before he came that the city's architecture would contain too much grandiose imperialism for his taste; he had yet to encounter the art nouveau buildings which were the ostensible purpose of his visit. The florid, wedding cake public edifices imitating the past on the Ringstrasse filled him with dismay, though that could have been partly due to a restless night in an unfamiliar bed after having driven twice around the Ring in order to find the turning to the small family hotel Anton had booked for him—the woeful end of a lamentable journey, eleven hours at the wheel, most of it on the ruler-straight autobahn through mind-numbing, disciplined Germany, being hooted at by manic German drivers.

Plus time for that shattering interlude at Melk, with the abbey shining in golden baroque splendour on its cliff above the sluggish river, while he heaved into the water the thing which had lain like an unexploded bomb in the boot until then. Where now, he hoped, it still lay, on the river bed. But possibly floating downstream towards the Danube, if the rocks he'd sought to weight it down with had torn through the plastic refuse sack he'd wrapped it in. Who could tell? All in all, it had been a nerve-racking experience. He still felt unhinged.

But there was no going back, not now.

Orlando had some time ago decided he disliked flying—or rather, that he disliked airports, and the loss of individuality they brought, all that humanity being herded together like sheep. Also, he had known he was going to need his car at some point or other on the journey . . . a point which, in the event, had turned out to be Melk, a purely fortuitous stop, when he had seized his chance . . . But, half-way through Germany, stalled in an accident tailback for an hour, he'd have given much for a steadying glass of scotch and a comfortable seat with British Airways, rather than the sausages and stodge which was all the next services had to offer. His breakfast here in Vienna had been cold ham and sausage, too.

He endeavoured to pull himself together. He couldn't spend the rest of his life looking at the world through jaundiced eyes, missing Sylvie. He would have to accustom himself to being without her. What was done was done. Perhaps tomorrow he'd feel different, when he'd had a good night's sleep and he'd seen the Karlsplatz and the Steinhof church for himself and not merely in photographs.

It was unforgivable of Anton to be so late—if he'd ever had any intention of turning up, that is, of keeping his promise to show Orlando the delights of his wonderful native city.

He ordered another coffee while he gave Anton the benefit of a further half hour, closing his eyes against the procession of plodding, weary old horses pulling open carriages filled with tourists, feeling the sun warm on his face as he sat at the small table outside the very café where the Secessionists were reputed to have met.

Otto Wagner . . . Orlando Williams . . . He had been entertained by the charming coincidence of them bearing the same initials, having already found so many other things to admire in the *oeuvre* of the Jugendstil architect who seemed to have much to say to him. To have created a work of art out of a railway terminus, to have designed those twin pavilions of the Karlsplatz to have built them in white marble, moreover, embellishing them in green and gold, as unlike a London Underground station as it was possible to imagine, seemed to Orlando nothing short of a marvel. He could barely wait to see them, and

48

the church at Steinhof.

Anton, likewise, had professed to admire Wagner's work, though Orlando knew now that this was expediency rather than true admiration.

Orlando himself had originally thought of qualifying as an architect, but the long training had defeated his half-formed good intentions. Instead, he had found a niche in writing and lecturing about late nineteenth- and early twentieth-century architecture, a period which had a special appeal for him. A book and several articles on the art nouveau period had put him on the lecture circuit up and down the country, where he was very popular on account of his cherubic good looks and the throwaway humour he brought to his talks, and had proved reasonably profitable, so far. He wasn't sure how long this could go on. For one thing, he had begun, if the truth were told, to weary of the sinuous decadence, the lilies and languors of the art nouveau period proper; it was one of the reasons he'd warmed to the work of Otto Wagner, who was, so to speak, the last fling of the movement, and was less flamboyant and excessive than, say, Victor Horta, the Belgian, less outrageous than the exuberant Spaniard, Gaudi, but also less severely ascetic than Charles Rennie Mackintosh. Indeed, he seemed to Orlando to exemplify the concept of restrained and decorative elegance, while embracing the doctrine of new artistic freedom equally as successfully as his friend, Gustav Klimt.

It was a Klimt design, an original but hitherto unknown mosaic panel in a copper frame, which had brought Orlando and Anton together, in London.

They had come across each other quite accidentally, or so it seemed at the time, a chance meeting at the Q Gallery, where Sylvie worked—if work was the right word—one of life's little serendipities of the sort that was wont to lift Orlando's spirits inordinately.

A remark from a stranger, both of them standing in admiration before the extremely valuable and recently acquired Klimt.

'But Otto Wagner, all the same,' had murmured Orlando, almost to himself, 'could never have been influenced by him.'

His overheard remark had an electric effect on the man standing next to him. 'Otto Wagner? You know his work?'

The man was foreign, that much was apparent. Given away not only by his accent and his long belted mackintosh, but also by the fact of his speaking to a stranger.

'Not to say *know*,' replied Orlando. 'Only from drawings, photographs . . . his reputation, you understand.'

'Ah, but the real thing! Nothing can compensate for that.'

This was true, Orlando knew, and he immediately began addressing himself to the question of why he'd never before visited Vienna in pursuit of architecture, and resolving to bestir himself and make good the omission.

'So,' said his new acquaintance. 'I am Anton Drucker, from Vienna. An associate of Mr Quarmby.' He held out a manicured hand. A tall, handsome man with a fit, athletic body and a narrow face, knowing eyes regarding him assessingly, a careless smile. 'You should see the real thing,' he repeated. 'As no doubt the charming Miss Sylvie here would advise.'

'Sylvie?'

He should have known, even then. At the time he was too preoccupied with trying not to laugh. Sylvie, who had only the vaguest smattering of knowledge about art and artists, and cared not at all. She was employed at the Q Gallery only to be decorative, to hover in the background and pass interested customers on to its owner, Jonathan Quarmby-Crump.

Everyone, even the customers, recognized she was featherbrained, but when Sylvie smiled, no one minded. She and Orlando had lived together for nearly twelve months, which was a long time for both of them, especially in view of their differences.

He'd so far put up with her faults because she was the most beautiful creature he'd ever encountered, long-legged and slim, with her white, pearly skin and her damson-coloured hair. To possess such a wondrous being had at

51

first seemed like winning the lottery twice over. But, by and by, inevitably, custom had begun to stale her infinite variety. His self-indulgent existence was no longer his own. He was used to demanding perfection in every area of his life, and here was one in which he patently wasn't getting it. Her faults, he decided sorrowfully, were many. Out of bed, they had no common meeting-ground: music, of the sort he listened to, sent her into cracking yawns; to her, a book was a copy of *Vogue;* the pictures and works of art that surrounded her all day at the gallery might have been posters for all she knew or cared. His flat was no longer his own: bottles of dye, from whence the damson colour of her hair emerged, littered his hitherto pristine bathroom; her clothes nudged his out of the wardrobe. She was wildly untidy. He might have been prepared to put up with this, but in addition, food, a matter of the utmost importance to Orlando, who was as greedy for this as everything else in life, scarcely mattered at all to Sylvie. Her nails were so long she dared not prepare a meal, much less wash up after it, in case she broke one. As a consequence of this indifference, she was so slim she was more than half-way to being anorexic. Faced with a beautifully arranged plate of mind-bogglingly expensive food, she would nibble at a truffle or a morsel of lobster and push the rest away, untouched, whereupon waiters, who knew how mightily the chef had laboured over the dish and feared tantrums when it was returned, would bob up with anxious questions.

'Delicious, thank you. Just not hungry,' Her dazzling smile made them hope the chef would forgive the insult. But Orlando, thinking of his pocket, and a future with a woman with whom he could share virtually nothing, found it less easy to forgive.

'I've cooked us *boeuf bourguignon,* darling!' she'd announced, hoping to astonish him that last night before she was due to leave, a day before his own departure. 'I know it's your favourite.'

'Thank you, my love.' For the effort of going to Marks and Spencer and buying it, for putting it into the microwave. Even though she hadn't got that quite right either. She could never get it into her head that nine minutes meant nine minutes, and not eight, or ten.

But for all their incompatibility, her flawed perfection, he saw now that he would miss her. He had loved her, as deeply as he was capable of loving anyone. Poor Sylvie, for whom a broken nail was the biggest tragedy life could inflict. Shallow Sylvie, flitting from one job to the next, one man to another . . .

He wished, quite desperately for him, and now too late, that she was here.

He looked at his watch and faced the fact that Anton was not going to come either, no longer pretending to himself that he had ever expected he would, accepting that he had never intended to be in Vienna. He would just have to find some other way of meeting him, some other place where he could kill him. Unless Anton killed him first when he learned what he had done. He wasn't sure which would be more preferable.

Meanwhile, Steinhof.

* * *

A few miles' drive took him to the City Psychiatric Clinic. There were guards at the gates, but they let his car through without any trouble when he told them he wanted to visit the church. If you hadn't been told, you wouldn't have known this was a hospital, a psychiatric one at that. If, that is, you hadn't seen the bars on some of the windows of the purpose-designed buildings on the wooded hillside as the road wound upwards like a serpent, or passed groups of poor, lost souls being escorted between the trees.

At the summit, Wagner's white cruciform church crowned the hill like the cross on Calvary. Looking a little shabby now, nearly a hundred years having passed since its erection, verdigris from the once-gilded bronze bolts streaking its white marble facing slabs, its huge copper dome turned green, but still marvellous in its simplicity and elegance.

Inside, space and light. Light everywhere.

White and gold and blue. The gilded angels on the golden dome over the altar glowing in the radiance of the sanctuary lamp. Light filtering through the stained glass windows on to white walls, while a woman played the piano to a small group of people gathered round her. Slow, haunting, discordant pieces. Schoenberg, who else? What other music could be more appropriate in this place designed to calm the unquiet, disturbed mind? Music that explored an interior world of violence, madness and despair.

He took his seat in a roomy, functionally designed pew, his eye drawn to the huge mosaic behind the altar with its elongated, haloed figures arising from convoluted curves that seemed to him to resemble the interstices of the human brain, while the atonal music dropped note by note into the hushed silence, into the concentrated listening of the people at the front of the church, and into his own consciousness. Its reverberations made him feel, for the first time, that he, too, must have been mad to do what he had done.

He was awed, and humbled, and profoundly affected by this place, one man's finest aspiration, conceived and executed nearly a hundred years ago. In the space of ten minutes he lived again the last few days, and the weeks that had led up to them, felt horror for the first time. It made him wish that he could go back and undo all that had been done, start his life again. Even now, he could not explain wherein had lain his motives. He had not given it thought; he had simply been propelled by a compulsion to do what he had done.

It had all stemmed from that first meeting with Anton, in the Q Gallery. Contrived, he knew now: Sylvie had asked him to meet her there as she finished work—knowing Anton would be there, too. That apparently spontaneous conversation—that casual invitation from Sylvie to Anton to join them for dinner . . . Orlando hadn't objected, had in fact welcomed the chance to talk to someone who proved to be both intelligent and charming. More than charming to the impressionable Sylvie, it became clear, as the friendship between the three of them grew, as Anton's visits to London became more frequent. Perhaps it was even then that Orlando had felt the first stirrings of anger against them both, sensing that she had begun to find him very dull by comparison with quick-witted Anton and the slight air of recklessness, the willingness to take risks, that he projected: a spice of danger had always excited Sylvie. Perhaps Orlando's failure had been to refuse to admit this until after the event, to having ignored his own sense of impending doom.

Until he was getting ready to leave for Vienna, in fact.

It would never have occurred to Sylvie that cleaning out the flat before going on holiday was preferable to coming home and finding it stale and in chaos. That Orlando might feel otherwise, and clean out the fridge, empty the garbage. Especially that he would hoover the carpet, and find what she had hidden under their bed, along with two pairs of laddered tights, countless used tissues and a shoe bill for two hundred pounds.

What business did Sylvie have with a parcel like that, nearly two metres long, done up in bubblewrap? Sylvie, who owned nothing in the world except clothes and make-up? Orlando had the answer to his own question immediately he saw it, without any need to undo the wrappings, but he opened it anyway. The story came back to him: the faulty burglar alarm at the Q Gallery which had gone off during the night some three weeks previously, the arrival of the police who had stemmed its clamour, put it out of action until it could be reset the following morning when the gallery opened. The discovery of the burglary which had subsequently taken place between the two times, without let or hindrance. The Klimt, found to have disappeared. Worth, what? A good deal, but it scarcely mattered how much. It wasn't going to set up Anton for life, but was probably only one in a long line of such acquisitions. It had been stolen, and that was all that mattered.

Everything else fell into place, doubts Orlando had shuffled to the back of his mind

57

for weeks were answered. He knew Anton had engineered the whole thing, and Sylvie had obviously been involved in plans for the disposal of the Klimt, though not the actual theft, since she had indubitably been in bed with himself, Orlando, at the time. He wanted to believe that she had been inveigled into the scheme unwittingly, but even Sylvie couldn't have been so dim as to pretend not to know what it was all about.

He hadn't thought to query his own actions when he perceived the nature of the parcel. His only thought was anger at how he had been duped, and an overwhelming need for revenge. He did not like to be thwarted, or made a fool of, and both had happened to him.

Someone slid into the pew beside him. He raised his head and saw Anton, treacherous Anton, beside him, his narrow face concerned, but concerned only because he had decided that was how it ought to look.

Orlando refused to move until the music finished, and only then stood up. Together, they went outside.

'So, you found the place yourself without assistance? I guessed you would be here—my apologies for being late. Where is Sylvie?' Anton asked, with a casualness that belied the urgency behind the question.

'In Tenerife, with her friend Angela.'

'Of course, of course. How could I have forgotten?'

How, indeed? Their idea had been for them to allay suspicions by carrying on as planned, even to the point of Anton meeting him here, and Sylvie supposedly holiday-making in Tenerife with Angela.

There was a pause. Orlando imagined the questions racing through Anton's mind: why had Sylvie not contacted him, answered the telephone? What had happened to the Klimt?

He thought of the explanations he could give, if he were so minded, of the quick telephone call he himself had made to Angela which had confirmed what he had suspected, that Tenerife had never been on the agenda. Of how he'd gone to the hotel where Anton had a permanent reservation, with no doubt at all in his mind that Sylvie would be staying there, too. Found that Anton had already left for Vienna, and then, having dealt with Sylvie.

But why should he tell Anton? Better to let him sweat, and not tempt fate by attempting to kill him, a fitter, dangerous and far more ruthless man than he. He saw now that it had never been a serious option. He would have no idea how to go about deliberately planning a murder, never mind committing it.

Sylvie had been a different matter. A matter of rage, a moment's loss of control. Even now, some hapless chambermaid might well be opening the wardrobe door and finding her body . . .

He thought there was every chance he

might get away with it. No one had seen him enter the hotel, or leave. He had known which room to go to, and Sylvie had answered the door. He would not easily forget her face when she had seen him, or forget his own sense of betrayal. She had lied, and cheated him in every possible way, and she deserved what she had got. Already the high moral tone of his thoughts back there in the church was receding. He felt no remorse.

Only regret for the necessity of ridding himself of the work of art, which, in a moment of aberration, he had put in his car, intending to keep it until he could find the right moment to put it on the market. Coming to his senses on that long motorway journey, he had seen it as the one thing that would surely prove his undoing.

It had cost him, it had cost him dearly, to ditch a work of art and leave it reposing at the bottom of a sluggish river somewhere in the Danube valley. He began to calculate.

Twice-wrapped, tightly, in polythene. Lowered into the scarcely moving water, at a spot he remembered well.

After a while, his spirits began to rise.

ANNE HATHAWAY SLEPT HERE

By the simple reason of being murdered on Christmas Eve, Mrs Muriel Endicott managed to cause all concerned as much trouble in death as she had in life.

It appeared very shocking at first, indeed scarcely possible, that such a terrible thing as murder could actually have happened in a quiet, rather dull little village like Kirby Purefoy—and on Christmas Eve, too—but the victim being Mrs Endicott went a long way towards removing incredulity. A plastic bag pulled over her head removed any further doubt.

Her body was found at half past ten in the evening, and the police doctor, whose duty required him only to certify the fact of death, did so as expeditiously as possible. Anxious not to spoil his Christmas, he then hurried on to the carol service in the village, which was followed by midnight mass. He did, however, out of the goodness of his heart, pray for Mrs Endicott's soul, an act of Christian charity which would one day earn him rewards in Heaven. He was probably the only one in the village to do so.

The pathologist, meanwhile, had also arrived at the scene of the crime, having reluctantly left his Christmas Eve party to answer the summons to examine the body. Declaring that in his opinion Mrs Endicott had been dead for about six hours and that she'd suffered a wound to the back of her head before being suffocated by the plastic bag, he pontificated further without adding anything to the already known sum of knowledge about the cause of death, and refused to do the post-mortem until the day after Boxing Day: his wife, he rightly concluded, would not care to have her slice of turkey, carved by him, after he had so recently carved up Mrs Endicott.

The thought of slicing up a turkey also caused a delicate shudder to run down the spine of Mrs Endicott's only son, Hugo, a plump, petulant and slightly balding person who dealt in antiques, but the shudder came only from the notion of such hackneyed Christmas fare. He had a friend staying with him, and had arranged a civilized Christmas *dîner á deux* in his luxury flat, with a brace of pheasant, a bottle of Margaux, and some fine ripe Stilton to follow. Since he'd already had his Christmas Eve interrupted by the arrival of the police, and by having had to identify the body, he saw no reason to postpone any further arrangements. His mother was, after all, in no position to object, and wouldn't have been eating with him, anyway. Hugo had not been fond of his mother, nor she of him.

She'd been about to enter her own front door when she'd been attacked. A window

62

at the back had been forced open, and it was thought she had surprised a burglar, causing him to panic. The door was unlocked and the key still clutched in her hand. Her Christmas dinner—a small chicken and a pre-packed individual pudding—plus a few other groceries, were scattered over the path, and the Sainsbury's plastic bag which had contained them was drawn tight over her head.

She was found by two venturesome young carol-singers, who'd been dared by the rest of the group to go and sing at old Ma Endicott's cottage. They'd have been better off not bothering, Hugo considered. They must have known there'd be no invitation inside to partake of mince pies, and that they'd be lucky if they came away with a five pence piece, let alone without having the door slammed in their faces.

The cottage was near the centre of the village, with only a narrow strip of garden and a picket fence at the front to separate it from the road, a space no more than three or four feet wide, which Mrs Endicott had kept filled with old pots that spilled over with cottage garden flowers in the summer, and ivies, ornamental cabbages and universal pansies in the winter. It was of Elizabethan vintage, low and white, with an old pantiled roof and windows with tiny, square panes. Roses and clematis bloomed around the door. It was much admired by the visitors who came to buy the plants she propagated and sold in the large garden at the back, having undercut the family-owned nursery garden on the main road by twenty per cent. The back garden had been small, too, when she and Hugo had first come to the cottage, but Mrs Endicott was always prudent, and in order to extend her acreage, she'd purchased the field behind from the farmer who owned it, getting it at a bargain price because he was going through a bad patch at the time.

When she discovered the interest paid to the cottage by her customers was nearly as great as that in buying plants, Mrs Endicott had begun to serve English Cream Teas at small tables set on the flagstones at the back of the house if the weather was clement, indoors, if not. Miss Pilgrim, who ran the Tudor Café, hadn't been pleased about this, but it proved to be a more lucrative and dependable source of income than that gained from selling plants, which tended to be unreliable in regard to damping off, greenfly and all manner of other annoying plant ailments. It led on to her offering bed and breakfast accommodation, which was very popular with visitors who preferred home comforts to the damp beds and leathery bacon and eggs which the Dusty Miller offered.

And after all, who could resist the appeal of staying in a house where Anne Hathaway had once slept?

Mrs Endicott had, shortly after acquiring it, renamed her cottage. Instead of being No. 5, Church Road, it was now Hathaways. Gullible visitors were intrigued by this, those who believed what they wanted to believe, and who were delighted to learn that Anne Hathaway had indeed briefly stayed there, before her marriage to William Shakespeare.

'Why do you tell such lies? There's no evidence she ever came near the place!' Hugo demanded pettishly of his mother.

'She might have. It's only a bus ride from Stratford-upon-Avon.'

'They didn't have buses in the sixteenth century, for God's sake!'

'They had good strong legs. Twelve miles there and twelve back, they thought nothing of it. And there *were* Hathaways in the next village at one time—that's a provable fact. They may have been related. Besides, there's the letter, isn't there?'

Oh yes, Hugo was forced to agree, there was the letter. But, not wanting to pursue this subject, he added, 'You'll be telling them next that the four-poster in the back bedroom is Shakespeare's second-best bed!'

'Now there's an idea—why didn't I think of that?' Mrs Endicott looked thoughtful. 'He did will that to his wife, didn't he?'

'Leave me out of it this time,' Hugo warned. 'That letter's bad enough. It'll get you into trouble one day.'

'Oh, rubbish! I've never actually claimed it was genuine. People put their own interpretations on it. Now, about that bed . . . '

But, meeting his scowl, she understood what he meant, and gave in. They had been blackmailing each other in this sort of way for years. It was how he'd got his antique shop started.

His mother was, if not exactly rich, worth a bob or two by now. She'd always had an eye to the main chance, which was why she'd married his father. Unfortunately, Basil Endicott, a minor civil servant of some promise, had disappointed her by inconsiderately dying before his promise could be fulfilled. And even more inconsiderately, by not leaving any money, so that the building society very soon foreclosed on the mortgage of their house.

In order to provide a home for herself and fifteen-year-old Hugo, she had been forced to take a position as housekeeper to a Mrs Neasden, the bedridden old woman who lived in what was to become Hathaways, with her sour-faced, resentful daughter, Vera. A necessity which had, in the end, proved to be a blessing in disguise. The old lady had taken a fancy to Muriel Endicott, who knew which side her bread was buttered and acted accordingly. Unlike Vera Neasden, she let it be seen that she didn't mind how menial or distasteful were the tasks she had to perform. When Vera took the huff about the favouritism her mother showed the newcomer, and to having a clumsy, disagreeable adolescent about the place, she upped and left, and old Mrs Neasden quickly came to see that her housekeeper would be a more worthy beneficiary under her will. She died soon after altering it, leaving Mrs Endicott everything she possessed. It wasn't a fortune, just the cottage, and a small sum of money, but it had marked the start of Mrs Endicott's upward mobility.

It was almost immediately afterwards that she'd seen the possibilities of the Hathaway letter.

Her only regret about her bed and breakfast trade was that she could offer but one set of accommodation at a time, even though the cottage, like the garden, had been extended. Originally three small labourers' cottages, over the years a wall or two had been knocked down here and there, a staircase removed, fireplaces opened up, doors stripped of their 1950s hardboard flushing and a damp course installed, so that now it was charmingly unexpected: low-ceilinged and dark-beamed, with cosy alcoves and floors at different levels to trip the unwary.

The 'letter' was a scrap of tattered paper which had appeared during the demolition of a wall, behind which was a tiny room, formerly used as a cold store in the days before refrigerators and freezers. Opening up the room considerably enlarged the living-area, but the storeroom having originally been built out into the rising ground at the back of the cottages, it was cold and dank as the grave, and gave off a peculiar smell. Hugo and his mother stuck it out for a while, but the wall was eventually reinstated and the door bricked up.

The torn piece of paper was stained with mould and covered in crabbed, faded handwriting with long s's, the lines sloping upwards across the page. The barely legible signature might, by an adroit exercise of the imagination, be construed as 'Anne Hathaway'. How it had remained intact for four hundred years, considering the damp state of the room where it was found, was not a question visitors were encouraged to ask, but if they did, Mrs Endicott was ready to explain its state of preservation as being due to the draughts which whistled through the cavity wall and had presumably preserved it, like a mummy. It had been framed, and now hung in the place of honour over the fireplace of the room set aside for serving tea, scones and home-made jam at four round oak tables.

Despite other grave faults, the late Mrs Endicott had been a woman of taste. She had a flair for reproducing the right atmosphere without allowing it to become twee. A comfortable casualness and mixing of periods was apparent in the furnishings of the cottage, yet they blended happily together against cream plastered walls and vibrantly patterned old rugs spread over the polished, original stone floors, her collection of old English porcelain adding distinction to the décor.

The collection had begun modestly with a couple of slightly chipped Derby figures and a few Coalport plates, but had grown enormously over the years and was now worth a tidy sum. She had an eye for a genuine piece. It was about this that she and Hugo had quarrelled violently on the morning of her death.

Much of her prosperity, he'd have been the first to admit, was due to hard work and determination. She could turn her hand to anything, and frequently did. She wasn't, however, at all fussy about how she achieved her success—and she was lucky. Only a few weeks ago, at a Sunday morning car-boot sale in the car park of the Dusty Miller, she'd picked up an old Chelsea figurine: the rumour soon spread that it was worth a sum that would have had Sotheby's swooning— much to the chagrin of the Cartwright family, from whom she'd bought it for a few pounds. But they were an ignorant and feckless lot, one of their number always in trouble of one sort or another. They'd have sold off their grandmother if she hadn't died the week before, leaving them with nothing but a load of old junk even they wouldn't give houseroom to. They wouldn't have recognized a Chelsea piece if it had jumped up and bitten them. Mrs Endicott got it for less than a song.

Hugo had no objection to that. It was fair game. But he considered such an extremely valuable piece of porcelain would be far better being offered for sale in his shop rather than kept on a shelf in the dark recesses of the cottage where it might, God forbid, get knocked off by that dozy Sharon Simmonds.

Young Sharon, the desperate end of Mrs Endicott's long line of disgruntled cleaning women, was hovering in the kitchen, languidly polishing silver, when she overheard this. Bridling indignantly, she made it her business to overhear almost every word of the following heated exchange, and what she couldn't manage to catch, she interpreted. Apart from anything else, Hugo had argued, his mother's china collection was beginning to go over the top. How could one fully appreciate fine pieces among all this clutter?

'Clutter?' Mrs Endicott had repeated dangerously, and they had gone on from there. Hugo to remind his mother of what he knew of her past but unspecified activities, and she to remind him, in her turn, of things he would rather forget. It had ended with Mrs Endicott informing Hugo that she was going to make an appointment to see her solicitor after Christmas to change her will.

Well! thought Sharon, whose boyfriend was Kevin, the middle Cartwright boy. Her mind boggled at what Hugo said the Chelsea figurine would fetch.

*   *   *

Speculation was rife in the Dusty on Christmas morning when the news of Mrs Endicott's untimely demise became public.

In charge of the investigation was a young woman detective inspector named Mary Treadwell, highly ambitious and unmarried, with no responsibilities other than presents to buy at Christmas. She had been going to spend Christmas Day with her family: her parents, two sisters and their husbands, plus five rumbustious children under five. She was quite willing to forgo these pleasures in the interests of her career.

Though it soon became aPparent to everyone in the village who she was, Mary preferred for the moment to retain her anonymity. Women drinking on their own were likely to be looked on with suspicion in the Dusty at any time, but especially on Christmas morning, when they should have been at home stuffing the turkey, peeling the sprouts, coping with overexcited children and putting the pudding on to steam. So she had with her a young police constable in plain clothes, a Scotsman who had volunteered for Christmas duty because his own celebrations were centred around New Year, rather than

Christmas. An easy-going type who knew he'd only been roped in as cover, he was content to drink his pint and leave the detecting to her.

The season of peace and goodwill didn't extend to being charitable about the late Mrs Endicott, Mary soon discovered, listening quietly in her corner. Though not overtly expressed, the general consensus of opinion appeared to be that she'd had it coming to her one way or another.

'It'll be that Hugo that has it coming to him now,' remarked someone. All that *lovely, lovely money*,' he mimicked, drooping a limp wrist.

Sniggers all round accompanied this jest. In the macho ambience of the Dusty, antique-dealers were apt to be thought quite likely to varnish their toenails.

'What about Vera Neasden, then? She'll be sick as a parrot to hear that. Wheresomever she may be.'

'Serves her right. Should've been nicer to her old mum in the first place.'

'Oh, I don't know. The old 'un led her a right dance, I reckon.'

'Two for a pair, then. Vera weren't above proof. Funny old business, that, though, her going off so sudden after sticking it all them years.'

'Who d'you think done in the old witch then?' asked the landlord, and the ensuing conversation became very interesting to Mary Treadwell. By the time she left, she'd added further names to Hugo's on the list of suspects: the Cartwrights, simmering under a sense of injustice about the figurine they thought Mrs Endicott had swindled out of them . . . the belligerent son of the outwitted nursery garden owners . . . Miss Pilgrim, who'd been forced to reduce the price of her afternoon teas, although her scones were *much* lighter than Mrs Endicott's. Not to mention Trowbridge the farmer, who considered she'd pulled a fast one on him over the sale of the field and swore, moreover, that she'd thrown fresh yew clippings over the hedge and poisoned his cows. If the cows were daft enough not to know what they couldn't eat, that was nothing to do with her, Mrs Endicott had retorted, but Trowbridge hadn't forgiven her. And she hadn't exactly been a favourite with the landlord of the Dusty, either, putting it about that his beds were damp.

Hugo met Mary Treadwell for the second time, this time at the cottage on Boxing Day, at her request. He didn't care for women police, or women at all for that matter, and this one he sensed was sharp and intuitive. He repeated his previous statement to her: Sharon had exaggerated the extent of the quarrel he'd had with his mother, whom he certainly hadn't seen again after that visit to her on Christmas Eve morning. Then, unable to stand it any longer, he made a beeline for the back recesses of the cottage and the shelf where the figurine

73

had stood. He gave a yelp. He cried in anguish, 'The Chelsea piece, it's gone!'

'What Chelsea is this?' Mary asked. 'Tell me about it.'

He launched into a precise and loving description. According to Hugo, it had been an exceedingly fine and rare composition, a pair of rustic figures on one simple base, a shepherd and shepherdess. Tears came into his eyes at the thought of it. Perfect in every respect, superb quality, of the much-desired Red Anchor period, with rich, bright colours that blended perfectly with the soft-paste glaze. Worth—oh, my God, Hugo couldn't bear to think about it!

There were other things missing, too, he added, looking round, bits and bobs, a few small pieces of silver . . .

'Is that so? Perhaps you'd give me a list,' Mary said casually over her shoulder, as though the framed Hathaway letter which she was facing and reading was of more importance. She turned round, smiling slightly. 'Where did you come across this?'

Hugo swung into the usual glib explanations, about finding the letter when they'd had the mistaken idea of taking down the wall, while she moved interestedly around the cottage interior, coming to a halt by the rebuilt wall, as the flow of words finally came to a stop.

'Well, I daresay it'll do for the tourists, but I

74

don't believe a word of it,' she said cheerfully.

'Oh,' said Hugo.

'You don't really expect people to swallow that, do you?' she asked, though plenty of people had. 'Cavity walls, for one thing—in a house this age?' she went on, laying her hand on the wall in question. 'Hardly likely, I'd have thought. Nice piece of fakery, though, that letter. Your own work?'

'It wasn't difficult,' Hugo declaimed modestly, after a small silence. But he was beginning to sweat, even though the forgery was harmless, nothing actually illegal, as his mother had said often enough.

The policewoman had bright blue eyes which regarded him with interest. She removed her hand from the wall, rubbing it fastidiously. 'Feels clammy. No wonder you bricked up the room behind again.'

Oh, God, this was it. Despite her apparent casualness he was suddenly, absolutely, convinced that she knew. Somehow, she'd sussed it out. The police never took anything on face value—she must have been listening to gossip in the village . . . His glance slid hopelessly away, and her eyes sharpened.

Hugo wasn't a clever man. Astute, like his mother, when there was money to be made, but not very intelligent in the long term. But it was apparent, even to him, that retribution, the thing he'd dreaded for twenty-five years, was snapping at his heels. He should have told the truth in the first place, never mind his mother's advice. Well, it was too late now for those sort of regrets, and his mind began to seek for other ways out.

Dimly, he reasoned that if the police knew he was being honest with them now over this, however belatedly, it would go better for him in the matter of his mother's murder. Better to confess rather than let them find out.

Because they surely *would* find out. He knew with terrible certainty that this woman inspector had put two and two together, and that they would dig under the flags of the room behind the wall, and when they did, they'd find the bones of Vera Neasden.

He hadn't meant to kill her. He'd been only fifteen. She'd been sniping at him and he'd pushed past her, a big clumsy youth who didn't know his own strength. And she'd fallen and hit her head against the iron-bound corner of the oak chest . . . The words tumbled out as he explained, years of pent-up guilt fell away. 'It was an accident,' he said, 'an accident.'

Mary Treadwell sat down abruptly on the nearest chair as he began, and thereafter listened in silence.

It had been his mother who'd said they must hide Vera in a cupboard at first, until they could think what to do with her, telling him that the police would never in a million years believe it had been an accident. Hugo would have done anything she said, he'd been so terrified. Then she'd come up with the idea of burying the body under the flagstones of the cold-store room, of pulling down the wall to give more credence to what they were doing if anyone should enquire, and at the same time gaining themselves a little more much-needed living-space. When the old lady asked what all the noise was, downstairs, his mother had replied, 'Spring-cleaning. I'm afraid Vera wasn't always as meticulous as she should have been.'

'It would seem there were a lot of things Vera wasn't. One of them was grateful,' the old lady said sharply, fingering the note her daughter had left behind, the note which, at his mother's command, Hugo had forged in Vera's handwriting. He'd always had the knack of being able to copy anything, had carried on a brisk trade at school in forged sick notes, dodgy bus passes, pop concert tickets, anything, really. It was a facility that had come in very useful later, too, when he began to deal in antiques, in faking documents of provenance and the like. But his success in fooling old Mrs Neasden had unfortunately given his mother the idea for 'finding' the Hathaway letter.

He'd always known that little piece of unnecessary deception would land them in trouble one day.

Unfairly, his mother, the instigator of it all, was beyond punishment now. Despite the fact

77

that it was she who'd forbidden him to go to the police when Vera died, had told him what to do and helped him to bury her. Despite the pillow she'd held over the face of Mrs Neasden as soon as was decently possible after she'd changed her will.

When the policewoman had questioned Hugo carefully over every detail, she was silent for a while, then asked him to accompany her to the station to make an official statement. 'Before we go, I must tell you that we're questioning Kevin Cartwright in connection with the murder of your mother. He left his fingerprints all over the place, and he's also confessed to breaking in.'

Hugo reeled. What had he done? Had he delivered himself into her hands—confessed to a crime when there was no need to have done so? With no guarantee that his claim that it had been an accident would be believed, either. He felt ill. His asthma was coming back.

'The Cartwrights started celebrating Christmas early, and Kevin was drunk enough to think he could get the Chelsea figurine back,' the inspector was continuing. 'He got in through the back window, but couldn't find what he'd come for. While he was searching for it, he heard your mother's key in the lock and rushed out, knocking her over. He thought she was only stunned, but he wasn't sure—'

'So he put the plastic bag over her head to make certain she wouldn't recover and name him,' Hugo intervened quickly

'Not quite. He couldn't find what he came for because it had already gone, hadn't it? You came back after your quarrel with your mother, knowing she'd be out doing her Christmas shopping, broke in at the back and lifted the figurine, together with more bits and pieces to make it look like a genuine robbery—'

Hugo's breathing became noisy.

'Then you heard Kevin getting in, kept out of sight while he began to search—until he heard your mother's key in the lock, in fact, and rushed out. You followed him, but by the time you reached the door, he'd gone and you found your mother lying there, unconscious. It was you who suffocated her with the plastic bag.'

He hadn't, after all, fooled Detective Inspector Treadwell for one minute by that clever piece of play-acting over the disappearance of the Chelsea piece. He didn't bother to ask her how she knew it had happened exactly as she said. Had it been anyone else, he'd have accused her of making wild and unfounded guesses, but you never knew with women. They had mysterious powers beyond his ken. Her instincts had probably told her, though he had to admit it was probable she had some sort of proof as well—his prints on the plastic bag, he supposed dully, he'd been in too much of a hurry to think about that. It didn't matter. All that really mattered was that he was for it, one way or another.

Hugo was crushed. Women had bedevilled him all his life. He'd never been able to follow the labyrinthine twists and turns of their minds, to understand in any way what they might be thinking. But now, he knew exactly how Anne Hathaway must have felt when she discovered she'd been left only her husband's second-best bed.

He'd risked everything for a piece of porcelain. Furious at his mother's threat to cut him out of her will, he'd returned to the cottage and taken the figurine and the other trifles, as the policewoman had guessed, reckoning on certain outlets he knew about where he could later secretly sell the porcelain.

He should have known better. Even dead, his mother had followed him and exacted her revenge. As he fumbled for his door key, the Chelsea piece had slipped through his sweaty palms on to the expensive, imported Etruscan tiles in the entrance hall to his flat, and smashed into a thousand pieces, utterly beyond repair.

'Shall we go?' asked Mary Treadwell.

PERIL AT MELFORD HOUSE

It was nearly six months since I'd last visited my elderly aunts, Marigold and Lydia, at Melford St Bede, and I was rather ashamed of the fact that it had been so long. I'd been so preoccupied with practising and studying for my final exams—not to mention returning my engagement ring to Freddie—that it only belatedly occurred to me I hadn't seen my family since Christmas, when I'd gone home to stay with them at Melford House and we'd spent the holiday as cheerfully as one could in post-war Britain, with shortages of everything still apparent, and food still rationed, despite the war having ended three years ago.

Lydia met me at Leverstead station with the car which she had, as usual, parked outside the station entrance, blocking the narrow High Street with lofty disregard for all traffic regulations. She seemed to feel she had a special dispensation to park wherever she wished, confident that the police would recognize the car and not make a fuss. And of course they could hardly fail to recognize it—a pre-war Baby Austin which Jimmy Cole at The Garage had resprayed a cheerful bright yellow to her instructions—and, naturally, they wouldn't make a fuss, knowing the car belonged to Miss Crowe from Melford St Bede. Since the war, people no longer doffed their caps to the gentry, Jack was as good as his neighbour, but here in the small town of Leverstead, just as in Melford village itself, people had long memories, and the Crowe family were still kindly regarded for their benevolence and their participation in local affairs. Even my grandfather, Nathaniel Crowe, irascible and autocratic as he was, had been respected during his lifetime, if not loved. It was only behind his back that Melford House had been referred to as 'Old Crowe's Nest'.

By the time Lydia had wedged her stout, tweed-costumed body behind the wheel and we had stowed my cello and my bags alongside a great deal of shopping and a large, ungainly parcel from Postleford's, the butcher's, there wasn't much room left in the tiny car.

'Shove that parcel to one side,' Lydia ordered, in her abrupt way 'Only sausages, and bones for Hector.' The statement was accompanied by a large wink, from which I understood the parcel also to contain something from under the counter to supplement the human rations, dragooned from Bert Postleford, or obtained in exchange for a hot tip for the 2.30: Lydia was mad about horses, hunting and racing, and her little flutters were a byword in the family. 'Wonderful to see you, Vicky!' she added gruffly, attacking the engine and setting us off with a kangaroo jump.

I glanced at her in surprise. My Aunt Lydia was not one to voice her emotions so openly. Her straight, iron-grey hair was cut short and brushed back from her face in the same old-fashioned, uncompromising style she'd worn for years, but I fancied the set of her chin was a little less determined than normal, and as we climbed the hill towards Melford I realized she was driving her car even more erratically than was her wont—which was to say I thanked the Lord above that we encountered no other vehicle.

Melford St Bede is a lovely village, standing on a hill overlooking a deep valley, and the road from Leverstead winds up through the woods that clothe the hill. We were nearly at the top, where the road takes a sharp right turn, when Lydia stopped the car and switched off the engine. I was happy that she pulled in to the side first and didn't simply stop in the middle of the road, as she was quite likely to do.

'Vicky' she began, 'something you should know. I've moved back to the Grange.'

'Goodness!' The Grange belonged to Lydia, a largish house in the centre of the village, with stables attached where she kept several hunters, but she'd returned to Melford House to live with Aunt Marigold since Marigold's stroke the previous year, and had seemed since then to accept the arrangement as more or less permanent. The Grange, though not the stables, had, in fact, been on the market for months. 'But why? What about Aunt Marigold? Why didn't you let me know? And what—?'

'Whoa, there, old thing—' she said, much as she would have addressed Winston, her favourite horse. 'One question at a time.'

'Well,' I said, more calmly. 'Which one would you like to answer for a start?'

'First one, I suppose,' she answered after a moment's pause. 'You asked me why. Why I went back to the Grange after Christmas. That was when he came.'

'When who came, Aunt Lydia?' I asked the question gently, and took her capable hand in mine, because it was, incredibly, trembling. A tear, even, rolled down her weatherbeaten cheek.

'Why, Malcolm Deering. Nurse Wilcox's stepbrother.' Her voice hardened, and she brushed the tear away angrily. 'But, of course, you haven't met him yet. Suppose you'll be like everyone else—especially Marigold—and think he's charming! Butters her up shamefully and she just laps it up, thinks he can do no wrong. Then I had an offer for the Grange, but when it came to the point, I couldn't face the thought of actually selling it, and then Marigold became impossible and so I went back home to live. Realized my mistake too late! Only thing to do now, I suppose, is go back to Melford House and stay with Marigold until all this is cleared up. Oh, Vicky, if only your mother had still been alive! Always the one who knew the right thing to do, you know. But you're so like her, I'm sure you'll be able to help.'

My mind reeled, trying to sort all this out. My mother, Grace, I should explain, was the youngest of the three Crowe sisters by many years, the only one who had married, though Marigold, I had always suspected, had had her moments when she was younger, even accounting for the exaggerated stories of what she liked to think of as her colourful past. My mother had fallen in love with my father, a penniless young academic, when the war came, he was chagrined not to be able to serve in the forces because of his poor eyesight, and had to be content with a job in the Air Ministry. We lived in a flat nearby, but soon the Blitz started and despite my protests, I was sent away from the dangers of London to live with my mother's family at Melford St Bede. Two months later, both my parents were killed when a bomb dropped on our flat and demolished it, and Melford House became my permanent home. I was fourteen years old, and I would never forget the love and kindness shown to me by my aunts during this terrible time—and even, in a less demonstrative way, by my grandfather.

Not that it was all sweetness and light, living with my relatives. My grandfather, as I have said, was an old curmudgeon, and tight-fisted at that. He enjoyed tyrannizing over his little empire and, as far as his two elder daughters were concerned, had seen off one suitor after another as not being good enough, or rich enough, though perhaps he also realized that neither of them was really cut out to make a good wife. Lydia was too devoted to her horses and dogs, and Marigold to herself. My mother, his youngest and his favourite, had been allowed to go her own way with only token objections.

As for the aunts . . . they had a great deal of affection for each other, but they could scarcely have been more different, and, needless to say, their temperaments often clashed. Their squabbles were usually short-lived, due no doubt to their very wise decision after Grandfather died to keep separate establishments, but there was always some ongoing drama between them which I believed they enjoyed as adding a little spice to life.

Marigold was the elder, though only by about eighteen months. She was devoted to the arts, especially to music, and I had her to thank for encouraging me to work for a scholarship to the Royal College of Music, as a first step towards making music my career. She was no mean pianist herself, and she also painted. Before the war, as she never

86

let anyone forget, she had been in with the Bloomsbury set, numbering Virginia Woolf among her friends; she had even, at one time, until stopped by my grandfather, attempted to surround herself at Melford St Bede with arty types, rather fancying herself as another Lady Ottoline Morell, I suppose. She had always been delicate, and was still very pretty, rather vain, and perhaps a trifle shallow.

Whereas Lydia . . . plain, blunt old Lydia, she was the one who'd worked tirelessly during the war with the Women's Voluntary Services, taken charge of the billeting arrangements for evacuees and done her stint as a firewatcher. When the war ended, she went back to occupying her time with her horses, her dogs and riding to hounds. Lydia in hunting pink was a sight to make strong men quail. She'd always been formidable, and to tell the truth there were times, as a child, when I'd been more than a little afraid of her. At the same time, she was eminently sensible, so that her attitude now was all the more disturbing.

'Oh, that woman!' she declared now, cutting into my thoughts. 'What a snake in the grass she's turned out to be!'

I presumed she was referring to Nurse Wilcox, which didn't altogether surprise me, since she was not a woman I naturally warmed to. She had been taken on following Aunt Marigold's stroke about a year ago, a voluble, irritating woman of about thirty-five, bossy as nurses are, with an enormous appetite, and always demanding endless pots of strong tea She had sandy hair, and a mole on her chin, from which sprouted a single, black hair.

Perhaps it was the thought of tea which made me say now, 'Let's go on to the Grange, and you can tell me all about it. I'll even have a cup of bonfire tea with you.' (My childhood name for her favourite smoky lapsang souchong.) 'You shouldn't be living there all on your own . I can stay with you just as well as at Melford House—'

'Lord, no! Wouldn't do at all. I'm quite all right, and Marigold's expecting you, and besides . . .' Her voice faltered to a close. She really was quite unlike her usual, confident self.

Besides, what?'

'I want you there to keep a watching brief.'

'A watching brief!' I tried not to laugh. 'You've been reading too many of those thrillers.' Gory pulp fiction with lurid covers constituted Lydia's bedtime reading, but they'd never before affected her clear thinking.

'Maybe I have,' she said quietly, 'but you can't put everything that's been happening down to my imagination. Nor to accidents, as Marigold insists. Something's going on, Vicky.'

'Good heavens! What sort of things?'

'They're trying to kill Marigold.'

There was a long pause. Had it been anyone else but Lydia, I might have thought this a leg-pull. But a sense of humour was never her strong point. I reminded myself of her age, and her addiction to crime fiction. 'Aunt Lydia! Isn't that going a bit far?'

'Ha! Maybe you won't think so when you hear what I've got to say. For a start, there was Benjie, and that finnan haddock Wilcox sent up for Marigold's supper. Shows what a fool the woman is, not to have listened when I told her how Marigold hates smoked fish. She fed it to Benjie, and an hour later the poor cat was stone dead.'

'He was very old, and he was ailing,' I reminded her gently. When Marigold had written to me, mourning his death, she'd said he was seventeen, which she reckoned was 119, in human terms. Be that as it may, he'd certainly been around for almost as long as I could remember.

'That's what everyone said. All the same, I wish I'd obeyed my natural instincts, had him down to the vet to see just what he did die of. She knows about poisons, that woman. She's supposed to be a nurse, after all. And it all began after Malcolm appeared on the scene, just after Christmas. Marigold should never have allowed him to stay, lounging about, doing nothing. Think they're on Easy Street, both of them.'

'If that's so, wouldn't killing Aunt Marigold defeat the object?'

She gave me a baleful look. 'Not now that

she's changed her will in his favour!'

'What!'

'Thought that'd make you sit up! As you know, through your grandfather's will Melford House goes to me after she dies, and there's nothing she can do about that. It's falling to pieces, going to rack and ruin because Father was too mean to spend anything on its upkeep, and Marigold really has no interest—but I don't mind about that.' Her face reddened. 'Fact is, I should mind frightfully if it were to go out of the family.'

I knew how much she loved the old house, though it wasn't a sentiment I could share. It was the dreariest old place imaginable, a hideous Victorian brick edifice, all high chimneys and unnecessary gables and turrets on the outside, and inside full of dark corners, gloomy, allegorical stained glass and heavy old oil paintings of dubious artistic worth. It had been built and furnished by my great-grandfather, who had been too busy making money from the manufacture of boots and shoes to acquire any taste, and had remained largely unchanged ever since.

'She can't touch the house, but she can leave her money where she wants—and she's left it all to Malcolm Deering! 'Fraid she's cut you right out, left you without a penny, old girl!'

This was a shock, but not the disaster Lydia seemed to think it would be. Money for its own sake had never appealed to me. 'I've quite enough as it is, Aunt Lydia . . . Certainly more than most of my friends. After all, Grandfather did leave me something—'

'A pittance!' she interrupted. 'Mere pittance! Because he meant me and Marigold to leave you something as well, don't you see?'

I vaguely recalled that Marigold, as the elder daughter, had come into the bulk of the Crowe fortune, such as was now left, but I'd never given it much thought. If asked, I would have supposed Marigold would leave her money to some artistic foundation or other, and Lydia to some charity for retired horses. But I was astonished that Marigold, who was quite sharp underneath all the fluff and frivolity, could have been so utterly foolish and uncaring of her sister, so taken in as to make a will in favour of a stranger, a young man virtually unknown to her, however much he flattered her. When I met Malcolm Deering half an hour later, I found it even more unbelievable.

But for the moment, Lydia was continuing with her story: 'There's more, Vicky. Only two days ago Marigold was nearly killed by one of those finial thingummies falling off the roof, though there was only the lightest breeze. Remember what happened when one blew down that time before? Shattered a York stone paving slab, no less! The rest should have been removed or made safe there and then. She was lying out on the terrace in a deck chair—only missed her by the purest chance.'

'Aunt Lydia. Just supposing anyone would try to climb out there on to the roof to push the thing over, the chances of getting it to fall in exactly the right position must be remote.'

'Ah, but it *is* possible to get out there. You know that, don't you?'

And, of course, I did. In a famous escapade, when I was about eight, I suppose, I had scrambled out of an attic window on to the roof with my cousin William, where we crouched behind one of the false gables and dropped tiny pebbles on to the grown-ups, who were drinking cocktails on the terrace below. We nearly fell off the roof with helpless laughter, which was how we were found out, and poor William took the brunt of the punishment because he was seven years older than I was and should have known better, they told him. Each of these false gables, of which there were many, was crowned by a heavy stone finial in the shape of a foliated fleur-de-lis. Lethal, if it fell on anyone's head. But even if the one above the terrace had become loose enough to push over . . . 'It's too much of a coincidence, Aunt Lydia.'

'Not when you remember the fish—and the rabbits.'

'Rabbits? Was there some poisoned rabbit stew as well?'

'You're not taking this seriously, Vicky!' she admonished, poking me with a sharp

92

finger. 'Well, maybe this'll convince you: yesterday, when Marigold was taking a stroll in the old rose garden, dear Malcolm was out potting rabbits in the copse, or so he said.' She plunged her hand into her capacious pocket and showed me what she explained was a spent bullet. 'First time I've ever known anybody go after rabbits with a revolver!'

I confess that one did rather take me aback. 'Does Malcolm own a revolver?'

'There's Father's. Never got rid of it,' she added unnecessarily, because at Melford House no one ever threw anything at all away, even unto the third and fourth generation.

'Well, he obviously missed,' I said lamely.

'Only just. She imagined it was a wasp zinging past her head, thought there must be a nest in the gazebo. A wasp! Went out and looked when she told me, and guess what? Found the bullet, of course.' She went on rather hurriedly, 'Bad business all round—and unnecessary, too. They've only to wait, after all, but they won't want to do that, in case she changes her mind again.'

'Aunt Lydia—what do you mean, they've only to wait?'

'Prepare yourself for a shock, Vicky. Marigold . . . her heart, you know. Doc Crampton's an old fool in some ways, but I suppose he knows his job. Says it can't be long before she cashes in her chips. Any day, in fact. Mind you, the best doctors have been wrong before now. She may go on for years.'

I was as saddened to hear this as Lydia evidently was, despite her gruff words, although it wasn't unexpected: Marigold had never fully recovered from that stroke. I really couldn't imagine what Melford House would be like without her—or even how Lydia was going to manage without their constant sparring. 'Know she can't help it,' Lydia added, starting up the car, 'best sister in the world, matter of fact, but one can't help thinking it's made the poor old thing a bit gaga.' I could think of nothing sensible or comforting to say to say to this, and so we drove the last couple of miles in silence.

'Anyway, it's not just me, Vicky,' she said, as we at last turned through the gates at Melford House and bucked up the potholed gravel drive. 'Your Cousin William thinks there's something fishy about that pair, too, yet he keeps telling me not to worry, everything will turn out right. Can't understand him. You should talk to him—he's joining us all here for dinner tonight.'

'Oh, then if William agrees with you, it must be so,' I answered tartly. 'But you're wrong if you think he'll talk sensibly to me. He still treats me as though I'm twelve years old, with a brain to match.'

William, (he of the pebbles thrown from the roof) was actually my second cousin, twice removed. We'd always been the best of

94

friends, but since he'd been demobbed from the Navy, and had gone back into his father's solicitors' firm, he'd changed for the worse. He wasn't fun any longer, though I suppose he could be excused, in a way. His father suffered from gout, an acutely painful and disabling condition which seems to provoke amusement in everyone but the sufferer, and consequently William had had many of the decisions and worries of the firm thrust on to his shoulders. He'd become pompous, at least when it came to advising me what I should or should not do, especially regarding my engagement to Freddie Fergus. He'd been right about Freddie as it so happened; he'd turned out to be just as ghastly as William had predicted, and I'd given him the old heave-ho several weeks ago, but I'd seen no reason to inform William of this fact and give him the satisfaction of saying 'I told you so.'

Why Lydia thought I'd be charmed by the man who came to the door to greet us as we drew up before the house, I cannot imagine: I loathed Malcolm Deering on sight. There was something just too good about his wavy hair and his moustache and the silk cravat tucked into his shirt neck, and his Errol Flynn smile. He was older than I'd imagined he would be. According to his sister, Nurse Wilcox, he'd flown Spitfires in the war, and been decorated for bravery, all of which I felt was an unlikely story, despite his handlebar moustache and his tedious use of RAF slang. 'Oh, jolly d!' he said, when we were introduced. Apparently, he'd had a nervous breakdown due to the traumatic effects of the war, and needed a long rest to recuperate. I didn't believe a word of it. I was more than inclined to agree with Lydia that he and his sister had found a cushy number at Melford House, and were trading on the fact.

But . . . just supposing it were true? That he *had* been brave and audacious? Not all heroes look like heroes. Did that mean he would also have the audacity to carry out these attempts on Aunt Marigold's life?

'You'll see a big change in her,' Lydia had warned, but as it happened I did not, for I was never to see my Aunt Marigold before she died.

She was resting in her room when we arrived, and slept on and on. It was only when Nurse Wilcox went in to rouse her to get ready for dinner that we realized why she hadn't put in an appearance. Yet another accident. And this time, it had been a fatal one.

'I'm not one to give in to hysterics, I'm sure,' the nurse said, after a third cup of fiercely strong tea had revived her somewhat, 'but it fair gave me a turn when I went in and saw what had happened. Not that I didn't warn her—I told her that great heavy portrait was downright dangerous, right over the bedhead—nasty old thing, begging your pardon, glaring out of that ugly frame!—what would happen if the cord gave way? "Good heavens, Nurse, that's my grandfather. He's been there as long as ever I can remember and he's never fallen!" she said, which didn't seem very logical to me, but then, that's what she was like! Not that you'll get me to say anything against her, she was one of the best patients I've ever nursed. Fussy about her food, but then, there's many a nurse would be glad if that was the only thing to complain of in their patients, I can tell you! Caught her right on the head, that frame did—but Doctor says even if it hadn't, the shock of it falling like that would have killed her, and I'm sure he's right.'

'Damn poor show, all the same,' Malcolm Deering said, walking across to the window and looking out over the lawn with what I couldn't help thinking was a sickeningly proprietorial air. Perhaps he didn't know that the house, if not Marigold's money, was now Lydia's.

It was at that moment that William arrived from Leverstead, having been informed by telephone of what had happened. He came into the room and I forgot that my relations with him had been on the cool side lately. Those nice, steady brown eyes sought mine immediately. 'Vicky.'

'Oh, William!'

He put his arm around my shoulder, and its clasp was oddly comforting. He included Lydia with an outstretched hand. At the moment, he wasn't being at all pompous.

Nor was he later, when he gave his father's apologies for not being there in person, and said to us all, 'He's given me permission to inform you of the contents of Aunt Marigold's will. I think you, Nurse Wilcox, and your brother, should hear it, too. It's soon told. She leaves one or two small bequests to various people. A pension for life and the tenancy of his cottage to Gornal, her old gardener. A legacy of a thousand pounds to you, Vicky. The rest of her entire fortune goes to you, Lydia, to pay off the mortgage on the Grange and to help with running Melford House as you wish it to be run. The house now, of course, belongs to you.' He paused. 'Oh, and in a codicil, she leaves fifty pounds each to Nurse Wilcox and Malcolm Deering for their kind attention to her over the last few months.'

The faces of Malcolm and his stepsister were a study. Lydia went brick-red. It was news to me that the Grange was mortgaged—but, after all, those stables of hers didn't run on fresh air, and it was well known in the family that her regular racing wagers more often than not demonstrated the triumph of hope over experience. But her embarrassment at her finances being made public was coupled with another expression I couldn't put a name to.

'I think that's a very fair and straightforward will,' concluded William, shuffling papers briskly together.

'Fair! A miserable fifty! That's a calculated insult, considering—' began Malcolm, only to be stopped by a vicious look from his sister. He subsided, but his languishing blue eyes were now smouldering with anger and resentment.

'Fifty pounds more than you deserve!' muttered Lydia.

'Oh, so that's what *you* think?' said Nurse Wilcox. 'Well, Miss Crowe had every right to leave her fortune as she wished, I'm sure. I've known patients to have stranger fancies than she had before she died, but all the same . . .' She glared at Lydia, then me.

'All the same what, Nurse Wilcox?' asked William.

'She gave us to understand she'd changed her will, entirely in favour of my brother . . . She said she was very fond of him, she said—' She paused in a curiously knowing sort of way, trying to stare us down. The black hair on her chin trembled visibly. She seemed about to say much more, but only added, 'She said he was like her own son.'

'Fine thing for a chap to find out he's been left nothing at all,' Malcolm put in. 'After all a chap's done for her.' His vacuous face brightened. 'That's it! There must be a will that supersedes this!'

'Be quiet, Malcolm!' Nurse Wilcox said sharply. He opened his mouth, looked at her, then decided to shut it.

'I assure you,' said William stiffly, 'this

was Miss Crowe's last will and testament, to which the codicil was added only last week, when you, Mr Deering, drove her down to my father's office.'

'She told me herself, in person, that she was leaving every penny to me!'

'There's a world of difference between saying what you're going to do and doing it,' William answered drily. I had no difficulty in going along with this, knowing Marigold quite capable of such dissimulation—deceit, if you like—in order to keep Malcolm and his sister dancing attendance upon her. But, if they had thought they were to benefit when she died— and Nurse Wilcox must have been aware of Marigold's critical state of health—why make those murder attempts at all? Lydia would be bound to contest a will made in Malcolm's favour, and allegations like that would not have improved their chances of success. They were an unpleasant pair, but I didn't think the sister, at least, was stupid.

Wilcox said threateningly, 'You haven't heard the last of this!' Just at that moment a nasty, horrid thought insinuated itself into my mind, and, as I looked at Lydia and finally identified the expression I had failed to recognize before, strengthened and grew. I felt rather sick.

An hour later, on the terrace, I found the opportunity to give my somewhat gabbled explanations to William, who listened with gratifying attentiveness until I'd finished.

'What you're trying to say, Vicky, is that *Lydia* staged those "accidents"?'

'Well, she could have done.' It was the last thing I wanted to believe, but it seemed horribly clear to me: Marigold had thought it wiser to let Lydia, as well as the nurse and her brother, believe that she'd made Deering her heir, for the simple reason that she knew Lydia well enough to realize she'd have been quite unable to keep up the sort of pretence she herself had done. And Lydia had believed what she'd been told—the result being those 'accidents'—a blundering attempt to make Marigold see the precious pair for what they were and presumably to persuade her to revoke that unfair will.

It occurred to me William was not exactly looking as bowled over by my theories as I thought he would be, and I saw that, as usual, he'd got there before me. 'I'll admit the same thing did occur to me,' he said, 'but—that finial just happening to become conveniently loose enough for Lydia to push over? No, that won't wash! it had probably been balanced there for ages, and some freak movement of the breeze finally toppled it. Mind you, I'm not saying it might not have given her the idea for a series of so-called accidents . . . poor old Benjie snuffing it, Grandpa's revolver being fired and the spent bullet being found—'

'It did,' interrupted a sturdy voice behind

us. We turned to see Lydia stomping out of the drawing-room, via the french windows. 'Damn fool thing to have done—though it seemed a good idea at the time to try and make Marigold come to her senses where that pair was concerned. Did nobody any harm. Except old Benjie, of course—but that was a kindness. Should've been put out of his misery months ago, according to the vet, only Marigold wouldn't hear of it.'

'But the picture?'

'Nothing to do with me, not that! You don't believe I would've done anything that might hurt old Marigold? She wasn't even in the garden when I fired that bullet—and I knew nothing on earth would make her touch that finny haddock.'

I was convinced she was telling the truth. Lydia might have been foolish, but she would never have done anything that could actually have killed her sister. 'No, I'm sorry I even thought it. Of course I don't believe that.' But I couldn't help thinking her schemes had planted a more sinister intention in someone's head.

'I've had a look at that picture,' William said. 'From what I could see without touching it, I'd say it's impossible to tell whether, the cord had simply rotted over the years and finally given up the ghost, or been helped on its way by being teased and pulled apart to the last strand. If it had been doctored, it had been cleverly done. What's more, there's not so much as a speck of dust on the picture.'

Even in the best-regulated households, of which Melford House was certainly not one, and never had been, even in the days of a sufficiency of servants, this was unusual. As everyone knows, when a picture has been hanging in the same place for years, dust inevitably accumulates behind it, so this one had obviously been taken down and cleaned before it fell, which had to be suspicious in itself. 'No fingerprints, then, not a shadow of proof,' I said.

And just supposing the cord *had* been tampered with, wasn't that an incredibly haphazard way to try to murder someone? The picture could have fallen at any time, when Marigold had not been in bed—or even in the room—though perhaps that was just the point. If it hadn't succeeded in killing her, it would just have been put down to another narrow escape. If it had succeeded, all well and good. Sooner or later, if these 'mishaps' continued, one of them had to be fatal.

'There'll have to be an inquest, won't there, and I suppose there's no doubt the verdict will be accidental death? That pair are going to get off scot-free.'

'Well,' said William. 'I'm not so sure about that.'

And, with the air of having saved the best until the last, he pulled a long envelope from his pocket. 'When Marigold made the codicil to the will last week, she left this letter with my father, not to be opened until after her death. It follows on from certain enquiries she'd asked us to make.'

If he expected to surprise us, he succeeded. 'What enquiries?' Lydia asked.

'About Malcom Deering and his sister. You couldn't understand, Lydia, why Marigold should be so taken in by Deering—but the truth was that she wasn't. Right from the first, she suspected him—with good reason, as she explains in this letter. She asked us to instigate enquiries, though neither my father nor I knew just why, until we read this.' He tapped the envelope and asked abruptly, 'How much do you know, Aunt Lydia, about Marigold's life when she lived in London?'

It was some time before she answered, and when she did, I thought she had already guessed where his questions were leading. 'More than enough. Rackety sort of company she kept, called themselves arty to justify acting as they pleased, without thought for anyone else.'

'She had a particular friend called Gayton Bulmer?'

'Friend! She actually told you about him?'

'In this letter, yes.'

'So you also know about—' Lydia broke off, studied the carpet, then looked up. 'Oh, well, water under the bridge now, but a terrible

104

thing at the time. To have a baby and not be married . . . the shame, the disgrace.' She sighed deeply. 'Poor Marigold. You're telling me they were blackmailing her over that?'

'More than that. Deering was claiming he was that child.'

'What!' She gave a snort of derision. 'Ridiculous!'

'Well, as you know, the baby was given up for adoption . . . Nurse Wilcox, who, incidentally, is no more Deering's stepsister than I am, but someone who nursed him just after the war in a hospital for nervous disorders, came across a photo of this Gayton Bulmer, and spotted what she thought was a quite extraordinary likeness to Malcolm Deering. She also found out that Marigold's friendship with Bulmer had been rather more than that—'

'Found out! By listening to village gossip, no doubt, and snooping around among Marigold's private affairs, for I'll tell you one thing—my sister never kept any photo of that rotter on display! Not when he'd damn near ruined her life—died just before the war, and good riddance!'

'Be that as it may, Wilcox brought Deering here as her stepbrother, on the pretext of his nervous exhaustion due to the war. Marigold let them stay here at Melford House, dancing to her tune, giving them promises of more to come in her will, while she took steps to discover their backgrounds. She let them think she believed Deering's claim to be her son, but, as she makes clear in this letter, she knew from the first that it was quite impossible.'

'Of course she did!' Lydia declared sturdily. 'She had the baby adopted, but that didn't mean she'd forgotten him. Always kept track of him. He joined the army when war broke out, and was killed in the western desert. Broke her heart.'

There was a silence.

'So why set up that business with the picture?' I asked.

'Yesterday morning, my father sent up details to Marigold of what our enquiry agent had established regarding Deering's real identity. I believe she confronted them with what she now knew to be the truth, and they realized time had run out. They could have faced charges for attempting to get money by false pretences—but remember, they still believed they were to benefit from her will— so they had to get rid of her before she could revoke it.'

'The portrait didn't fall by accident, then,' I said, hating to think of it.

'If it had been prepared, it would take only a sharp tug when Marigold was sleeping to bring it down. Or—'

'Or it could have been lifted down and Marigold clobbered with it,' Lydia finished. 'Especially, if she'd been given something to make her sleep like she did. Well, a post-mortem will soon find that out.'

We fell silent, each of us unwilling to face the prospect ahead, though thankful that, one way or another, the two miscreants were not going to get away scot-free. Presently, Lydia left us to go and see to her horses, and William and I were alone. When he took my hand and pulled me to him, I didn't object. In the circumstances, it was very good to feel the warmth and comfort of his arms around me.

'And now,' he announced masterfully, 'about that ass Fergus. You're not going to marry him, Vicky. I won't let you.'

'Oh, you won't? And why not?'

'Because you're going to marry me. You've owed me that ever since you let me take all the blame for throwing those pebbles from the roof.'

'In that case, it's about time I paid my debt, isn't it?'

FRESCOES

He fell in love the instant he saw her, though it wasn't until much later that he identified the exact moment.

'You must be Andrew St John, the art expert from the Heritage people.' A slight young woman with unkempt sandy hair, she put down her garden fork, scrambled to her feet and extended a grubby, unselfconscious hand.

'I've come to look at the frescoes, yes. And you are Miss Landers?'

'Oh, Meg, please.' Despite the tatty old jeans, working-boots, deplorable T-shirt, and the hair, which looked as if she'd cut it herself with her gardening shears, he liked her at once. Her grip was firm, her eyes steady. Moreover, she'd pronounced his name correctly, 'Sinjun' and not 'Saint John'. He was predisposed towards people who took the trouble to get it right, feeling they must take him more seriously, and believe him older than his open-faced appearance might at first lead them to do.

'This is an amazing place.'

Her eyes lit up. 'Did you walk up the drive?'

'The taxi left me at the main gates.'

He'd been warned it was a long walk, but worth it for that first glimpse of the

108

house, if the weather was fine, which it was, unseasonably so. A little heatwave had arrived suddenly, and might have made him regret the dismissal of the taxi, had the walk not been so magical. The neglected drive wound upwards through thick stands of cool woodland, with beeches showing the fresh green translucency of their young growth and groups of deer standing at a distance under their dappled shade. At one point, he had been stopped in his tracks by the sight of bluebells spreading as far as he could see, wave upon wave. The deep, mossy banks either side were massed with the pale, greenish clusters of late primroses. And then the trees opened out and the Palladian house was suddenly before him, much smaller than he'd expected: Margent House, built of the soft, creamy local sandstone two hundred and fifty years ago. At closer proximity, it could be seen that the stone was somewhat crumbling now at the edges, seemingly a metaphor for the whole house, which, he'd been told, was sinking fast through neglect into not so gentle decay.

Meg Landers was now the sole owner of this.

It had come to her as the last remaining member of the Cortis family, and she had immediately perceived the incredibly foolish notion of not only occupying it, but also restoring it to its former glory and one day opening house and garden to the public—with no other qualifications for such an optimistic undertaking than having been trained as a landscape gardener. She had, in point of fact, been pulling weeds when he'd appeared, no doubt in an attempt to reveal the original pattern of the once immaculate parterres, and hadn't noticed him for several minutes. He had stood and watched her, unwilling to disturb the moment.

She—the only living figure in the landscape—and the stillness of the hot afternoon, imparted a strange, dream-like quality to the whole place. Pale against the rising background of thick, forest trees, perfectly proportioned and symmetrical, the house stood as it had done for two and a half centuries; the heavy scent of some unseen rose hung on the air, rampant climbers weighed down broken pergolas. The empty basin of a large circular stone pool showed ancient, dried cracks under the sun, its fountain silent. A stone urn, long fallen from its pedestal, lay smashed among the weeds in the gravel. Bees droned. He could, for two pins, have sat down on one of the curlicued iron seats and slept.

But Meg Landers had looked up and seen him and approached, anxious to forward the business in hand, and the dream was broken.

'You think I'm a fool to want to keep this up, don't you?' she asked forthrightly a few minutes later, pausing at the great front door to unlace and remove her boots, revealing small feet in pink socks.

'I think you may be deeply disappointed in the end, if you try.'

'I might have known it, you're like all the rest! But I know I can do it if I have faith.' She sounded very young. There was a crusading light in her eyes.

Andrew was perhaps five or six years older than she was, but he was a young man intent on cultivating his own *gravitas*. 'Faith isn't enough on its own,' he reminded her, only wanting to prepare her, but colouring up in the face of her direct gaze, suddenly hearing himself. Sounding, and feeling, middle-aged.

'So,' she said, 'it all depends on you, then.'

'The Heritage Foundation, not me.'

'But they won't give me money if I don't agree to pull the orangery down—unless you recommend otherwise.'

That was true. Only there were other problems with the house, besides that of the orangery, just as serious. His visit was a mere formality: he was the bearer of ill news.

'I didn't like your Mr Montgomery-Hines when he came to see me. He's a pompous prat.'

Andrew grinned spontaneously, and in a moment lost the air of importance he strove so hard to project. Very nearly, he congratulated her on her perception, almost told her that not liking Montgomery-Hines definitely put her on the side of the angels, but of course he didn't. Still, she smiled back at him, showing she'd understood what he hadn't said, anyway. The smile illuminated her. She had a scattering of freckles across the bridge of her nose.

Her feet made no sound as she padded in front of him, leading him through a series of rooms where damp spread maps of unknown continents all over the walls, where parts of plaster cornices had fallen away from the ceilings and carpets were worn to the threads. Mice scuttled behind the wainscoting and there was a sweetish, fungoid odour of dry rot above the smell of the dust which lay thick everywhere. He wondered why she'd bothered to remove her boots.

Watching him with small, sideways glances and noting his dismay, she said rather breathlessly, 'Better to reserve judgement until after you've seen the frescoes.'

The orangery was a Victorian addition, tacked on to the back of the house; a fussy building of no architectural merit that ruined the clean lines of the main house. It had a series of long windows on three sides, but still looked more like a chapel, or even a folly, than an orangery. Among other disasters, reported Montgomery-Hines, the roof timbers were riddled with woodworm, and Andrew immediately appreciated the extent of the problem: the Foundation didn't have unlimited funds, and the amount of money

112

necessary to restore this part of the place alone would knock the whole project on the head.

'I thought it could eventually be used as a tearoom. Bring back the orange trees. You know,' Meg was saying wistfully.

His heart, not normally a volatile organ, leaped in sudden sympathy with her. But there was no point in raising her hopes. He began to look for the frescoes.

She was going on to say something else, but he scarcely heard. Turning, his eyes had been drawn straight away to the shorter side of the orangery, the one which abutted on to the house, which until now had been behind him. In the centre of the wall was the wide, high, deeply recessed door through which they'd entered. He now saw that it was framed by the frescoes, seven in all, which occupied the rest of the wall.

Each had its own painted border, but they were set closely. Together they made a great wall of living colour, vibrant and almost as fresh as the day they had been painted. Which was, he knew, some time during the summer of 1937, when the artist, Lillie Cortis, was twenty-two.

'Incredible!' he murmured, stunned, momentarily at a loss for anything more to say.

'Aren't they just?'

They were incredible not only because of their intrinsic beauty, but also because, from

113

studying what little was available of the work of Lillie Cortis before coming here, it was quite evident to Andrew that in these her art had taken on a new and important direction.

Flashes of brilliance in her early work had been evident from the start, but, like many of her contemporaries, the young artist had spread her talents too thinly while in search of her own 'voice'. Pencil sketches, watercolours, oils on canvas, woodcuts remained, but her death at such an early age had meant that not nearly enough had been left behind for the now eager Cortis collectors, especially since she'd had a reputation for carelessness and such disregard for her own work that she quite often recklessly gave it away, forgot to sign it or lost track of what she'd done with it. Nevertheless, she'd achieved a certain posthumous fame. She was currently fashionable.

And here, in front of him, was the glorious evidence that she had far exceeded anything she'd ever done before. Why had these frescoes never had the attention they certainly deserved?

Well, it wasn't only, he thought, answering his own question, that the climate of opinion of those days had needed to change before they could be evaluated and fully appreciated, though that was certainly true. She'd been too young to have built up a solid reputation before she died—and more significantly, the frescoes had remained in obscurity until now. No.one with sufficient authority to pronounce on their merit had ever examined them. Lillie Cortis had been tragically killed almost immediately after they had been completed, and this house had then gone to a distant cousin in Ireland who had not wanted it. It had remained unoccupied and been allowed to fall into near-ruin for over sixty years before the cousin had died and left it to Meg Larders.

Gazing at the frescoes, Andrew had already made up his mind. Their excellent state of preservation proved that the school of thought which said that frescoes could not last in the British climate was entirely wrong. Mercifully the orangery, for all its decrepitude, had remained dry, and only a little restoration would be needed to make the panels as good as the day they were painted. They must never again be left to survive as best they could. Forget Montgomery-Hines and his woodworm. The orangery would cost a small fortune to repair, but it must be done, or failing that, pulled down and another building erected around the frescoes, for their protection.

Andrew began to feel very excited.

The first stunning impact over, he became absorbed in the technical details of the work, the painterly qualities, the strong lines of the drawing, the pure colours, the balanced calmness and serenity of the compositions.

He was—and made no apologies to himself for it—reminded of the one he considered the greatest Old Master of them all, Raphael, and the simplicity and power of his Sistine Madonna.

The theme of the frescoes was the Seven Ages of Woman. Against intricately depicted and finely finished backgrounds of fields, foliage, flowers and small animals, starting with spring and moving through the months towards winter, each age was shown: rosy baby, sturdy child, budding adolescent. Next, a radiant young woman gazing towards her lover, shown as a tall figure in breeches, with his back to the viewer; then, a madonna-like mother nursing an infant—followed by a mature grandmother, surrounded by her children and grandchildren. The seventh fresco depicted not, as might be expected, an aged crone *'sans* teeth, *sans* eyes, *sans* taste, *sans* everything', but a figure forever young, lying prone and encased in ice, hands crossed on her breast.

Lillie Cortis had been twenty-two, he reminded himself, when she had painted these. Twenty-two.

'I know nothing about art, but I could just gaze at them for hours.'

He had been so absorbed he'd forgotten the woman behind him. 'Tell me what you see, Meg?'

She thought for a moment. 'An affirmation

of life?' she ventured, rather shyly.

'Don't you see death, too?'

'Yes, of course, if you look closely, you can't fail to see that.' She shivered.

In each picture, there was indeed a representation of death, so tiny and concealed that one had to strain to look for it: a skull and crossbones; old Death himself, with his scythe; a hanged human figure; a coffin, a skeleton, and what he took to be a mummy. Six *memento mori*. But in the seventh panel, above the door, Andrew could find no such. Instead, he discovered water gushing from a spring, an obvious symbol of life which then, however, turned into the frozen ice block around the dead figure.

Amazing! Yet . . . the more he looked at the painted panels, the more oddly disturbing Andrew was finding them. Disturbing, and puzzling. Perhaps the feeling was caused by those intimations of mortality, that last ice-enclosed corpse eerily foreshadowing Lillie Cortis's own death. Astonishing as they were, he found himself revising his earlier, rash comparisons with Raphael.

'She must have died soon after completing these?' They had been, as far as he knew, her last work.

'Yes, two weeks later she was dead. So sad, such a waste.'

'It was an accident, wasn't it?'

'A flying accident, horrible. Neither she nor

117

the pilot survived.'

She didn't seem inclined to elaborate, but his reading before he came had given him the story, which had made newspaper headlines at the time. During the year before her death, Lillie Cortis had been involved in a scandalous affair with a man called Johnny de Souza, whom the gossip columnists liked to describe as a rich playboy and philanderer, already twice divorced and on his third marriage. Drink and cocaine were variously put forward as the reason why his small aircraft, while heading across the Channel towards Le Touquet with himself and his passenger on board, after having been waved off from his private airfield, should have crashed into the sea. Nothing of the wreckage had ever been recovered.

Andrew dragged himself away from contemplation of the wall. It was time to concentrate on practicalities. Meg Landers was watching him anxiously, and said abruptly, obviously misinterpreting his long silence, 'They'll have to deal with Richenda before they pull this place down.'

'Richenda? Who is she?'

'Richenda Leigh.'

The name bobbed about on the edges of his consciousness for a while before he could capture it. Then he had it. Richenda Leigh had been another artist of the same generation as Lillie, lesser-known, now almost forgotten.

'She was Lillie's greatest friend, and she's still painting, you know. She's rather—well, eccentric. I'm not really qualified to judge, but her work seems lovely to me, though that's not something she can accept. She comes in here and looks at Lillie's frescoes then goes back to her rooms and destroys what she's done.'

'She's still painting? Good God, how old is she? And she lives here?'

'She's nearly ninety, though you'd be hard-pressed to believe it. I think she's holding on because she's afraid if she dies, there'll be no one left to care or protest about the orangery being demolished, and the frescoes with it. But she's no need to fear. The house belongs to me now, and there's no question of them being destroyed.'

He wanted, very much, to help her, touched by the combination of vulnerability and courage, perhaps stubbornness, the unexpected steeliness that wouldn't even admit the possibility of defeat. But how could she contemplate coping with the weight of all this? He'd been told that, in addition to the house, she'd been left a small inheritance—which the house was certainly capable of swallowing whole. The frescoes themselves, *in situ* as they were, could not be realized for cash—and it had to be admitted that, exciting as they were to him, and would be to Cortis aficionados, they weren't of such overriding interest to the general public as to draw in big crowds.

'But why,' he asked, 'hasn't Richenda Leigh ever made known the existence of her friend's work? She obviously recognizes its virtue.'

Meg studied him cautiously, assessingly. 'She might tell you herself. She was staying here when the frescoes were done, and she's lived here since Lillie died. No one ever told her to go, she says, so she just stayed on. Come on, she knows you're coming.'

They left the orangery the same way they'd entered, by way of the recessed door in the exuberantly painted wall, and came eventually into a set of rooms which Meg told him had once been used as the servants' quarters, and where Richenda Leigh had lived her reclusive existence ever since Lillie's death more than sixty years ago, venturing out only once in a blue moon, her wants now attended to by a woman from the village, who brought in her supplies.

Richenda Leigh was tall and thin, her gaunt frame clad in cotton trousers and a shapeless sweater, a woman who fell into that category of persons who seem ageless. She could never have been beautiful, but might have been handsome once, in a dark, gypsyish way—her hair, even now, was not white, but iron-grey, and her eyes were still luminous, dark and full of a bright and somewhat intimidating intelligence. When she spoke, it was with the voice and the vitality of someone much younger.

Meg said, 'Do you want me to make the tea before I leave you, Richenda?'

'You're not staying, then?'

'You told me you didn't want me to. I will if you've changed your mind.'

An unfathomable look passed between them. 'Please yourself.'

'Well, then, I will.'

Meg went out, and came back presently with a tray. But it wasn't until after the tea had been left to draw thoroughly and then poured that the old woman showed any signs of being willing to talk about the reason for his visit, and began to speak of the summer when Lillie had painted the frescoes.

'So, what did you think of them?' she interrupted herself. Andrew manfully sipped the now dark and bitter tea. 'I thought them—extraordinarily beautiful.'

She became very still. 'Did you now?' For a long time she was silent, then she said, 'I helped her, you know. I don't know if you're familiar with the technique of fresco painting?' He was, but she went on without waiting for an answer. 'Well, you have to work with watercolours on to wet plaster, so you must arrange to do only as much work in one stint as you can complete. First of all the cartoon of the whole conception, complete with every last detail, has to be sketched on to the plastered wall, then the section to be worked on is chipped away, replastered the next day, and the painting done straight on to it while it's still wet, joining up to the parts still to be painted—and so on. We'd been in Italy earlier in the year, studying techniques, but oh, it was hard, mucky work, I can tell you! Enormous fun, though. We worked from scaffolding, did the plastering ourselves. You have to finish each day's painting before the plaster dries—that way, it reacts chemically with the paint and becomes durable, unlike paint on dry plaster. She worked like one possessed; we both did. She was like that, you know, absolutely filled with passion for something and then letting it drop. Besides, she wanted the work finished before she went off to France with de Souza.' She paused to drain her teacup, then gazed unseeingly out of the window. 'We had never been so happy.'

There was a silence.

'Who gave her permission to paint the frescoes?'

'Permission?' She laughed, then shrugged. 'Lillie owned the house. Her father had died six months before and she couldn't wait to cover up what she called that indecently naked wall as soon as there was no one to stop her!'

'Do you have any more of her work?'

A guarded expression replaced the smile. 'A little. But I won't sell, you know.'

'I'd just like to see what there is, if I may.'

122

Another long silence. At last, she indicated a portfolio leaning against the wall. When he'd placed it on the table beside her, she laid a hand on it in an unconsciously protective gesture.

Even now she seemed undecided, then she began to hand him an assortment of work— pen and ink sketches, woodblocks, designs for book covers, several portraits done in pencil or in oil. Andrew looked through them with a mounting sense of disappointment, even bafflement. Most of them were dated and signed, and spanned several years from when Lillie must have been still at school, through her years at the Slade, right up to her death. Like the other work of hers he'd seen, they were unusual and appealing, but with little to hint at that sudden glorious blooming into maturity, evident on the orangery wall. Yet some of them were dated the same year as the frescoes.

The old woman was watching him with an inscrutable glance. She must always have been a deep and unknowable person with secret thoughts. He closed the portfolio, thinking that either Lillie's had been a somewhat uneven talent, or the frescoes had provided some sort of spur she'd been needing to express herself properly. 'What happened? To make her suddenly able to paint like that?'

She only asked, after a while, 'Are you going to recommend their preservation, then?'

123

It was his turn to avoid a direct answer. 'Before I go, will you show me some of your work, as well?'

'It's not for public consumption. I don't keep much anyway.'

The silence which followed was as uncompromising as the words themselves, until Meg broke it. 'Oh, rubbish! At least let him see those you showed me yesterday.'

Richenda gave her a severe look, but as if belatedly recognizing the need to placate this man from the Heritage Foundation, she changed her mind. 'Very well, if you must. On the table by the window. But they're of no account.'

Andrew crossed the room. Watched by a huge, malevolent tortoiseshell cat occupying the outside windowsill, he turned over the paintings and drawings in the big folder—strong, bold colours and sweeping lines, forceful work of the sort he might have expected from her. But he wasn't prepared for the shock of realization that hit him. He finished examining them and stared through the window, so hard that the cat jumped off and ran away. He looked blankly over a neat kitchen garden with brick paths and flourishing rows of lettuces, clumps of herbs and a row of peas and beans, probably Meg's doing, he thought inconsequentially. He understood several things—above all, the significance in one of the frescoes of the figure of the lover, the tall young man with his back to the viewer.

'Well?' Richenda demanded. He turned to face her. She was dunking a ginger biscuit, and as she sucked in the sloppy result, her cheeks hollowing, he felt how old she really was, saw the skull beneath the skin, the dark hairs bristling on her chin, the cunning old eyes. She was not a woman he would ever have trusted.

He said, speaking with great care, 'You're an exceptionally gifted artist, Miss Leigh. What made you give Lillie Cortis the credit for painting those frescoes?'

An old-fashioned clock with a loud tick measured the seconds away. 'Since you're so perceptive, I thought you'd have known,' she said at last, in an attempt at mockery which didn't succeed. Over sixty years had passed, and something still hurt, very much.

He shook his head. 'No, I can't imagine.'

'It was the least I could do.'

Did she mean as a tribute to her friend? The figure of the lover in the frescoes, yes, its back to the viewer, might well have been either a young man, or a woman. He had thought that the face common to all the female representations was perhaps Lillie's own face, a self-portrait, though he hadn't been sure, having only seen one grainy photograph. Now he knew for certain that it was Lillie's face— but it was not Lillie who had put it there.

'If I'd said I was the one who'd painted them, who would care?' The bitterness was

125

evident in her voice. 'But consider what Lillie's work is fetching nowadays, how popular she's become! There are people who'd do anything to save whatever she created.'

Deliberate obscurity was not, in Andrew's experience, a condition which most artists willingly sought. He still couldn't understand why Richenda had chosen to hide her talents all these years; he was appalled at the waste. Above all, why was it so important to her now that the frescoes be saved?

Later, when she lay in the hospital bed, her face drawn sideways in a stroke, he was to regret that he hadn't chosen his words more carefully. At the time, he just spoke as the thought came to him:

'It isn't the frescoes you want to keep, is it? It's the wall.'

*   *   *

'Did you know, Meg?' he asked as he was walking with her at the front of the house a month later, two days after the second stroke had killed Richenda.

She was wearing plimsolls. She kept her eye on them as she spoke, pushing the gravel forward into tiny hillocks as they walked.

'I wondered. But I couldn't work it out,' she said at last, looking up to meet his eyes. 'And even after she'd told me everything, in the hospital, I wasn't sure of her reasons; I'm still

126

not. I did guess it was Richenda who'd painted the frescoes. Apparently Lillie had asked her—she knew Richenda was the better artist, the one capable of executing something like that.'

'Were they lovers?'

'Richenda and Lillie? I don't know. I think Richenda . . . yes, perhaps . . . but Lillie . . . ? It's hard to say. She was certainly heavily involved with this Johnny de Souza character, and she'd quarrelled with Richenda over going to France with him. But in the end, by the time she met him at his private airfield, her better nature had prevailed and she'd told him she couldn't go to Le Touquet with him after all, that she must keep her promise to Richenda to help her with the fresco painting as she'd agreed. The scaffolding had been set up weeks before, with Richenda waiting for the go-ahead, camping in the empty house. It would have been a tremendous job to tackle without any help, and she decided she couldn't let Richenda down. Whatever de Souza felt, I suppose he realized there wasn't much he could do about it. His mechanic saw them both get into the plane and saw it leave, and that's why it was assumed she'd been in the crash with him. What no one except Richenda knew was that Lillie had persuaded him to land on the big field beyond Margent House and leave her there. Even Richenda hadn't known she was coming until

127

she arrived.'

They said nothing for a while. 'I wish she'd never told me, Andrew.'

He wished that, too, or that he himself had never made that fatal utterance, which had come from Lord knows where. But Andrew never repined at what might have been. Meg, and what she felt, were more important. Encouraged by the unconscious pleading as she put her small, square, capable hand on his sleeve, he took hold of it and drew her down to sit on the edge of the empty stone basin. Sparrows, using it as a dust-bath, flew away in a chirruping cloud, affronted. 'Don't go on, if you'd rather not.'

'I'm all right.' She brushed away damp tendrils of hair from her forehead. It was hot, out here in the sun. 'Well, they began on the frescoes . . . but it was far from the fun Richenda made it out to be when she was telling you. In fact, they ended up having what seems to have been a humdinger of a row, something to do with Johnny de Souza. They were working on top of the scaffolding at the time and she says Lillie was so angry she stepped too far back, fell off and was killed.'

And so Richenda had broken into the space which had been created years before when a new brick facing was built in front of what had been the outer stone wall of the house, in order to make a new, smooth, inside wall for the orangery. She had put Lillie's body in the cavity, bricked it up again and plastered over it, afterwards covering the whole wall with that vibrant creation.

'Or that's what Richenda *says* happened, Meg.'

'It's possible. She must have been a strong woman then, she had the expertise. She'd already completed the cartoon on to the wall, so she'd only have needed to chip away as much of the last panel as necessary and then work at the brickwork until there was enough room to push Lillie through. Brick it up again, replaster, redraw that part of the cartoon, and continue the painting as though nothing had happened.'

'I'm not questioning that it's possible—but why did she need to do it, if Lillie's fall was an accident, as she says? Don't you think it's more likely the quarrel ended with her somehow killing Lillie, in a way that would leave no room for doubt if ever her body were found? But then, when she heard of de Souza's plane crash and the report that Lillie had apparently been killed with him, she knew she'd only have to pretend—if it were ever queried—that Lillie had painted the frescoes before she left with him.'

Meg stared into the empty pool basin as if seeing her reflection in imaginary water.

'Who's to know now what the truth really is? Except that she must always have been terrified that one day the orangery would be dismantled and Lillie's remains found—proving Lillie couldn't have painted the wall. One can almost pity her—it stopped her from ever letting her own work be seen—after all, anyone who saw both and knows about such things would have seen straight away they were the work of the same person—as you did. She's had to live with what happened all her life—she couldn't have lasted much longer and she probably thought she was going to get away with it. Then I came along. Her only hope was that the frescoes being attributed to Lillie would provide a good argument against destroying the wall.' She paused, and trailed her fingers along the friable stone of the basin, gave him a quick glance. 'And it will . . . Won't it?'

Richenda's tortoiseshell cat, which had been moping and become much thinner since her removal to hospital, strolled around the corner, found a bed of nepeta, rolled ecstatically around in it and then came to brush against Meg's legs, finally acknowledging new ownership. It sat at her feet in the sphinx position, its slitted eyes blinking in the sun, smelling of catmint.

'Are you saying what I think you're saying, Meg?'

'Why not?'

'Because—' He stopped. He thought briefly of his small, one-bedroom flat in one of the nicer parts of Belsize Park, his carefully organized ambitions, and knew he had been committed to Meg Landers and this crazy, quixotic enterprise she was determined on almost from the first moment he'd set eyes on her. He considered the concepts of justice and truth, and one woman's wasted life. He thought of the ruined frescoes.

She repeated her question.

He didn't really see why not.

THE UN-DEAR DEPARTED

Gordon McGregor would never have forked out all that money for his wife's new dress if he'd known she was going to die before she'd had the chance to wear it. But that was something which hadn't been decided upon at the time.

It wasn't that he was mean, of course not, despite his Scottish name and ancestry, just that he was careful, and abhorred waste.

'Bought it early enough, haven't you?' he grumbled, reluctantly adding the amount to her monthly housekeeping. 'The firm's dinner dance isn't until September, and it's only April.'

'It was too good a bargain to miss, from that new shop off Princes Street in Edinburgh. Surely you don't begrudge it! And don't forget, the Brodies will be at the dance,' Carrie added cannily, knowing that Gordon would never risk being thought niggardly by his boss in the matter of his wife's clothing allowance. 'Morag spends ten times this on her clothes.'

Which was probably why Donald Brodie had ulcers, along with his MD's chair. But Morag Brodie didn't need to spend money on clothes, she would have looked good in a sack. Even better in the sack, thought Gordon, with a rare touch of humour and more than a touch of envy.

He looked at Carrie, parading around in the new dress—an original model from the twenties, scarcely worn, she enthused—in olive green, beaded georgette, knee-length and with handkerchief points. She did a Charleston kick and twirled the long amber beads she'd bought to complete the outfit. 'Like it?'

'Very nice,' Gordon said, untruthfully. It was terrible. And second-hand! But then, she'd never had any taste. The colour was awful, and it was straight up and down, which Carrie certainly wasn't.

Sensing his criticism, she added quickly, 'It'll look even better when I've lost some more weight—it's coming off very nicely, hadn't you noticed?'

Gordon looked at her more closely. He knew all about Carrie losing weight; she'd been trying to shed the pounds throughout their married life. But he saw that this time the diet, or whatever, was working, she was indeed quite a bit slimmer than she had been. Though there was still a very long way to go. And the green of the frock did bring out the reddish lights in her hair—or had she had it tinted? Good heavens, she was looking quite—

'Pretty' was the word that came to mind, and might have been applicable, had she not just then done another chassis that made the floor shake. No one could be pretty, galumphing around like an elephant in a dress that would only have looked good on someone forty pounds lighter—someone like Morag Brodie, for instance.

He fetched up a sigh. He was a realist and knew that whatever Morag looked like, she wasn't a good wife for a man. Whereas Carrie—well, it had to be admitted that he was the envy of the colleagues whom he invited to dinner on a rota basis, in the interests of oiling the wheels of good working relationships. To do her justice, she was a capable hostess and kept the house shining and spotless, and she was an excellent cook (this was half her trouble—she enjoyed her own cooking too much). But there was more to marriage than that.

The truth was, he had made a big mistake— one of his few mistakes—in marrying her. They were no longer on the same wavelength, if ever they had been. He enjoyed serious music, whereas it only sent her to sleep; he liked to take long cycle rides out of Edinburgh and into the country, but she was too fat for cycling nowadays; and he read widely, mostly political biographies, for which pursuit she lacked the intellectual capacity. A bit of gardening and bridge every Tuesday afternoon was about her limit; both, in his opinion, a trivial waste of time. And she talked too much, about nothing that was important. She had got into a rut, she could no longer surprise him. But divorce was out of the question, Donald

134

Brodie was a 'Wee Free', a member of the Free Presbyterian Church, a religious fanatic who disapproved of divorce.

His reverie was cut short. 'You've been so generous about this dress, Gordon,' Carrie said, her eyes filling with tears. 'I—I've been thinking, maybe we ought to do things together more. It's not good for you to spend so much time alone. I've decided to go with you to the Highlands this year. I could do with a holiday, and the exercise will help me take off a few more pounds.'

He felt as though he'd trodden on a step that wasn't there.

His twice-yearly solitary walking holidays in the Scottish Highlands were beacons lighting the boring dreariness of his life with Carrie. He pored over maps and planned his routes for weeks on end. He had sussed out a series of small hotels, unfashionable and sometimes remote, but where the whisky was excellent, the food plentiful and hot baths were readily available to soak his pleasantly weary limbs at the end of the day. But often he took a tent in his backpack and slept in the heather, so that he could make long, circular trips over difficult, testing terrain rather than having to walk just so far and then turn back. The memory of the wonderful silence and solitude of the high hills and the deep lochs between, the sense of freedom, was what kept him going throughout the rest of the year. He wanted no companion with him, least of all his stupid, chattering wife.

'We can stay near Mallaig as we did last time,' she said with that silly, breathless laugh that got on his nerves. 'We'll take the car into Fort William to the shops, I'll get some lovely woollens, perhaps a kilt ...'

The thought of Carrie in a kilt nearly eclipsed his surprise at remembering they had indeed once been accustomed to spending their holidays together in the Western Isles. But that had been years ago, when Carrie was more active than she was now—and anyway, the walks they'd taken even then along the lochsides had been tame, without any sense of achievement, compared with the tough, boulder-strewn ascents he now attempted.

He could, however, think of no reasonable excuse to prevent her from accompanying him, which was why, in May, before the midges made life a misery, he found himself duly installed with Carrie at a small hotel with all mod cons, in a double bedroom with *en suite* bathroom, dressing up for dinner every night, on Carrie's insistence, though the hotel had a relaxed dress code and he was usually the only man to wear a tie.

The weather, as it so often was during May, was glorious, and every day they walked— walks; however, that were to Gordon so gentle they were little more than a limbering-up. He grew ever more frustrated at wasting his precious holiday puttering about when he could have been covering miles, legging it out to the top of some distant mountain, perhaps in the Cairngorms. Now, it was hardly worth donning his walking gear, his favourite old boots.

There was some compensation in that the hotel faced the sea, and he was able to slip out, blessedly alone, and walk along the shore every evening before bed, while Carrie put up her aching legs and read her magazines and wrote postcards and letters in the hotel lounge. He was happy enough to leave her to those long, interminable letters, while outside, where it was light enough to read a newspaper until after ten, he watched the magnificent sunsets behind the chain of blue islands across the bay, behind Eigg and Rhum and Skye, and thought his dark thoughts. Small brown dunlins and elegant oystercatchers waded at the edges of the glassy-calm sea, brooding cormorants stretched heraldic wings; there was total silence, save for the gentle splash of a wave on the white sands. Occasionally a magnificent stag could be seen on the skyline of the hills that swept down to the shoreline. Once, he caught a glimpse of the round, wet head of a sea otter.

Gordon wondered if he could bring himself to do it.

Towards the end of the first week—another week to be got through, my God!—Carrie played into his hands by deciding she was ready for something more strenuous than the four or five miles a day on the flat which had hitherto been as much as she could manage. They would make a sentimental journey, a round trip, one which they'd made many times in their younger days.

It was a complicated arrangement, which involved Gordon parking their car at a strategic point alongside one of the lochs, and walking several miles back to the small railway station where he had left Carrie to wait. One of the very few trains of the day would then take them to the point where they could board the mailboat which plied beween the outlying homesteads, following the rugged coastline. The next sea loch probed far inland, and at a tiny bay they would be rowed ashore in a small boat, thence to climb over the hill and down to the original lochside. A long walk back to their car ensued. Complicated, yes, but it might suit Gordon very well.

The path they took, after they'd been put ashore, zigzagged and switchbacked up and down to accommodate the lie of the land, but Carrie wasn't deterred. She set off in fine style as they climbed higher and higher, chattering happily and exclaiming at the blueness of the sky, giggling as she slipped and slid on the rough scree in her light, inadequate boots. 'Whoops!'

'Save your breath and watch your step,'

Gordon told her dourly. 'The path gets gey rough ahead.' It never took him long to lapse into broader Scots whenever his feet touched Highland soil. 'And it's boggy where it turns away from the lochside.'

'I can see why it has to,' Carrie said, panting gamely on. 'You'd never get across some of those rocks. They look terrifying.'

'You have to cross them at some places,' Gordon reminded her, 'so keep your mind on what you're doing. One slip and you'll be down in the loch.'

Which was reputed to have temperatures in which no one could survive for long, to be deeper than Loch Ness, and to shelter a monster older, twice as big and three times as fearsome.

'No thanks,' Carrie answered with another laugh, 'I'll take care. How about a rest and some lunch?'

A rest? They hadn't been going more than an hour! And they were progressing nowhere near as fast as Gordon thought they should be. In order not to have to keep hanging about waiting for Carrie to catch up, he was bringing up the rear—and what a rear! He averted his eyes from the solid rump in unflattering trousers and bent to drink from one of the bright, narrow streams that gushed down the hillside. He had just cupped a handful of the wonderful, icy water when Carrie turned and screamed, 'Oh, don't! It might not be safe!'

139

'Safe?' Gordon gazed at the clear, peaty water trickling from his fingers.

'You never know, a sheep might have—well, you know—in it, higher up. You might catch something horrible, like liver-fluke or scrapie. Anthrax, even.'

He knew he'd never be able to drink from a mountain stream again.

She had found a patch of sheep-bitten, sun-warmed grass in front of a granite outcrop above a sheer drop to the loch, where they could sit and eat their refreshments, with the sun on their faces. She was blessedly silent as she ate her pot of cottage cheese and an apple, then poured coffee from the Thermos. Presently, she closed her eyes.

Gordon sat with his gaze on the hills opposite, grey-green and treeless, looking smooth and innocuous, but wickedly deceptive as to the reality, with pockets of snow where the sun never reached still lodged at the summit. He'd walked up there, one autumn day, leaving even the sheep behind, up into deer country, where the wind had been so strong it had lifted the liquid coffee straight from his cup. Coming down, he'd walked into damp mist and lost his way, mistaken a sheep track for the path and nearly walked into a bog. As he paused to reorientate and get his bearings, the wind had blown the mist away and the sun came out brilliantly, in the sudden way it did in these parts. And there in front of

140

him was a small, hidden, silver lochan, fringed with reeds, reflecting light from the sky, with a golden eagle riding the high, empty air above. A sight that pierced his heart, never to be forgotten. Och, that was what it was all about . . . How he envied that eagle! If he had no encumbrances, no Carrie, no office politics, no Ian Cameron (his assistant at the office who was just waiting to cut his chair legs from under him) . . . If only. How many times had he thought of giving it all up, buying a croft miles from anywhere and spending the rest of his life here, alone . . .

'I think,' said Carrie, 'I think I should try to find some green one-bar shoes with Louis heels—'

'What?'

'To go with my dress. Perhaps I could have them dyed to match.'

People had been murdered for infinitely less.

'Shall we go?' He stood up, breathing heavily, repacked his haversack with all the gear he thought it necessary to have with him and slung it on his shoulders, and Carrie did likewise with hers. 'Come here,' he said. 'Let me adjust that, it can't be comfortable the way you have it.'

She came and stood meekly with her back to him. He reached out to grab her shoulders, ready to push, and at that moment she stepped sideways. He lurched forwards and, top-heavy

141

with his backpack, began a slithering career towards the edge, his heavy boots offering no purchase on the thin grass. For a moment he floundered, a second later he was gone. There was one hoarse cry, like the sound of a gull, and then silence.

Carrie cautiously approached the edge. Gordon was a big man, his backpack was heavy and his old-fashioned walking boots weighed a ton. The water was clear, right down to the bottom. She could see the outline of the rocks and Gordon lying on them. There was no way she, or anyone else, could get down to help him, even if it hadn't been too late. The rescue services would have to come in by boat to recover his body, after she had contacted them.

It was a long walk back to the car, but there was no hurry, and she had plenty to think about on the way there. In particular the good news she had to give Ian Cameron when she wrote to him as usual that night. About how easy it had been, after all. About the time it would be prudent to spend as a sorrowing widow. Until the annual dance, perhaps, when she, newly slim, supposedly through grief, would allow herself to be persuaded to accompany him, wearing the olive-green dress that he'd helped her to choose for the occasion.

TIME'S WINGÉD CHARIOT

Retirement had loomed large for Spencer Harrison during the last twelve months, and considerably more so for his wife, Eunice. Inevitably, it was now here, and to celebrate, Spencer had put two bottles of champagne on ice. He and Eunice lay on garden chairs in the hot sunshine, waiting to drink them. The salmon mayonnaise and the raspberries and cream to follow stood ready in the fridge.

'I think,' Spencer said, 'I can run the track fairly easily round that maple.'

Eunice wasn't listening. She lay back in the garden chair, hoping they could get this business over quickly so that she could go back to her summer pruning. Leaning over, she tugged at a daisy between the paving. The state of her hands was deplorable, but she didn't care for wearing gloves. She enjoyed the cool, green feeling of tiny plants and the sensuousness of sweet, crumbling earth between her fingers. She was large and placid, with a fair, bland face and a patient, plodding walk.

The garden had daunted other buyers, twenty years ago. Disproportionately large in relation to the size of the house, and encompassing to one side a steep and desolate jungle, bramble and weed-infested, where once stone had been gouged from the hillside, it had, however, rejoiced Eunice's heart with its challenges and possibilities. Spencer had bought the house for Eunice even before his first wife—Eunice's best friend, as it happened—had astonished him and left him, without so much as a word or a note, but at least sparing him the inconvenience and expense of the divorce he would never have got around to asking for.

Behind the house now stretched smooth lawns and herbaceous borders, while to the side the old quarry cascaded with rock plants in season, intersected by winding paths. High up, a small ornamental bridge crossed a narrow crevasse down which a bright, natural stream tumbled from above, providing moisture for the heathers, rhododendrons and azaleas which bordered it. All the work had been done by Eunice. She was a strong woman and lifted large rockery stones or wheeled heavy barrowloads of timber for constructing the bridge more easily—or at any rate more willingly—than Spencer would have done. He did not share her obsession.

The garden was indeed beautiful, but above all it was quiet, blessedly quiet. Apart from the gentle splash of the stream, the sounds were all of bees buzzing, leaves falling, birdsong in the springtime and the wind in the trees. Not a clock within earshot.

If Eunice's passion was gardening, Spencer's was clocks. Twenty-three at the last count, disposed in various parts of the house: the grandfather—which she must remember to call the longcase clock—in the hall, the Viennese wall-clock half-way up the stairs, the French carriage clock whose moods varied with the temperature, the sheep's-head country clock whose wooden works were riddled with worm, the skeleton clock in the dining-room, the hideous black marble and ormolu mantelpiece set. Spencer was incapable of doing things by halves.

The clocks were the only things ever seriously to disturb Eunice's placidity. The relentless chimes and strikes counting and measuring out the quarter-hours of her life drove her mad, while their constant ticking was like the Chinese water torture to her. Throughout the day, throughout the night, they ticked and chimed and struck, the silvery tones of the walnut bracket clock vying with the loud bong of the kitchen wall-clock and the double strike and the slow, measured thunk of the grandfather—the longcase—not to mention the Westminster chimes on the landing and the Whittington ones in the study.

It was no use stopping them while Spencer was out at work, because starting them again put the chimes and strikes out of kilter. Spencer's rage when this happened made even the noise of the clocks seem easy to bear He had been a British Army sergeant once, and still wore a stiff moustache and a bristly haircut. He was compact and muscular. His temper was nasty when roused.

The years with Spencer had, after all, been no big deal, and Eunice sometimes wondered if the clocks were a punishment for the wrong done to his first wife. But at least now she was spared the worst atrocity of the lot: a wooden wall-clock decorated with garish Highland scenes and 'A Souvenir from o'er the Border' painted around the face, with the long and repetitious tune of 'The Bluebells of Scotland' marking the quarters. Several years ago they'd been burgled and it had been lost, along with some ugly Victorian silver that had belonged to Spencer's mother. The police, thank God, had found neither clock nor silver.

Spencer lifted the first bottle of champagne from the bucket, uncorked it faultlessly and poured it so they might toast his future retirement. He could have stayed on until he was sixty-five, but he'd elected to go at sixty. 'Well, you please yourself,' Eunice had said, 'but you, retiring at sixty? You're a young man yet!'

He wasn't going to disagree with that, but she hadn't fooled him. She didn't want him under her feet all day, keeping her from her confounded garden. Their garden, upon which his own eye had now lit.

He wasn't going to be idle, he told her. He had plans for his retirement. Weekly trips to the library. Auctions where he might find the odd clock bargain. Visits to stately homes. Railway museums. He didn't mention the holidays abroad, he knew she'd never be persuaded to leave her garden.

He was full of the little economies they might make, too, and began to list them as the wine loosened his tongue—Eunice could dispense with the services of Mrs Cathcart, who presently came twice a week, because he wasn't a man who was afraid of turning his hand to a bit of help with the housework. And he would make their own wine, he added, gazing reflectively into his Sainsbury's champagne-type bubbles. Of course, they'd get rid of Eunice's car—not that they'd get anything for it, B-reg and all that, but they'd save on the tax and insurance.

Eunice, who'd heard all this before and had succeeded in coming to terms with what was going to happen by so far ignoring it, sipped her wine. She was totally unprepared when Spencer dropped his bombshell. 'I think,' he remarked, evidently continuing something he'd begun earlier, 'the track can run along there'—pointing to her herbaceous border—'and come along to the tunnel which I'll make here.'

'There' appeared to go smack through the middle of the magnificent clump of lilium regale that had taken years to establish. 'Here' was just where the small rockery was, a little beyond the flagged path outside the French windows. Looking at it, Eunice's heart, not normally a volatile organ, jumped about like a wild thing inside her ribcage. She felt sick. The moment she'd dreaded for years was here.

'Track?' she echoed faintly. 'What track?'

'My steam railway track. I knew you weren't listening.' He repeated what he'd said before and outlined its proposed route through the peonies, skirting the Japanese maple, with a little station, maybe, at that point, there . . . where this year Nevada excelled herself in a huge arched spread of white fragrance. 'I've always wanted a steam railway, ever since I was a lad.'

Eunice's horrified mind took in the enormity of what he was saying, and what she was going to have to do. She looked around at her beautiful garden. 'You have? I never knew.'

'Oh, yes, dear, I've been planning it for years,' he said.

*   *   *

The next morning, Eunice went into town to do some shopping. Before she went, she announced that if the track was to go through the rockery by the French window the stones and some of the plants would need to be moved, and she'd do it on Tuesday.

'Isn't it a bad time of year for moving plants?'

'I'll settle them in plenty of peat—they

148

won't realize they've been moved. There's a nice shady place for them on the other side of the bridge.'

Spencer was very busy while she was out. Afterwards, he cleaned up the tools and put them all back in place so that she wouldn't notice they'd been used.

It was raining the next day, but that didn't prevent Eunice starting on the job. He watched her from the kitchen window, monolithic in a shapeless old waterproof garment and gumboots, patiently trudging up the steep, narrow path of the quarry with her first barrowload of stones.

He knew how she hated his precious clocks, though she'd long ago given up saying so. After that burglary, in fact. She'd been very shifty about it and he'd suspected for years why the police had never been able to trace any of those stolen goods—the Scottish clock and the silver, taken while he was away on a business trip. It had been fairly obvious, knowing Eunice as he did, that to get rid of them she'd bury them somewhere in the garden, but where, in a garden this size? He'd known that one day, if he waited, she'd give herself away and he'd find out what she'd done with them.

She'd gone white when he'd mentioned tunnelling under that rockery.

There was the second bottle of champagne left from Sunday, nearly full. Eunice had suddenly seemed to lose her taste for it after

149

his announcement about the rockery. He'd corked it up again with one of those gizmos that was supposed to keep it drinkable, and put it back in the fridge. It shouldn't be too bad.

He took it out and poured a glass, holding it in readiness as Eunice came to the bridge with the heavy barrow. She paused and lowered it, and he began to sweat. She wasn't going to cross after all. But, after a moment, she lifted the barrow again and moved. When she reached the middle, the planks he'd loosened yesterday gave with the heavy weight and he watched his wife, jerked forward and off balance as the barrow tipped, tumble down the steep crevasse of the stream, with the barrowload of stones on top of her. He smiled and lifted his glass. Now he could go out and finish the job she'd started. No chance of salvaging anything much of his clock by this time, but at least he'd have proof of her perfidy, and justification for what he'd done. He tipped the glass and drained the champagne.

The clocks all over the house began to chime eleven o'clock as Spencer Harrison died from the Paraquat put into the champagne bottle by his wife. Outside, under the aubrietia and alyssum and miniature junipers by the French windows, the first Mrs Harrison, put there by Eunice before she constructed her rockery twenty years ago, slept on undisturbed.

150

JOURNEY'S END

The train was just about to leave Platform 9 at Euston station when the boy with the backpack loped towards the open doors and with great energy sprang on board.

'Excuse me, sir,' he asked, sticking his head into the carriage and addressing the passenger in the nearest seat, 'but is this the train for Milton Keynes?'

'I hope so,' said Eliot Voysey. 'That's where I'm going.'

'Great! Thanks.'

The boy stepped further inside, seconds before the doors closed and the whistle blew. He struggled to separate himself from his gigantic backpack and heaved it on to the rack as the train began to slide out of the station, before throwing himself down opposite Eliot, taking the aisle seat and politely folding his long legs out of the way of the old man's walking-stick. 'Close!' he grinned. A wide, white smile. Not a whit out of breath. He was broad-shouldered, tanned and had a clean-cut, college-boy appearance. American, or possibly Canadian, thought Eliot, acknowledging the remark with a smile of his own before going back to his reading.

Five minutes along the line came the announcement, 'Ladies and gentlemen, this is the 14.04 train from London Euston to Milton Keynes Central, calling at Harrow and Wealdstone, Bushey, Watford Junction . . . '

The boy laughed outright as the disembodied voice droned on, and the train forged ahead. 'They always do that?'

'Hmm? Do what?' asked Eliot absently, looking up from his proofs.

'Wait until the train sets off before they tell you where it's going? I mean—too bad if you're on the wrong one after all!' And then he blushed, as though his frank amusement might be taken for criticism.

'Frequently,' replied Eliot drily, who did his own share of criticizing a chaotic system he was forced to endure, despite his age, on a regular basis: almost every time he came up to London to see his publisher, or for his medical treatments, in fact. 'Fortunately the next station's not far. One could always alight and get a train back.'

'Oh, right.' Obviously reassured by Eliot's ironic tone that he hadn't put his foot in it, unwittingly transgressed some code of British etiquette, the boy's embarrassment receded. He relaxed and leaned forward, hands clasped loosely between his knees, seemingly fascinated by the unedifying prospect of the north London suburbs now flashing past.

'You've been to Milton Keynes before?' Eliot asked after a few moments, abandoning the small print as too difficult to read in the swaying train. The lad seemed likeable and inclined to talk, there was an hour to fill to the end of the journey, and at this time of day they were the only passengers in the carriage. Later, in the rush hour, every train in this direction would be packed to suffocation with commuters and their infernal mobile phones.

'No, it's my first visit . . . and while I'm there, I've a mind to see the place where my grandad was stationed during the war, though I never knew him. As a matter of fact, neither did my father. He was killed just before Dad was born.'

'Air crew?' There had been American Air Force bases locally.

'No, he wasn't killed on operations. He—er, died in an air raid on London, went up on a weekend pass and never came back.' Unexpressed was the youthful wish that he'd been able to claim a more heroic end for his unknown grandfather—that he'd been a bomber or a fighter pilot, maybe, going down in a blaze of glory—and he didn't notice the sudden tightening of Eliot's hand around the knob of his stick. 'Though I guess he did his share,' he added fairly. 'He was in the Canadian Air Force, but he was one of those what you call 'ems—boffins?—attached to that hush-hush place. Bletchley Park, wasn't it called?'

'Was he indeed? Then you've reason to be proud of him,' Eliot said quietly. 'What was he—a cryptanalyst?'

'A mathematician. Actually, I guess he was pretty bright.'

'He wouldn't have been there if not. Only the *crème de la crème* were recruited to work there.'

The boy looked pleased at that. 'You knew it during the war?'

Eliot nodded. 'I lived nearby. I'm still not far away.'

The question took him back more than fifty years. To when the small town of Bletchley and its surrounding villages had suddenly found themselves bursting at the seams with people billeted in every house that had a spare bed, the railway station was thronged, the pubs in the evenings packed and noisy. There'd been little petrol for private cars in wartime, and mostly you had to rely on clapped-out buses and bicycles for transport, but the sound of motorcycles revving through hitherto sleepy villages had been heard night and day, with dispatch riders bringing, as was revealed later, secret messages for the Park.

For Bletchley Park, a Victorian mansion then owned by the Government, otherwise known as Station X, had formed the hub of British wartime intelligence. Few people had known the full extent of its operations at the time—not even those who worked there— not then, or for thirty years afterwards. It had been the most famously guarded wartime secret in the British Isles. In fact, the work done there was now generally accepted to have shortened the war by several years, through its breaking of enemy codes and ciphers, notably the fiendishly complicated Enigma code, which the Germans had arrogantly believed unbreakable. Proving them wrong had been a momentous achievement which provided the chief means of gaining access to the enemy's secrets. In order to accomplish this daunting task, hundreds of men and women had been recruited, the brightest and best brains in the country: academics, linguists, teachers, promising young luminaries from universities, experts from the armed forces. They were forbidden by the Official Secrets Act to talk about their work, and they did not. Considering that the numbers who were eventually employed there grew into several thousands, this was scarcely less amazing than the scope of the work itself.

Rumours had, of course, flown around among the local populace as to what exactly was going on at the Park. All those fit and able young men with cushy jobs, when they should have been in uniform, on active service, tutted the old biddies of Stoke Peverel, knitting scarves and balaclava helmets for all they were worth. At the vicarage, next to the Norman church, where Eliot lived with his aunt and uncle, one or two intelligent guesses were put forth which, many years later, turned out to have been not so far off the mark. But at the time, no one involved could be drawn to comment on the nature of their work.

'May I ask your name?' Eliot asked the boy, somewhat abruptly.

'Ian Sutherland.'

Sutherland. So. It didn't, after what had already been said, come as a surprise. Eliot felt he'd always known this time would arrive, one day, and likely when he least expected it. At his age, he had long since ceased to believe that coincidences don't happen, but—the chances of meeting this particular person here, at this precise time? It was unfortunate, to say the least, in view of what Eliot was now expecting to occur hourly, and had been ever since he'd seen the first men with their theodolites, measuring up for the new housing estate near Stoke Peverel. The letter in his wallet, still unread after its receipt three weeks ago, felt to be burning a hole through his pocket.

A pause had fallen while these disturbing thoughts passed through his mind. The boy, who was looking at him curiously, evidently wondering at the effect of his name on the old man, broke the silence by saying uncertainly, 'My folks left Scotland and settled in Vancouver, way back.' An explanation seemed to strike him. 'Hey! You didn't by any chance know him? He was Ian Sutherland, too. I was named for him.'

'Indeed I did,' Eliot was bound to admit,

falling silent again while the boy registered his amazement at the coincidence, the train drew into busy Watford, and he himself gathered his wits against the onslaught of questions that was sure to come, the battering of memories and emotions he'd tried to ignore for over fifty years. 'It's not so surprising, really,' he said eventually, waiting until a couple of passengers entered the carriage, but passed through into the next one. It was a stopping train, no more than five minutes between stations now. He'd have done better to wait for the through train—and then he wouldn't have met this young man and been faced with things he would rather not have faced. But it was impossible to extricate himself now, there was more than half an hour to go, and Sutherland's grandson had a right to know what little could be told. 'I came to know quite a lot of those who worked at the Park. My name's Voysey, by the way—Eliot Voysey.' He extended his hand which the boy gripped warmly.

'Did you work there too, sir?'

'No, no! I'd just left college and come back to live with my aunt for the duration, to replace a teacher in the village school who'd enlisted for the Navy. I myself was never called up because of this.' He tapped his lame leg. He had long ago lost the frustration, the shame of not being able to do his bit for his country, like his peers, but he could still remember how it had felt. 'My aunt and uncle kept open house at the vicarage for any of the people from the Park who cared to drop in after church on Sundays, and quite a lot of them did, and on other evenings as well. Sandwiches, you know, bit of cake or a biscuit, cup of coffee. God knows how my aunt did it with the rationing, but she was a redoubtable lady, and people helped out . . . Your grandfather used to play the piano for us, quite beautifully, I remember. He had hands just like yours.'

He nodded towards the boy's large, powerful hands, like his grandfather's, big enough to be able to span an octave and a half, no doubt. And he remembered the first Ian's hands around Leonie's waist as she stood on tiptoe to let him kiss her goodnight, before mounting her bicycle and riding off to the big, rambling old manor house nearby where she was billeted with dozens of other Wrens.

She had a tiny waist, not disguised by the trim, crisp WRNS uniform, the white shirt, neat navy jacket and skirt, the saucy hat, much preferable to the lumpen uniforms the WAAF or the ATS were compelled to wear. Perish the thought that she'd chosen to join the WRNS simply because of the uniform— but there was no denying it was very becoming, and emphasized her delicate colouring, the pale skin, the dark brown hair, the only truly deep violet eyes he had ever seen. Eliot, twenty years old and fathoms deep in love, knew he would never love anyone else, and realized bitterly that his passion must forever remain his own secret—though if all the circumstances had been otherwise, he might have been encouraged to hope things could have been different. For he and Leonie shared the same sense of humour, enjoyed discussing the books they'd read, she encouraged him in his ambition to believe he might have a worthwhile future as a historian when the war was over—a faith in him which had been more than justified.

Ian was saying, ruefully, 'I'm afraid I haven't inherited my grandfather's talent for math, but I play the piano, too. I'm over here on a music scholarship, as it happens. I—I'd really like to know what you remember about him, sir.'

'Mostly his piano-playing,' Eliot replied, which was being a little more than economical with the truth, considering that the events of those last few days were engraved on his mind as if on tablets of stone, embedded in the silence of the years. And those other thoughts, which flowed like a dark, subterranean stream under the surface, things for years forgotten, or deliberately not remembered . . . those hot summer evenings, the windows open to the scents of the vicarage garden as the sun went down (had ever roses smelt as sweet since?), no lights switched on because of the blackout regulations, just the glow of the sunset filtering into the shadowed room as Sutherland played Chopin, Beethoven sonatas, Schubert. Able to conjure up magic from the piano keys, unable to take his eyes off Leonie, in the dusk pale and insubstantial as a moth. Martin Youlgreave watching them both, and he, Eliot Voysey, quiet, bookish, destined to be nothing but the watcher of them all. Up to a dozen people, besides himself and his aunt and uncle, might have been there at any one of those times, but Eliot only ever remembered these three.

Being physically handicapped guaranteed a certain anonymity, Eliot had already come to acknowledge with some cynicism, as if his brain must be as imperfect as his body. None of them, he was sure, realized how much he knew, or saw. Sutherland, in particular, was careless in his presence. And Youlgreave, brilliant and mercurial, who only came to these little gatherings because of Leonie, patronized him.

Eliot had been almost preternaturally aware of Youlgreave's jealousy, the level of emotional intensity radiating from him as if he had a fever. He couldn't believe Leonie wasn't aware of it, too. Perhaps she was. At any rate, she rather too pointedly ignored Youlgreave, all her interest being focused on the big Canadian in his smart uniform, though he was no oil painting beside the romantically good-looking Youlgreave, a floppy-haired Byronic figure in civilian shirtsleeves and open neck. Every woman in the vicinity—according

160

to Aunt Edith, who was a sharp observer of human nature—was ready to throw herself at the feet of this personable young man, especially since he was the proud possessor of an old Alvis, which was a great draw for the girls. But he scorned them all. His sights were fixed on Leonie . . . and might as well have been fixed on the moon, with Sutherland on the scene.

But even before Sutherland, Martin Youlgreave could surely never have meant more than a passing wartime fancy to Leonie Devenish, daughter of a wealthy upper-class family who had a large formal house in the country, and had owned another in London until the threat of war had forced its prudent sale. A debutante who, had it not been for the war, would have been dividing her time between coming-out balls, lunching at Claridge's, dining at the Savoy, shopping in Knightsbridge, wearing Schiaparelli frocks, and being seen at Henley and Ascot. Expected to be on the lookout for a husband from within her own class. She had, in fact, worn an engagement ring when she'd first joined them at those evening get-togethers, but her fiancé was never mentioned, and later the ring was not in evidence.

However, Leonie was not a natural social butterfly, but a clever girl who had been well and expensively educated, and when she'd joined the WRNS, was snapped up immediately for work at Bletchley.

How could Martin Youlgreave, handsome and intelligent, but far below her in the social sphere, ever have believed that anything lasting could come of a relationship with her, at a time when social distinctions mattered enormously—more than they ever would again? But he could, of course—his ambition was in every way as boundless as his conceit. He had emerged from Cambridge as one of its most brilliant mathematical minds, his future assured, already a star, and had been one of the first of those approached to work at Bletchley. Perhaps this had encouraged him to forget that his humble origins (he was a grammar-school boy, whose father was a clerk in local government in a small Midlands town) would forever preclude him from anything more than a casual romance with Leonie. It was as doomed as Eliot's own hopeless passion for her.

Eliot had never been sure how far the affair between them had progressed before the arrival of the Canadian, if indeed it had progressed so far as to be called an affair at all. But it was patently obvious that Youlgreave now mattered no more to her than did Eliot himself, who reflected moodily that at least Youlgreave and he had that one thing in common—although to Eliot, Leonie was always kind. But kindness was not what Eliot wanted from any woman, much less Leonie.

He had felt crushed with the weight of his hopelessness. Until the night he had overheard that conversation.

He became aware that young Ian, who seemed possessed of the transatlantic passion for facts, was now asking eagerly about the ruins of the moated castle which appeared unexpectedly beside the railway line as the train pulled into the next station. Eliot was, historically speaking, on firm ground here, his own territory: Berkhamsted Castle was where William the Conqueror had accepted the surrender of the Saxons in 1066, he informed the boy.

'Wow! I'm impressed. Is Milton Keynes as old as this?'

Eliot smiled. 'It could scarcely be more different!' He explained that until the 1960s Milton Keynes had been a small village which now stretched out its tentacles to encompass neighbouring villages until they were suburbs of what had grown to be a substantial city, a New Town purposely designed to accommodate the housing shortages still felt after the war. 'And they're still building. Round my own village, too. One of these days, there'll be no space left between. They'll have joined up.'

And once again, Eliot's heart jumped at the thought of those flattened acres of farmland around Stoke Peverel, destined to become another prestigious housing development,

163

together with the ancient tithe barn whose owners, after many years of wrangling, had obtained planning permission for its conversion into a dwelling. Now neglected and derelict, fifty years ago it had stood in a field, a secluded trysting-place where lovers often met.

Eliot had never been a violent young man. His disastrous fall at the age of ten, out of a tree from which he'd been scrumping apples, laming him for life, would in any case have precluded violent encounters of a physical nature, but he was basically peaceful and retiring. He'd never asked anything more than to live the quiet and studious life he'd planned, though paradoxically, when the war came, he found it a terrible thing to feel so useless, not to have the chance to fight for his country.

However, whether Eliot was violent or not, the conversation he had overheard that evening had enraged him to a degree not known before or since.

He had been reading in his aunt's garden, lying propped on his elbow, on the lawn under the big copper beech, when Leonie and Sutherland had come outside, carrying their coffee. They had seen him there and moved away to talk—but Sutherland had barely bothered to lower his voice, which had a carrying quality and was quite audible to Eliot. He'd made no effort to get up—with his disability, getting to his feet was an undignified proceeding, best done when no one else was

164

there to see him, or worse, offer to help. He had always hated pity. But anger made him stay where he was, as well—the assumption that he was of so little consequence to Sutherland that what he had to say to Leonie couldn't possibly concern him.

It was the mention of the hotel which alerted Eliot and made him listen unashamedly.

Brundell's, he heard, recognizing it immediately as the hotel where his aunt had always stayed on her visits to London, before the war. Shabby in a genteel way, all faded cretonne chair covers, dusty velvet curtains, sagging armchairs, rather worn carpets and elderly waiters, renowned for its unimaginative but reliable cooking. Aunt Edith had once taken him there for tea on his birthday—numerous dainty sandwiches, of which he'd made short work, in true schoolboy fashion; scones and jam, crumpets with lashings of butter oozing from the holes, cream cakes and chocolate eclairs . . . he had felt slightly sick in the train on the way home, but it had been worth it.

And now, over ersatz coffee and austerity rock cakes made by Miss Mottley and other ladies of the village, Brundell's was being discussed, in a way that left no doubts in Eliot's mind.

Turning his eyes from contemplation of the quiet, unremarkable countryside that was

165

now flashing past, Eliot's young companion remarked, 'Someone wrote to my grandmother when my grandad was killed. They said the air raid on London that night was one of the worst of the war, the hotel he was staying in was flattened, not a single survivor, not a trace of anyone. I guess,' he said slowly, 'it might have been you who wrote?'

'No, no, I believe it was my uncle.'

The good Revd Bowen had felt compelled to write, having known Sutherland and entertained him as a guest at the vicarage, and having received in return the immense pleasure of listening to his music. Afterwards, he said it was one of the hardest letters he had ever had to pen: there had never been any indication, until after he died, that Sutherland was married, much less that his wife was expecting their child. When the truth was learned from his commanding officer, it had somehow seemed like a betrayal of trust, though perhaps, excused the vicar, it had simply been that they had known him such a short time, that their acquaintance had really been of the most superficial. Certainly the unworldly vicar had never suspected anything between Sutherland and Leonie—and it had somehow escaped even shrewd Aunt Edith's notice. Or had it? Eliot was to wonder afterwards. He himself had always preferred to believe that Leonie had not known the true facts, either.

166

Later that last evening, when the final notes of the 'Pathetique' had died away, Sutherland had announced that he had a forty-eight hour weekend pass and would be spending it in London, pooh-poohing the danger of air raids. He had never before visited the capital and, war-torn as it was, there were places he wanted to see in case they disappeared for ever.

'You must go and hear Dame Myra Hess, too, at one of those lunchtime piano concerts of hers—I hear they're becoming quite famous. I wish you a pleasant, or at least an interesting, time,' said the vicar, excusing himself to go back to his study, being very much preoccupied at the moment with the funeral on Friday of Bert Havelock, the sexton, and his replacement as gravedigger, general factotum, school caretaker, ARP warden for the village, and sergeant in the Home Guard. He had been leader of the bellringers, too, though sadly they no longer rang, being silenced for the duration.

Leonie, too, it transpired a few minutes later, had four days' leave coming to her, but she would be spending it at home, she said, in Norfolk.

'What a journey you'll have, my dear, the trains so full, and so unreliable!' Eliot's aunt had declared, looking up from turning the heel of a khaki sock and giving Leonie a steady look. 'Must you go?'

No stauncher patriot existed than Aunt

Edith. She had an undaunted belief in eventual victory—but only if everyone implicitly obeyed every government exhortation, such as, Is Your Journey Really Necessary? Not to mention the fact that one might well, have to stand all the way, with trains so jam-packed there was often no room even to sit on suitcases.

'I feel I should. I haven't seen my parents since—'

'My dear, how foolish of me! Forgive me.' Aunt Edith paused. 'Of course, you must be so anxious to see them. Your sense of duty does you credit.' Her knitting needles resumed their clicking. 'And it will do you good, too.'

Leonie had the grace to blush.

She had recently suffered the personal sadness of having two brothers killed in action, and she hadn't seen her parents since the last one, her eldest brother, had gone down with his ship when it was torpedoed. At that time, too, the war was going badly, while activity at the Park was increasing and personnel were working in three shifts round the clock. The strain was telling. Anyone who cared to notice couldn't help but see that Leonie, like many more, was living on her nerves.

'Oh. Oh, yes, well . . . Yes, I think it will buck my mother up to see me,' she said lamely.

Eliot felt sick at heart at her duplicity

It wasn't until later it occurred to him that, simply by informing Youlgreave of what he'd overheard, and where Leonie was to meet Sutherland the following night, he had in fact engineered the perfect crime.

He hadn't envisaged murder, certainly, or ever dreamed that jealousy would go so far. But who could tell what had been in his young, heart-sore mind at the time? That Martin Youlgreave would knock Sutherland down? Quite likely. That he would shame Leonie out of the clandestine weekend? Possibly. The war had made young people more willing than ever to kick over the traces, and even some of the older generation had become more tolerant, but, though standards of behaviour were slipping, there were still nice girls—and he liked to think Leonie was one of them—who cared about their reputations. There must have been gossip already, of course. The pretty, clever little Wren and the big Canadian—their attraction for one another couldn't have gone unnoticed, nor the coincidence of their going on leave at the same time. But then, they weren't the only couple to plan a weekend together. Life could be short, and time was precious.

'Will you give Ian this letter, Eliot?' Leonie had asked him breathlessly the following day, dropping off the waiting 'jolly boat', as the small truck used for transport was known to the Wrens. 'I couldn't find him, and I must catch the next train or I'll never get to Norwich.'

About to leave for Bert Havelock's funeral, Eliot had, after several moments spent wrestling with his conscience, torn open the letter. When he'd read it, he saw it was as he'd thought, that wiser counsels had prevailed after all. Leonie had decided against the weekend in London, and wouldn't be meeting Sutherland as they'd arranged. It had obviously been easier to say something like this in a letter than to tell him in person. Eliot thrust it into his pocket and conveniently 'forgot' all about delivering it to Sutherland.

That he subsequently bitterly regretted this petty and malicious action, and was to be ashamed of it for the rest of his life, made no difference. Especially now, when he knew what the builders must find among the accumulated debris of years as they moved in to begin restoring the old tithe barn. Old bones, scraps of clothing, uniform buttons perhaps. For Eliot had known that Sutherland, still expecting Leonie would be there, would go to keep his rendezvous with her. He could never have left for London the next morning. He was already dead by then.

Unable to sleep with his uneasy conscience that same, hot, airless night, listening to the drone of heavy bombers leaving for Germany, Eliot had at last gone outside in search of coolness, limping along the unlit village street towards the stream that crossed it and ran alongside the churchyard. He found

Youlgreave leaning against the stone parapet of the narrow bridge, looking down into the slow-moving water. He had a cut lip and the makings of a black eye, he was filthy, and it was evident he was very, very drunk. He would not otherwise have spoken to Eliot as he did, albeit in a largely incoherent fashion—about Leonie, about upstart Canadians and the bloodiness of life in general. Before staggering away to his waiting car, he had confessed: 'Well, I've done it at last. Finished it once and for all.'

And that fateful bombing of Brundell's Hotel had, in fact, provided the perfect cover-up for Sutherland's murder. No survivors, bodies damaged beyond recognition, no records left to show who had registered there, or who had not. Eliot knew he should have informed the police of the true facts, but he found it impossible, then or afterwards.

The train was gathering speed as Leighton Buzzard was left behind. Eliot checked his watch. Less than fifteen minutes before the arrival at their destination, where his wife was meeting him with the car. He felt slightly embarrassed that there hadn't, after all, been much he could tell the boy about his grandfather, but young Ian seemed satisfied. Eliot began gathering together his unread papers, putting them into his briefcase while Ian talked about his plans to stay in the area for several days. Did he expect to be offered a bed? People across the Atlantic were so hospitable. But Eliot knew he couldn't ask that of his wife. Perhaps he should ask him to drop in for a cup of tea when he visited the Park? No, he didn't think that, either. He found himself greatly relieved when the boy confessed he was going to stay in Milton Keynes with his girlfriend who, he suspected, had every minute planned.

'Thank you for talking to me about my grandad. My grandma will just love to hear about it.'

'I hope it won't bring back unhappy memories.'

'Oh, she doesn't mind talking about him. She married again, you know, and she's had a very happy life.'

'I'm glad to hear it.'

They shook hands and said goodbye, and in a few moments Ian Sutherland and his backpack had disappeared from Eliot's life.

Eliot didn't go straight to the car park, but made his way into the station waiting-room. Once there, he took the letter from Youlgreave out of his wallet. He sat for several moments with it held in his hand, bracing himself to read it.

He'd last seen Youlgreave on television a few weeks ago. Lord Youlgreave, he was now, having gone into politics and taken his seat in the Lords after receiving a baronetcy in the New Year's Honours list some years ago. Tall and handsome as ever, over eighty though he was, his trademark the white hair that flopped untidily over one eye, reputedly a millionaire several times over, he was a popular media figure who could always be relied on for an amusing quote or an outrageous opinion. Martin Youlgreave had achieved even more than his early ambitions could have envisaged. Monetary success and recognition had come early. Moreover, the social revolution which had taken place after the war had allowed an interaction between the classes that no one could have dreamed of—and he had, in the end, married the daughter of a penniless peer of the realm. She was rather a pretty young woman, nothing on Leonie for looks, but they made a handsome couple.

Eliot had watched his progress, noted his undiminished self-esteem, and wondered how the man could have lived with himself all these years.

At last he opened the envelope and began to read the thick, black, confident handwriting:

Dear Voysey,
Of course I remember you, but I must confess I am at a loss to see the point of your communication.

You must recall that I was very drunk the last time we met—I freely admit that—and perhaps said some unwise

173

things, though I cannot recall exactly what I did say. However, to suggest that I confessed to murder—my dear Voysey! But no, I have not taken umbrage at the suggestion—in fact, I find it amusing rather than offensive.

I can understand how you jumped to conclusions, totally unwarranted though they are, after what I said to you that night, and it is true that we had an argument that developed into a fight, that Canadian officer and I, but such encounters often serve to clear the air. We were both hot-blooded young men, and Leonie was after all a very beautiful woman. However, I can assure you Sutherland was very much alive when I left him. There must have been someone who saw him before he caught the train for London the next morning—although it is, of course, unlikely in the extreme that anyone will now be found who remembers doing so, so many years after.

So, dig as they may, no skeleton, no uniform buttons will ever be found in that barn, for the simple reason that Sutherland was not killed there. Unfortunate though it was, he certainly died when that bomb fell on Brundell's Hotel.

Poor Leonie. I did hope she might have turned to me after that, and it was a bitter thing to find that she did not, that I might as well have not been there for all the notice she took of me. Ah well, we were all young and thought love was a once and only thing! I wonder what became of her after the war? If ever you should meet her, give her my kindest regards.

Yours

Youlgreave.

Eliot folded the letter, put it back in his wallet. He sat motionless on the dark-blue perforated metal seat in the stuffy waiting-room. The smug confidence of the letter, the certainty that the remains would not be found, baffled him. Yet . . . was it possible that he, Eliot, had been wrong all these years, that Sutherland had, after all, gone to London and perished in the air raid?

Or—his mind began to race . . .

For suddenly, in a flash of bewildering clarity, he remembered, in the way his memory sometimes worked nowadays, recalling events which had happened half a lifetime ago more clearly than those of last week. He was there, that night, on the bridge, with the dark stream moving slowly below, Youlgreave's car pulled up on the verge, the churchyard behind and Youlgreave himself, with his damaged, dirt-streaked face, his hands, arms and his white shirt caked with soil. It all fitted in so perfectly that he knew beyond doubt he was right.

There had, after all, been no need to go digging up the floor of a barn to hide a body when there was a freshly dug grave waiting, only needing to be dug a little deeper, the body carried from the barn in Youlgreave's car, thrown in and covered over . . . until the legitimate occupant, Bert Havelock, was lowered in and the grave filled up the following day. It was not the first time in history such a thing had been done.

Eliot thought for a long time about the letter he held in his hand, and the man who'd written it, but any ideas of doing something to bring him to justice died at the moment he came to that last sentence. Sutherland was dead, and however he had come by his death was unimportant, compared with the living . . . All those concerned were now old; no one would be better for raking up past miseries during the time that was left to them, for the sake of so-called justice. Better to let sleeping dogs lie.

He stood up, left the waiting-room and the station, and walked across the car park to where his wife was sitting in the car, reading.

'Goodness, how late the train is again, darling!' she remarked, kissing him affectionately and raising her deep violet eyes to his; she was a still-beautiful woman, despite her age. 'What was it this time?'

'Oh, nothing much, Leonie dear, nothing that matters now. I met an interesting young man on the train, but that's all,' said Eliot. 'Perhaps I'll tell you about him, when I'm not quite so tired.'

But he knew he never would.

ACCOUNT RENDERED

The man with the curved scar on his face, the man called Hans Meyer, left his car and carried his grip to the hotel.

The Hotel des Chevaux Blancs was so hidden in a fold of the green mountains that it could easily be missed. It was shabby, its paintwork was blistered by the sun, the stone façade blended indistinguishably with the rock, so that visitors had almost passed the entrance before they saw it, but to those who knew it, it was a pleasant place to stay.

Old Pierre polished the glasses behind the bar perfunctorily. It was too much to ask one to work in this heat. And besides, he was still aware of the good *choucroute* he had eaten for lunch—and the bottle of wine that had accompanied it. He yawned pleasurably in anticipation of his afternoon snooze.

Hans Meyer walked smartly through the open door. 'A room if you please, monsieur.'

Pierre snapped his jaw to in the rest of the yawn. 'Certainly, monsieur. A single? And for how long?'

'A single, yes. I am not sure how long I shall stay'

Pierre pushed over the register, and watched while Meyer signed. 'You will enjoy your holiday here. We have many German visitors.'

'I am not German, I am Swiss.'

'A thousand pardons, monsieur. I am not usually mistaken.'

He called his sister's grandson, Jean-Paul, from his play outside and directed him to show the visitor to his room. Though he looked fit, M. Meyer too was an old man, and it was time the boy learned that there was more to life than daydreaming about and watching insects and wildlife. The child talked of nothing else, and was delighted that in M. Meyer he had a captive audience. 'I'm going to be an entomologist, monsieur,' he announced, proud of the word, as he humped the visitor's bag upstairs. Pierre watched them thoughtfully.

The register stated that M. Meyer was from Montevideo, which would account for the deep tan and the fine white wrinkles around his eyes where the sun had not reached. So, he did not live in Switzerland. Trouble, perhaps? A man with the look that Pierre had seen in M. Meyer's eyes certainly had trouble. Probably women—they were without doubt the greatest source of trouble in the world. With one exception . . .

For a moment the tough old man held his breath against that ancient pain, then he reached out his hand, almost blindly, to grasp the passing Yolande's plump, yielding waist. 'Come, mon *petit thou*,' he whispered. 'There will be no more visitors . . .'

There was still one way—even at his age, thank God—of obliterating a memory he could not bear to think about, even now.

But this time, Yolande made a pretence of pushing him away. 'You old goat! Who is the German?'

'He's not German, he's Swiss.'

'Which is lucky for him, eh? You do not take kindly to our German visitors.'

Pierre picked up a glass to wipe, twisting it so viciously that its stem snapped. 'I do not forget, that is all.'

Meyer had been given a room which looked out directly on to the road leading to the top of the mountain. The pastures on both sides were lush and dotted with flowers, the pines and oaks were thick, deeply shading the road. But nearer the top, the trees thinned out and on the summit there was nothing but sparse grass, where in winter the wind would sweep the snow into deep drifts.

Meyer shivered, despite the heat, and turned away. He began to unpack his grip, stacking his belongings methodically in the drawers and wardrobe. Then, with slightly shaking fingers, he took his tooth glass and poured into it from the bottle at the bottom of his bag a large quantity of spirits, which he drank straight off, as he needed to do when his nerves were on edge.

* * *

He stood apart from the coachload of tourists who were grouped around the guide, outside the bare, lonely, beautiful little church.

'It was built, *m'sieur-dames,* to replace the old one which was bombed during the war. You will please look here . . .'

Meyer hadn't noticed that the old barman, Pierre, was behind him, until he spoke. 'He does not tell them, of course, that it was their countrymen who bombed it. That, *naturellement,* they would not like to hear. You observe, they are for the most part Germans. I cannot myself understand why they come here.'

Meyer turned away from his contemplation of the valley where once a village of some four hundred souls had stood. 'You were here in the war?' he asked.

'I was here, twenty years old and fighting with the Maquis. One day, I came home and found that my village, down there, had disappeared. In one single bitter winter night the Germans had murdered its inhabitants, the old, the sick, women and children.'

'Murdered?'

'What other name is there for it? The next morning they ordered those few who by some miracle or other had been spared to pack up and go to the next village. They wanted the place totally evacuated, you understand, so they could raze it to the ground. The people were forced to pack up what belongings they could carry, and to set off. Half-way there, machine guns were turned on them . . .'

Eighty of them, lying like scraps of torn paper in the snow. Red blood, and white snow, and the red, white and blue of the defiant tricolours they had carried.

'And there was something else, too. That night the wild horses were heard.'

Meyer's face, which had up till then retained its controlled lack of expression, twisted. 'All horses are basically wild, my friend.'

'You do not like them, eh?'

'I have worked with them for most of my life in South America.'

'Nevertheless, you are still—afraid of them?' Pierre asked shrewdly.

'Let us say, rather, that I have respect. You must have respect for anything that can do this to you.' He touched the livid, crescent-shaped scar that ran from his brow to his temple. 'But what of *your* wild horses?'

'Three hundred years ago, a troop of them roamed free as the wind on the Pass. Alas, they died out—or so it was said. But we in our village used to put out hay, apples, a little sugar. And always the next morning the offerings had gone. Yet no one ever saw the horses, except for that night. They were heard, whickering and neighing all through the hours of darkness. The sound of galloping hooves echoed through the streets. There are some who say they still roam, and will not cease until vengeance has been extracted for that time of horror.'

White horses, that might have been flurries of snow in the moonlight, though no one seriously believed that, galloping, swerving, with manes and tails flying, eyes rolling, nostrils aflare . . .'

Meyer mopped his forehead. The day was already hot, it would be stifling by nightfall. There was a hint of thunder in the air. My God, he could do with a drink.

'M. Meyer, the soldiers who did that were animals, and worse—but they were acting under orders. Who could have given that order?'

Who indeed? Hans Meyer turned his eyes away from the lined, weatherbeaten face of the old man in front of him, and looked down into the valley. A young officer, not much more than a boy, homesick and lonely and too drunk to remember *what* orders he had given? Too sodden to recall anything the next day except the night-long beating and drumming of the wind that had turned itself into a nightmare of stampeding horses?

'Why do you stay here?' he asked Pierre.

'I am waiting.'

'For what?'

'For the man who did this thing. He was sent away, immediately afterwards, but he will return. I feel it, I know it, here.' He touched

183

his breast, and looked Meyer full in the face.

'But sixty years can change a man, can it not?'

'However much he has changed, I shall know him.'

'And if you did recognize him, what would you do?'

'I should kill him. One of those villagers was my young wife of six months.'

That night, Pierre served his guest with a dish of mountain blue trout of such delicacy that the taste was like angel food on the tongue, and a bottle of Riesling so rare that M. Meyer was tempted to take a little more than was wise. He was already more than half drunk when he retired to his room, raised the bottle of spirits to his lips and drained it.

*   *   *

Pierre drove back to the hotel with Yolande, who had been spending her day off in the town. She sat with her hand on his knee, until she found it necessary to use both hands to keep her balance. The parcels on the back seat, which he had paid for, jumped every time he wrenched the steering-wheel round another zigag of the road. He was too old to be driving, she thought, but judged it better to keep the thought to herself. He didn't take kindly to references about his age.

Pierre knew he was driving badly. It was

184

because he was angry. 'Why the hell did you let Jean-Paul go off this morning with that German?' he demanded.

'You said he was Swiss.'

'Swiss, German, it's all the same, you know what I think.'

'But they are such friends. He tells the boy such stories—and he's given him a camera. They went out to take butterfly pictures.'

'Butterflies? Friends? How can you say that? You know nothing of this Hans Meyer. He might be anything—a rogue, a murderer!'

Yolande sighed patiently. 'Pierre, you are letting your imagination run away with you again.' It was not the first time she had heard something like this from the old man, and not the first time he had been mistaken. 'Monsieur Meyer is a kind and gentle old man. I cannot think why you dislike him so much.'

The dusk was closing in and Pierre switched on the headlights; the trunks of the pine trees glowed redly.

'Do not forget that I am responsible to my sister for Jean-Paul. If anything happened to him, she would never forgive me.'

'You worry too much,' she said, hoping to distract him with the hand she laid back on his knee, which he ignored.

'Even you must admit how strangely he acts, staring down into the valley—and the amount he drinks, *mon Dieu!*'

She withdrew her hand, but said softly, 'But

men have many different ways of forgetting, have they not?'

'And of remembering.' Pierre swung round the last bend but one before the hotel.

Here, the road led straight upwards before the last bend, at which point it curved almost at right angles and led directly through a short tunnel which had been blasted through the rock. It was a highly dangerous spot, and there, in the full glare of the headlights, stood Meyer, just in front of the tunnel, his back against the sheer rock face. Without thinking, without conscious effort, Pierre put his foot down and drove straight towards him.

He had never imagined that when the moment came, he would be reluctant to do it.

For years he had conjured up such a moment as this, savouring it, rolling it around in his mind like good wine on the tongue, now, he broke out into a cold sweat and had to force himself on, conscious of Yolande with her hand to her mouth, petrified with fear, and the figure of Meyer, like one of Jean-Paul's butterflies, against the rock. It was only at the very last second that some reserves of strength, or sensibility, enabled him to swerve the car away.

But as the car veered across to the left, the figure of a small boy darted out from that side. Pierre jammed on the brakes, something large and heavy flashed across the windscreen, the car met it with a violent impact, and there was a long, shuddering scream.

Jean-Paul lay like a broken doll in the road, a wing of dark hair across his forehead. Pierre walked stiffly towards him, knelt down at his side, and the boy opened his eyes. The blood drained from Pierre's heart, leaving him weak and giddy with relief.

The boy's eyes fell upon the shards of glass and plastic by his side. 'Oh, my camera!' Then, frightened, 'Monsieur Meyer!'

Pierre stood looking down numbly at the body of Hans Meyer. Or was it Hans Meyer? The face was waxy white in the car's headlights, and the anonymity of death had already spread over the features.

There was a soft, distant sound of what might have been thunder, that might have been the galloping of retreating horses, and Pierre crossed himself and backed away fearfully as he noticed that the hoof-shaped scar on the dead man's face was slowly disappearing.

PORTRAIT OF SOPHIE

Waiting for Daniel to arrive, I pulled my car off the road and sat savouring the view across the familiar stretch of bare Pennine moorland falling steeply away a few yards from where I was parked. On the opposite side of the valley was more moorland, rising in the distance to hills that were a deep teal blue on the skyline. Two pewter-coloured reservoirs could be glimpsed deep in the folds of the descending hills, and right there in the horizontal cleft where their slopes met at the bottom tumbled the swift-running river. The sky was duck-egg blue. Larks sang. It was good to be back, after all.

I'd left the heavy, continuous stream of traffic behind on the motorway and come over the tops, taking the road across Ingshaw Moor. Once an ancient packhorse track, it wound sinuously downwards towards the first straggle of houses and the hairpin bend hiding the small-town industrial sprawl in the valley. The first of the houses, whose slated roofs I could just see to my left, had been home to me since I was eight years old, when my grandfather had brought me there after my mother died.

Built towards the end of the nineteenth century for a woollen clothier, the house stood above a steep, narrow drive that led off the road between two stone pillars, bearing the two words, left and right, 'Ingshaw House'. Its solid Yorkshire stone was now darkened by natural weathering and by the industrial pollution that used to emanate from the valley's mill chimneys during the bad old days. But it was handsome and solid, not so big as to be uncomfortable, and with plenty of scope for accommodating the Brereton furniture-making business, and secluded enough to satisfy my grandfather's solitary inclinations while remaining accessible for business purposes. The outbuildings where the work went on gave no indication at the moment of their present function. The yard was quiet and still.

I looked at my watch and sighed. Daniel was late, but he never did have much sense of time.

Impatient, never one to sit still for long, I seized my coat and climbed out of the car to stretch my legs, took a few paces forward and nearly jumped out of my skin when something dark and sinister flapped up out of the harsh, wind-blown grass right at my feet with a hoarse *kok-kok-kok*. But it was only a moorcock, disturbed by human presence, more scared than I was. It flew away on a clatter of wings, and I turned up my collar and wrapped the folds of my coat around me, leaned against the car bonnet and looked down into the dip of the valley, a prospect of home that was never far from my mind when I was in London, where I presently lived, worked and quite often felt I couldn't breathe. The air here was like champagne. I filled my lungs deeply.

And as my gaze drifted back again to the house, a woman came out and took the flagged path to the side gate set into the high stone wall surrounding the garden, scarf flapping, hair whipped back from her face. Two tall, lightly built golden salukis pranced beside her, with long fringed tails and silky ears laid back by the wind. Stylish animals, a mirror of her own taut elegance.

Cluny.

Younger than I'd expected when I'd first met her, she was still a stranger to the community after two years, contemptuous of opinion. It seemed to me those hounds, exotically foreign to the Yorkshire moors, just about summed up her abrasive, take-me-or-leave-me attitude. But that same sharp mind and acid wit made her stimulating to be with— sometimes, anyway. If you didn't take offence at the occasional barb aimed in your direction. As I watched her striding effortlessly through the heather and bilberries, I tried to suppress my misgivings. I'd only stayed a few times in the house since Grandpa had married Cluny van Doelen, and never since his death.

* * *

The work of my grandfather, William

Brereton, had once been featured in a glossy magazine under the heading 'Heirlooms of the Future', alongside another entitled 'Thomas Chippendale—Heirlooms from the Past'. The article pointed out the differences between the two men's work—no ornate, rococo carving or wide-bottomed Georgian chairs for William, no Chinese latticework: a Brereton design was simple, honest and unadorned—apart from the minute bee, his trademark, his signature, which appeared discreetly somewhere on every piece. But solid craftsmanship, and an instinctive feeling for line and form linked the two men. Also, they were both Yorkshiremen, self-made. And, like Chippendale, William Brereton knew the value of his work. Those who bought from him weren't over-charged, but they didn't buy cheaply. If the two men had ever met, they would have had a great deal in common, said the writer.

But Chippendale had been dead for over two and a half centuries, and my grandfather for barely two and a half months.

He'd died by breaking his neck in a fall down the stairs on a January day, missing his footing and tumbling from top to bottom because he wasn't accustomed to using a walking-stick, and hadn't placed it squarely when he began to descend. He'd been alone when it happened, a fit and able 78-year-old, and the worst of it was that the stick had been nothing more than a temporary measure to

191

help him over a bout of lumbago caught by sitting too long in a draught.

After his body was taken away, Magda told me that Daniel had seized the stick that lay next to William on the floor, and as though it were entirely to blame for the accident, snapped it across his knee like firewood, and hurled it into the heart of the flames leaping in the great open fireplace. It was a quite uncharacteristic fit of rage, but then, Daniel had worked for the Old Man for fifteen years. William had been a stubborn, unyielding old cuss at times, but there'd never be another like him.

Magda Lutz was William's housekeeper. She'd looked after him for over fifty years, ever since the loss of his first wife (and with pressed lips had continued to do so since his second marriage). Since his death, she'd been bereft, wringing her hands and uttering woebegone *mittel*-European lamentations. What was to happen to her now that she was left alone at the mercy of the second wife?

Cluny herself, returning from a visit to the vet with her dogs to find her husband dead, had wound a scarf round her head, called for the salukis, who accompanied her everywhere like familiars, and gone out again into the bleak, iron-grey afternoon, taking the pathway beside the beck, straight down to the house where Stephen Baines, a lawyer working in the firm acting as William's solicitors, lived.

Well, William had been twenty-five years older than Cluny, and had long passed man's natural span, and his dying was bound to cause her problems, legal and otherwise. Twelve months ago, a heart condition had been diagnosed, and he'd semi-retired and handed his business over to Daniel. He had died possessed of little more than his house and contents, and he hadn't left a will.

As for me, I grieved for him and wondered why he'd thought it so important for me to have that portrait.

This oil painting, handed to me at the funeral by Magda, who insisted that William had told her he intended me to have it, was the only thing I had to remember him by, but I'd never had expectations of a great inheritance from him, anyway. His furniture might have been sought after by those in the know, but it hadn't brought him a great deal of profit. He'd despised commercialism and had never taken on board the principle of diminishing returns. As far as he was concerned, he quoted what he estimated a fair price for each individually designed piece, and from then on it took as long as it took, regardless of time or money. In the absence of a will, his estate would pass naturally to Cluny. I had no problems with that. All the same, there were one or two small family treasures I'd dearly have loved as keepsakes. And it *had* been surprising, and had rather hurt me if the truth be known, that he hadn't thought to leave me something he'd made with his own hands. Just a chair, perhaps, or a small table, would have been nice.

Instead, I'd found myself in possession of the painting. A portrait I hadn't seen before. Hadn't even known existed.

*   *   *

The feeling grew, as I waited, shivering beside my car, that this impulsive visit of mine probably wasn't the best idea I'd ever had, and I might even now have climbed back into the driving-seat, turned and headed back to London, if the four-by-four hadn't appeared on the horizon and a moment later screeched to a halt beside me.

Daniel leaped out. 'Zoe!' Two strides and I was enveloped in the old, familiar bear hug. I breathed experimentally. It was OK, my ribs seemed intact.

He overtopped me by a head. His open, good-natured face beamed and I smiled up at him. Daniel Souter had a natural charm, he was the sort you instinctively liked and trusted, and because he was laid back and good-humoured, people were apt to underestimate him. I'd never make the same mistake. There was a lot more to Daniel than you might think at first sight, much more than a personable face, humorous brown eyes and dark tousled hair. I'd known him a long time, right up until I'd moved away and become a PA to a media person.

His hands stayed on my shoulders, big, shapely hands accustomed to lifting huge pieces of furniture and heavy planks of wood, yet capable of wielding a fine chisel or an adze with tremendous skill, and sensitive enough to draw and execute the precise designs he conceived. That combination of artistry, practicality and love for his subject was what had first endeared him as an eighteen-year-old to William, who'd recognized him as a natural heir to his own craft and had taught him everything he knew. But he'd always had his own ideas, and had gradually moved away from the strong, plain, almost monolithic Brereton designs, into making his own creations, something altogether lighter and more flowing. William had let him have his head, knowing that these sorts of skills were something beyond his own abilities.

'Come and sit inside, where it's warmer,' he said, adding truthfully, if not tactfully, 'your nose is turning blue.' He slid the door of the Discovery open for me. I needed no second invitation. The fitfully bright, blowy afternoon indicated that spring might just conceivably be on its way to this part of the world, but you didn't argue with March winds like this, not up here on the moors. Enough was enough, even when it was champagne. I settled in the warmth and we half-turned to face each other.

'Good to see you, Ms Kennedy. Looking very—Londonish.' I was suddenly awkward with the hairstyle that had cost me an arm and a leg, the knots of gold in my ears, my short-skirted designer suit, all things I took for granted nowadays, but which might, very soon be things I could no longer afford. 'What time are you expected at the house?'

'Around tea-time.' I hadn't said precisely. Better to arrive in my own time, I'd decided, thus pre-empting any fuss.

'First things first, then. Tell me about the painting.'

'Right. Well, I've had it professionally valued, as you suggested. It's beautifully executed, they say, and has a lot of appeal, but it's unattributable to any one particular artist, so it would fetch less than if it had been by someone well-known. Plus the fact that portraits apparently aren't too popular, I don't know why. They wouldn't commit themselves, especially since it's been messed about.'

'Someone's been having a go at cleaning it,' the precious young man at the art gallery had tut-tutted when I'd taken it in, only that morning, on, my way here, *'and that's not the original frame. Nice enough, but new. Takes off the value.'*

'Yes, well,' Daniel said, when I repeated this, 'the old frame was falling apart, so the Old Man made a new one. I guess the object

196

was to make it look presentable, not to preserve its possible value as an antique.'

'They still think it might fetch five thousand, even six, all the same. Always assuming I wanted to sell it—which of course I don't.'

'Five thousand? That all?'

'It's more than I thought—and it doesn't matter anyway, I don't intend to sell it.'

'OK, OK, just a thought, not serious!' He grimaced slightly and stared through the windscreen, over the coarse, tussocky grass, permanently bowed down by the prevailing wind. 'But it isn't a joke, not really, is it, Zoe?' he said gently. 'There's something all wrong about that portrait. I mean, about why he particularly wanted you to have it. And don't tell me you don't feel the same.'

He'd been aghast when William, normally a conscientious man, had died intestate, unable to believe that he'd treated me in what Daniel regarded as a very shabby manner. There wasn't even the excuse that the Old Man had felt there was no hurry to make his will. At his age it couldn't have escaped him that time was fast running out, and that in the absence of any legal documents, everything of which he possessed when he died would go to Cluny, whom he'd met and married only a couple of years before. Daniel's hope, although slight, had been that the painting might turn out to be extremely valuable and would help remove some of the guilt he personally felt at having done better out of the Old Man than I had—never mind that the business at the time of the handover hadn't been looking too healthy, William's way of running it having left precious little in the coffers. And for me, his only living relative, nothing but a mediocre painting. If indeed it *had* been his wish that I should have it. There was only Magda Lutz to say it had.

'I'm not ungrateful to him, Daniel,' I said. 'I shall treasure the portrait—if only because it obviously meant something to him.'

'I can vouch for it that it did. He said so when he was making the frame. He thought she had a look of you.'

Actually, the ingratiating type at the auction house had said the same thing, but I'd put that down to his general smarminess, though it was true that I'd felt an uncanny frisson myself when I'd first seen the face in the portrait, an unexpected recognition I found difficult to explain. 'And does she?'

I recalled the portrait of the young woman in the plum-coloured costume, her face framed by a high fur collar, the blonde curls of an Edwardian fringe peeping from under the brim of a matching velvet hat. A composed, heart-shaped face, clear hazel eyes, a closed smile and an air of poise and self-containment. Whereas me—well, I had fair hair, too, but otherwise I had only grey eyes, a nose I preferred to think of as *retroussé* . . . No way could I be said to look like her.

Daniel evidently agreed with me. 'Not really. She looks a bit po-faced to me. Well, OK, then, maybe there is a *bit* of a resemblance. Something about the chin.'

'Too sharp, you mean.'

'Firm.' He grinned. 'Determined. Or stubborn—if we're being honest.'

Knowing exactly what he meant by that, but not wanting to pursue it, I refused to rise to the bait. 'Do you really think we might be related? Who *is* she, I wonder?'

'*Sophie in a Velvet Hat,* by someone who for some reason gave it a title, but didn't sign his name. But that's what you're going to try and find out, aren't you? Isn't that why you're here?'

I might have known he'd see right through the excuses I'd made to Cluny about collecting the rest of my stuff still remaining at the house. 'Partly. But I do want to pick up my things as well.' I took a breath. 'I'm coming back, Daniel. I've got a new job, in Leeds, and I'm looking for a place to live.'

For a moment, his eyes blazed. 'Leeds?'

'Why not? City of opportunities. Exciting place nowadays, they say.'

'Is that what you're looking for, excitement?'

'No, I just think it's time to come home.'

We faced each other, unspoken tensions again between us. He'd never wanted me to go away, and I hadn't forgotten why. It would have been so easy to let myself feel the same way, but I'd needed to try my wings, I'd been eager to feel the taste of freedom before being sorry I'd never experienced it. What that had actually turned out to mean was the disastrous, intense involvement with Murray, my then boss, which had all ended in tears, as I'd realized too late it was bound to. I'd got over that now, as one does, in the end, and here was Daniel, still unattached. There'd been one or two flings, I'd gathered, but nothing serious.

Of course, I'd known Daniel too long to expect to be swept off my feet by him. But I'd grown up since those early days, when heady romance seemed everything; I'd learned the value of truth and steadiness . . .

'I thought you'd never do it,' he said softly, 'find where your priorities lie.'

Suddenly, he reached out and, not taking his eyes from my face, put his big warm hand over my still-cold one. A flood of sensations washed through me, a painful awakening of something long dormant, so unexpected that I felt totally disorientated. I didn't know what to say, and clutched wildly at the only safe option I could think of, 'Yes, well—going back to Sophie—I must admit she intrigues me. Though if Cluny won't let me look through the papers, old photos and things that Grandpa left, I don't see how I can possibly find out who she was.'

Not only Sophie, but the rest of my family too, was the thought never too far from the back of my mind.

While William had been alive, the rock in my life, the one person who was always there, it hadn't seemed to matter how little I'd known of my background. My mother had been embittered by her divorce, and reluctant to speak of the past in any shape or form to a young child, and William only ever referred to my grandmother as his lost wife, as if she were a pair of spectacles he'd carelessly misplaced. It wasn't until he died and Magda handed over the portrait that I began to question whether all families were like this—and to realize how urgently I wanted to find out more about my own.

I reached for the door. 'Time to be making tracks.'

'Hang on. I asked you to meet me here before you go to the house because I think there's something you should know first, Zoe.' He was suddenly very serious.

My heart plummeted. I knew what he was going to say. I'd been expecting it, it was what I'd feared ever since Grandpa had died. 'Cluny's going to sell Ingshaw,' I said flatly.

I was surprised by how much I disliked this, I who'd left my home for the delights of London and had sworn never to return, not permanently. Well, I'd changed my mind about that, but I hated the idea of Ingshaw not being there to come back to whenever I wanted, or needed, it.

Of course Cluny would sell, as soon as she legally could. She'd be short of money, and she had no allegiances to the place. I thought guiltily of the portrait and what it was worth. Did I have a moral obligation to hand it back? But I'd offered it once, after the funeral, and she had given it one cursory, rather denigrating glance and said take it by all means.

'Whoa, steady! No, it's not Ingshaw, though I'm sure she'll put it on the market like a shot as soon as she can. Trouble is, there aren't many people about who'd be willing to buy a house with business premises attached to it.'

'Which would mean you moving out?'

'Unless I can raise the cash to buy it myself, and use it as a showroom and for extra office space. Fat chance of that.'

I suppose having to move an established business and find new, more expensive, premises just like that entitled one to feel gloomy.

'It's nothing to do with the house. Prepare yourself for a shock. It's Magda.'

'Has Cluny given her the sack?'

'It hasn't come to that, not yet, though it might well do, especially if Magda carries on as she is doing. No, Zoe, it's something else entirely.'

* * *

Inside the house, the hall was dark and
202

unwelcoming at first sight, without the bright fire that had always been kept burning in William's day. I tried to avoid looking at the foot of the stairs, where his body had crashed down on to the richly coloured encaustic floor tiles. Tried not to believe that his tall, upright figure would appear at any moment. The steep staircase down which he'd fallen, with its Turkey-patterned carpet, rose directly opposite the front door, branching off either side at the top. On the landing, a Victorian stained glass window of immense gloom and ugliness cast a dull, yellowish light downwards. There was a plate rack filled with blue and white china. A tall Satsuma vase with peacock feathers and pampas grass stood sentinel at the foot of the staircase, several murky looking pictures of no distinction hung on the walls. It looked as though not a thing had been moved since the day it was first placed there, maybe a hundred years ago.

When he was just starting his business, William had bought the house from an elderly spinster, complete with the furniture she'd inherited from her father, primarily because its nostalgic ambience had appealed to him. Showing potential clients around, using the house as a sort of showroom, had served to emphasize the point he was trying to make—that his furniture was timeless and fitted in anywhere. Each room in the house held at least one of his pieces. Here it was a huge table in heavy, dark, gleaming rosewood, its simplicity of design revealing the beauty of the grain, making it look almost silkily alive. I always wanted to stretch out a hand to stroke it.

A draught came through from the dining-room, shivering the papery petals of a bowl of golden-eyed white narcissi on the table. Mrs Sugden, who came to clean, had left the window—and doubtless all the other windows in the house—wide open, as was her wont. In a moment, Magda would appear and go round shutting them, clucking her disapproval, but for now the gusts of sunlit air blowing in lifted the curtains, wafted around the delicate scent of the flowers and brought the cold breath of the moor indoors. Due to Mrs Sugden's unwavering belief in the natural symbiosis of cleanliness and godliness, everywhere was relentlessly clean; if anything could be polished, it was. You walked across those coloured, shining tiles at risk to life and limb.

Magda came into the hall with a rush of the exuberance that characterized all her actions, arms thrown wide. She was fair and buxom, a big woman in every sense, huge emotions, generous impulses. Being engulfed in that wide, all-encompassing embrace was a bit like being swallowed by a marshmallow. At last she stood back and regarded me, her huge blue eyes brimming. 'Oh, my *dorlink*, I'm just so, so glad to see you!'

Although Magda was given to dramatic gestures and utterances, her command of English was normally excellent and idiomatic. She'd found herself in England just after the war, a bewildered refugee, one of those who were then called Displaced Persons, and had counted herself lucky to be employed by William to act as his housekeeper and to look after his motherless little daughter, Elisabeth, my mother. She'd been with him ever since and had taken me to her bosom when I in turn arrived motherless at Ingshaw. Now it was only in moments of stress that her faultless pronunciation deserted her, when the rhythms of her native tongue asserted themselves. 'You have told her, then, Daniel?'

He had come in with me, but I was the one who replied. Yes, Daniel had told me. I'd been stunned when he had, and it must have showed on my face now, for Magda said sadly, 'And you don't believe it, either?' Normally one who bestowed smiles like blessings, she looked so downcast, so obviously at her wits' end that I hugged her again.

'Magda, it just seems so—'

'You don't have to take my word for it. Come with me.' Picking up a large flashlight which was standing on a bookshelf, obviously in readiness, she beckoned us to follow. '*She* won't be back yet. She's gone down to that solicitor fellow, Baines. Again.'

Daniel and I exchanged glances and

followed her up the thickly carpeted steps to the top, where she knelt down beside the ugly majolica jardiniere and shone the light on two tiny holes in the oak skirting, roughly the same distance above the floor, either side of the staircase.

'What do you make of that?'

I saw what I was meant to make of it, that a string had been stretched across between them, forming a tripwire. But I couldn't believe it—I wouldn't! That my grandfather had been made to die like that. Cruelly, and without grace, or dignity. That he had, as Magda was convinced, been murdered.

*   *   *

But it was no use, nothing would persuade Magda that a strong nylon thread or something similar hadn't been deliberately fastened across the top of the gloomily lit staircase, causing William to trip and plunge to his death.

'There! If only I'd thought of looking straight away! But everyone—the police included—took it for granted it was an accident, an old man falling because he wasn't accustomed to a walking-stick.'

This was the first I'd heard about any police. 'What were they doing there?'

'Routine, when there's a sudden death,' Daniel assured me.

'I should have known!' Magda moaned. 'He hadn't been himself lately—that lumbago was the last straw. He wouldn't have missed seeing something like that otherwise. There was nothing wrong with his eyes.'

I knew Daniel had heard all this before. Like him, I could see it was no use pointing out that those two holes proved nothing, how they'd got there was anybody's guess— they could have been woodworm holes for all anyone knew. And hadn't I, often enough, pinned garlands and streamers down the length of those gloomy walls at Christmas? Evidently the police hadn't been suspicious, and I couldn't see how they might prove an 'accident' had been staged even if they had been, but I was pretty sure they'd need less flimsy evidence than that.

'Magda, if anything of that sort had been rigged up, then someone would have had to remove the string or whatever afterwards, and there was no one in the house when it happened.'

'So we've been told—but remember who found him! Don't forget, I was conveniently given the day off. I was at the January sales in Leeds with Rita.' She sniffed. 'At least she agrees with me.'

The redoubtable Rita Beardsall, Magda's boon companion. Until her recent retirement, owner of the busiest hairdressing establishment for miles around (it was no coincidence that Magda was still improbably blonde, at her age) and in a prime position to be arch-priestess of local gossip.

Daniel put his arm around Magda's plump shoulder 'We're all upset, but think about it, Magda—that's a pretty haphazard way of attempting to kill anyone; there's no guarantee they'd actually die. More than likely he'd just have been badly injured.'

'An old man like that, with his heart condition? The shock alone would have killed him! Anyway, it was worth a try, especially when he hadn't made a will—'

'No one could have known that!'

'You believe that, do you—with that woman thick as thieves with his lawyer? A man like that? As Rita says, if he's such a hotshot as he makes out, what's he doing working here? Don't tell *me* they didn't know!' She paused for breath, and added deliberately; 'Or maybe there *was* a will—'

There'd never been any love lost between the two women—perhaps because Magda had hoped no second Mrs Brereton would ever come on the scene to challenge the way she'd always cared for William. Cluny reacted only by remaining aloof, unlike Magda, who was never able to keep her feelings to herself.

This, however, was more dangerous. Not only was she accusing Cluny of attempting to murder her husband, but she was also accusing Stephen Baines, suggesting serious professional misconduct at the least, of suppressing a will.

I'd always believed Grandpa was trying to protect me -mistakenly, perhaps—by refusing to be drawn into discussing what was past. Or that the failure of my parents' marriage, my mother's early death from cancer, the loss of his own wife, had been too painful to speak about. I'd never pressed him, knowing what an intensely private man he was. It wasn't until he astonished everyone who knew him by remarrying that I realized with a shock he might have been a lonely one, too.

For this reason, if none other, I'd tried to be glad that he'd found Cluny, so much younger, but willing to share his latter years. Still, I was amazed at such hidden depths in my grandfather, and I wasn't the only one. Tongues wagged . . . old William Brereton and this stuck-up, spiky lady from nowhere, who would have thought it? With all those willing widows and well-preserved spinsters who'd been after him for years and would have been only too happy to provide him with home comforts and no hassle? As for her, what had brought her here, and made her stay, in this climate, after sunny Africa, married to a man old enough to be her father?

William, as usual, had ignored the gossip, and Cluny had lifted her chin a little higher, smiled her ironic smile and let them wonder.

And as if to confound them all, life

at Ingshaw had gone on as quietly and uneventfully as usual. Cluny, unlike other local wives, didn't entertain, accept invitations, join local societies, or even play bridge. She made no friends and seemed content to live a life as self-contained and independent as William, becoming a familiar topic of speculation, driving around in her open-topped car (whenever the weather allowed) with the handsome salukis sitting disdainfully upright in the back seat.

Magda said now, dejectedly, 'Well, I've done what I can. All I wanted was justice for him, but—' She laced her fingers together and took a deep breath. 'I'm leaving, anyway. My wages were paid three months in advance when I started here, and it's nearly three months since he died, so I'm free to go next week.'

'What?' I was shocked to the core. Magda had lived here all her life since coming to England. 'Magda, you can't leave! Where will you go?'

'I'm going to live with Rita.'

The idea of Ingshaw without Grandpa was bad enough, without either him or Magda it was inconceivable. But Rita had recently sold her hairdressing business for a very comfortable sum, and bought a luxurious chalet-style bungalow in a highly desirable new development on the outskirts of the town. She and Magda had known each other for thirty years and been bosom chums from the moment they'd first met.

Perhaps it would be the best solution, after all.

*   *   *

I couldn't help feeling relieved when Cluny later made her apologies for not being in for supper that evening. The prospect of sitting opposite her, with Magda's accusations still ringing in my ears, wasn't one I'd looked forward to. But Magda was furious, since she'd arranged with Rita to make up a four for bridge, and she wouldn't leave me alone, she declared, on my first night back.

'Don't worry about me, I'll be fine,' I told her. 'I'm tired after the drive, all I want is a sandwich and an early night. I'll see to myself.'

Through the window, I could see Daniel's Discovery parked outside, and lights in the workshop showing he was still working. Sensing Magda was beginning to waver, I went out and crossed the yard before she could change her mind again.

I never felt as though I was really home until I'd been into what I still thought of as William's workshop, the central hub around which Ingshaw House had always revolved. The first thing I'd done, every day when coming home from school, was to pop in, just to say hello. As I entered the big, brightly lit space now, I was welcomed by the familiar scents of new wood, linseed oil and glue, mingling in the thick, dry air with the sharper ones of shellac and turps. Sean, the boy who worked for Daniel, was still here too, hand-planing a piece of timber, his feet lost in rich blonde curls of wood shavings. Daniel had great hopes for this seventeen-year-old, had chosen him from a long list of applicants as one who really wanted to *learn* a craft, rather than simply get himself a job, in the same way that William had chosen Daniel himself.

We hadn't met since Grandpa's death, and the lad greeted me a little awkwardly, as if unsure whether to offer his sympathies, but he relaxed as I exchanged pleasantries with him for a minute or two, enjoying watching him as he finished the job. His hands on the plane were strong and sure. He'd been taught well. 'Daniel's in the back,' he told me, blowing the dust away, smoothing the piece of walnut with loving hands.

Daniel was telephoning and signalled he'd be with me shortly. I wandered over to the shelves where designs and sketches were fastened on to drawing-boards with large-headed draughtsman's thumbtacks, and brochures with photographs of finished pieces were stacked next to the design and pattern books going back to when William first started on his own. Furniture was still being made to some of his earliest designs. Idly, I picked up a leather-bound folio that was lying on the long, sloping drawing-table beneath. The front cover was decorated with a tooled and gilded design, showing the initial 'B', garlanded with honeysuckle, the flowers and foliage almost hiding the tiny bee, the Brereton trademark. I began to flick through, but saw immediately that the designs weren't drawn by William. Master of his craft as he was, creating articles of furniture powerful and strong enough to last until the next millennium, he was incapable of the sort of delicacy I was seeing here, in the turn of a leg, the curve of a backrest, that wonderful marquetry. Clearly, these designs were Daniel's.

I turned a page, and a sheet of paper sailed to the ground. As I bent to pick it up, my own name jumped out at me. *My dear Zoe.* The forceful, upright handwriting was unmistakably William's. What was a letter from him, addressed to me, doing in one of Daniel's pattern books? Why hadn't he given it to me? Daniel put the telephone down and without thinking too much about what I was doing, I thrust the paper into my pocket.

'That was Magda ringing from the house. She wants me to come and eat with you tonight to keep you company. She says she'll leave us some food.' He closed the book casually and slipped it back on to the shelf.

'Oh, Lord! I've told her—a sandwich is all I want.'

213

'A sandwich! I'll bet you've had nothing to eat all day. We can do better than that. There's a very good Indian restaurant opened down by the viaduct—not to be compared with the heady delights of a night out in Leeds, of course! But if that doesn't appeal, we could eat at my house. I do a mean bolognese.'

'Thanks, but no thanks, Daniel.' I summoned a smile. 'I'm tired, not feeling very sociable.'

An evening alone with him, before I'd had time to come to terms with the shock of what had happened between us out there on the moor, was the last thing I needed. Especially to be alone with him in the blissful house further down the hill that he'd converted himself from a tiny, former Methodist chapel—small for a chapel, that is, but as a house spacious and airy, full of light. Peaceful. I was far too relaxed and off-guard there at the best of times.

'OK. Another time, huh?' he said lightly

*   *   *

Cluny was pleased when I told her I meant to have a quick snack and an early night. 'Now I needn't feel guilty about going out myself.'

Where was she off to, all glamoured-up, her eyes secret? Head to toe in black, simple and unadorned but definitely not of the mourning kind, her only jewellery two small diamond

214

ear-studs. She looked stunning, but surely over the top for an evening out locally? Even with this Stephen Baines, as it apparently was. Her relief seemed equally overdone. Could it be that she'd arranged to go out because she was as nervous of us being alone together as I was? Cluny could be an amusing companion, when she was in the mood, but tonight she was brittle and edgy. Her green catlike eyes glittered and her smooth tawny hair caught the light as she bent to caress the narrow head of one of the salukis. Her tension seemed to have communicated itself to the dogs, whom she called Jewel and Gold. Despite their speed and alertness to any intruder, the beautiful creatures were of a nervous, gentle disposition, and they padded around uneasily, quivering every time a gust of wind howled down the chimney.

Cluny shivered too, in her thin dress. She'd always been enviably slim, but now there wasn't an ounce of spare flesh on her body. Even her face seemed thinner, there were shadows under her eyes and hollows sculpted under her elegant cheekbones. It could be put down to stress, a natural reaction after the last few weeks, but try as I would, I couldn't believe she had been as emotionally involved with my sober, elderly grandfather as all that . . . though would that thought have occurred to me, I checked myself, shame-faced, before I'd heard Magda's accusations?

But my guilty thoughts were soon turned to indignation by her careless shrug when I asked if I might look through William's papers. 'That old stuff? Oh, do what you like with it. I was going to burn the lot anyway when I got around to it.'

My face always reflected too much of what I felt. Cluny responded with a long, level gaze. 'I have to get rid of all the clutter, Zoe. I'm going back. To Harare. I'm going to fight for what was mine, for what my husband Stuart and I built up over the years.' She looked suddenly hard.

'Oh,' I said, taken aback. 'Well, good for you.' Cluny's previous life was mostly a closed book to me, but I did at least know that she'd fled Zimbabwe, after escaping from Mugabe's insurgents when they'd killed her first husband and lain waste to the farm it had taken half a lifetime to build. It was a brave, perhaps foolhardy, decision to go back and try to reclaim what she'd lost. And to carry out such plans she'd need money—but I couldn't yet bring myself to ask if she intended to sell Ingshaw.

*　　　*　　　*

In spite of my assertions that I wasn't hungry, I did full justice to the hearty soup Magda insisted on leaving. I found an orange and then made coffee. This big, old-fashioned kitchen was my favourite room, with its polished flagstone floor and red curtains, and always warm from the heat of the stove. Nothing matched, the cupboards were original to the house and the kitchen appliances were out of date, but it was comfortable and unpretentious. Only somehow I didn't feel quite so easy there tonight. I was aware as never before of the distance between Ingshaw and its nearest neighbour, and quickly drew the curtains. I switched off the lights, except for the lamp on the dresser, and sat near the stove on a rush-seated chair with a cushion at my back, feet up on the rung of another chair, a mug of coffee on the table, my patience rewarded. I'd steeled myself to wait until I was alone and unlikely to be interrupted before reading the letter, which had been burning a hole in my pocket ever since I'd picked it up in Daniel's workshop.

It was undated with many crossings-out and alterations. *My dear Zoe,* it began, *This letter is going to be hard for me to write, but I'll do my best, hoping it will make up for things I ought to have said to you before. I know I've fobbed you off whenever you've asked me about family matters, though God knows I'd ho wish to hurt you by doing that, just the opposite. I've never been much of a one for talking, as you know, nor have I ever seen any good in raking up the miseries of the past, but I can't have long to live now, and recent events have made me feel you have a right to know, if only to be prepared for what might come. If the telling seems bald, I hope you'll forgive that too, lass. I'm not good with written words, either, but here goes.*

It all started with Sophie. Sophie when she was young, the girl in the portrait, not the woman she was when I first met her all those years ago, in London. Or perhaps it went even further back, to Benjamin Temple, her father.

Sophie, in the plum-coloured velvet hat. Why had Daniel claimed to be as ignorant of her as I was when he must have seen this letter? Of course, it was possible that he might *not* have seen it, that it had only come to light by an accidental flick of the pages of that folio, I told myself, but despite the warmth from the stove, I shivered and felt the goose pimples rise on my arms.

But for me the beginning was when I married your grandmother. We met when I was in the RAF, and married a month later, a couple of reckless young kids in wartime. It was a mistake for both of us. When the war was over, I brought her home to Yorkshire, but she couldn't settle. She hated everything—the climate, the poky house we had to live in, the shortage of money. Life here was too tame for her, but more than any of that, it was me she found fault with. I'd changed, I was no longer the devil-may-care fighter pilot, one of the wild bunch, living for the moment because literally tomorrow we might be dead. She'd fallen in love with a madcap RAF officer scarcely out of his teens, and found herself

218

married to a dull and unambitious bloke who wanted only to forget the war and the horrors of seeing his comrades shot down in flames. I asked nothing more than to spend my life quietly here, making furniture, and I won't upset you by relating the hell our life became during the two years we were together. She had the Temple genes, she'd inherited her grandfather's, temper, and I retreated into my shell when I should have tried to understand her more, but

And that was it. There, at the bottom of the page, the writing stopped, maddeningly, mid-sentence.

I couldn't believe this was all there was. What about the rest of it? The minutes ticked by, my coffee stood beside me, stone-cold, while the usual asthmatic wheeze of the longcase clock in the hall heralded the hour. I waited for the ten unmusical bongs that would follow. They echoed eerily through the silent house, and I shivered. I'd have been glad of company, even the dogs, but they'd sprung into Cluny's car, as usual, the moment they heard the engine start.

After a while, I knew what I had to do.

All William's possessions, all the personal clutter of his daily living that had previously lain around the house, had been cleared away. His clothes, his music, his spectacles, his Fisherman's Friend lozenges, plus everything in his study, had all disappeared—within a week, Magda had reported. Clearing out

219

personal belongings is a painful task that has to be done when anyone dies, but the speed and the ruthlessness Cluny had employed suggested that either this had been the first move in an immediate decision to leave, or there was, as Magda had suggested, a less acceptable explanation.

From the hook behind the door, I selected the keys to the attic.

Forbidden territory up here, only previously visited under William's supervision, because he'd declared that the narrow stairs were unsafe. But as I looked around, I realized now that this reason had been nothing more than an excuse to keep the place secret. It was like a young boy's den. Piles of books with titles such as *The Boy's Wonder Book of Science*. A box containing a clockwork Hornby train set. An old box Brownie camera, a cricket bat. This new view of my unsentimental old Grandpa, his boyish treasures scattered amongst the sort of detritus that any family with a long occupation of a house and a big attic inevitably accumulates, very nearly unravelled me. I pulled a dust sheet from an old, buttoned chair, minus a few buttons, its rose velvet faded to stripy rust, and sank down on it.

Somebody had been up here, and recently. The dust on the floor had been disturbed, and in the middle of it was a not very large cardboard box. William's papers, evidently. I'd expected more.

I was on my knees, delving into the box, when I thought I heard noises. Faint but distinct, from below. Rubbish, it's all in the mind, I told myself firmly. All the outside doors were locked, and unless Magda or Cluny had come back much sooner than intended, I was alone. But the sounds were unmistakable, and coming nearer. Footsteps. I held my breath. The hairs on my neck lifted. The knob on the door at the foot of the stairs rattled.

The footsteps were real, and they were beginning to ascend the attic stairs. Dry-mouthed, I reached out blindly and my hand found something heavy and cold lying abandoned on top of a boxful of discarded kitchen utensils. It was a flat iron, ungainly to heft as a weapon, but I held on to it for dear life. I reckoned I could always throw it if necessary. If I used both hands.

'Hello, anybody there?'

'Daniel!' Relief made my knees buckle. 'Oh my God, you scared the wits out of me! You're the last person I expected to see.'

He took one look at the flat iron and raised a fending-off hand. 'Sorry—and I know, I know, you said—early night and all that. But I was locking up before going home and when I saw a light in the attic, the rest of the house in darkness, I thought I'd better investigate.'

Stupid of me, I should have remembered he had a key, for just such emergencies, and that he often worked until all hours, forgetting time existed.

'What are you doing up here, this time of night?' he went on. 'And before you answer— I'd feel a lot safer if you'd put that thing down.'

I was only too glad to comply. Those poor women who'd once had to iron huge piles of shirts and sheets and starched petticoats with contraptions like this! 'Good thing you called out. I might have bashed you on the head with it—or broken my wrist. I was just moseying around, that's all,' I said, as casually as I could, but thinking quickly. After reading that letter from my grandfather, my earlier intentions not to be alone with Daniel were doing a reverse. For one thing, I wanted to challenge him with why a private letter to me had been hidden in one of his design books. 'If you haven't been home, you haven't eaten yet.'

'Quick thinking.'

I let that pass. 'Come downstairs and I'll get you something.'

He gave me an old-fashioned look, no doubt suspicious of my sudden change of attitude, but after a curious glance around the attic, he followed me downstairs into the kitchen, sitting at the table while I put on fresh coffee and found some ham in the fridge. Reaching out to the biscuit jar, he took two, comfortably at home in a kitchen where he'd always been welcomed as one of the family. 'Wonder who first invented chocolate biscuits?' he mumbled, his mouth full. 'Hope they got the OBE.'

'Lay off them or you'll never eat this.'

'Want to bet?'

He munched away while I sliced the ham thickly to make him a mighty sandwich, not forgetting the mustard he liked. It made me think of other sandwiches I'd made for him, other times like this. Or not quite like this. I'd never before felt uneasy or unsure with Daniel. Betrayed was perhaps a better word.

I put the plate on the table. 'Daniel—' I began after a while.

'Mm, fantastic,' he said appreciatively, through big bites of the sandwich. 'Daniel, what?'

'Oh, nothing.' Wasn't I making mysteries where they didn't exist? I'd never before had reason to suspect him of anything remotely like dishonesty. Yet that folio of his had been lying open on his desk, and he'd put it away pretty smartly when he saw I'd been looking at it. Should I confront him, or let my instinct to trust him take over? I really didn't know. My judgement where he was concerned seemed to have deserted me totally; mixed-up didn't begin to describe how I felt.

I cut him a slice of Magda's rich, homemade fruitcake, poured coffee, and pushed a mug and the plate across to him. I poured some for myself. I might need sleep tonight, but I needed caffeine more, right at this minute.

'Don't be infuriating, Zoe. What were you going to say, and what *were* you doing, poking

223

about in the attic?'

I ignored the first question and, watching for his reaction, told him about my conversation with Cluny, and her intention to burn all William's papers and photographs.

'That's gross! Insensitive, even for Cluny.'

I said slowly, 'I don't believe she sees it like that. I think she's just a bit obsessed about clearing the decks to get back to Zimbabwe. She didn't want the picture, either, by the way, even when I told her what it was worth. Magda says it's guilt compensation.'

'Oh right, yes, Magda.' He finished the cake, then propped his elbows on the table. 'Look, Zoe, I'm having this problem . . . There's not a chance in hell of proving the sort of accusations she's been throwing around, about Cluny and Baines. Murder—just for this house? The stakes aren't high enough, for that. All the same, under the drama, Magda's not really the hysterical type . . .'

'You're not saying you believe her?'

'I don't know. It's just that I get a knot in my guts every time I think about that will. Or non-will, I suppose is nearer the mark. As far as you can ever know anyone, I reckon I knew the Old Man. He could be an old so-and-so, but it's just so out of character for him to have let Cluny come in for everything, even by default, Zoe, when you were the apple of his eye.'

I swallowed an iron lump in my throat. 'He didn't need to leave me money to show me that. What amazes me is that he didn't provide for Magda.' Whatever else, William had always been fair-minded, yet Magda had received not even a token acknowledgement for over fifty years' loyal and devoted service. She'd never so much as mentioned it, but I wondered how far that had contributed to her suspicions that Cluny and Baines had conspired to destroy the will, and then . . . to get rid of William himself.

I shuddered, and the silence lengthened as I thought about that, and the letter from him that I'd just read, seeing again the untidiness of it, and the crossings-out. It had looked like a rough draft—

Yes, I thought, yes!

William rarely read anything but newspapers, and when he did it wouldn't be long before his hand reached out for the nearest handy scrap of paper, to sketch a rapid design idea that had just come to him, or to jot down some reminder to himself. Then quite often he'd have a total memory lapse as to where he'd put these notes. They'd turn up on old envelopes, bills, petrol receipts, and once, memorably, on the back of a cheque for several hundred pounds. So why not an unfinished draft of a letter left in a pattern book he happened to be leafing through when the idea of writing it occurred to him? Afterwards forgotten—or even, since it was so obviously of importance to him, left there purposely as being as good a place as any to hide it away from prying eyes, since full pattern books could lie there for months, even years, without being opened. And then he'd died before he could return to finish it. The rest of the letter, if he ever had completed it, could be anywhere—in any one of the books and stuff Cluny had already got rid of, for instance. In which case I might as well forget it.

I thought about William. Taciturn, keeping his own counsel, stern, even harsh, at times, people thought him uncommunicative, but I knew his other side. If he'd been secretive, he'd had his own good reasons—and in that letter, he'd begun to open his heart and show them to me. If only I could find the rest of it, I thought, I should almost certainly discover the whole truth, including the reason why he'd wanted me to have that portrait. Which might simply have been because it was worth—not a fortune, but certainly a good deal more than any of the other pictures in the house. On the other hand, I was in no doubt now that Sophie, whoever she might have been, had some special significance, other than some real or imagined resemblance to me, that she was part of that family history of ours that I wanted so much to know about. And what, I asked myself, were those 'recent events' he'd referred to, which had made him change his mind and decide to talk about the past?

'So,' Daniel said at last, 'it's certain Cluny

will be putting Ingshaw on the market?'

I remembered with a jolt his personal involvement if the house and his business premises were sold. 'I'm afraid it looks like it. It won't seem right, no Ingshaw, but it's no longer my home, anyway. I'm going to start looking for somewhere to live tomorrow, for when I start my new job.' Commuting to Leeds while living here was a feasible proposition that would enable me to rekindle old friendships, with people who still lived here, at least. My special friend Rebecca worked for an estate agent, whom she was going to marry shortly, and would be able to help me find something I could afford on a salary lower than I'd earned in London.

I stirred my coffee. 'I've never known exactly how Cluny and Grandpa met.'

'Someone recommended him when she was looking to buy a chair. William took her round the house to show her one or two examples, as he used to do with customers, they got talking—and that was that, I suppose.'

'Do you think it was Baines who did the recommending? If she knew him before, that could be why she'd decided to settle in Yorkshire. It would explain a lot. I mean, why Yorkshire, of all places, if not?'

But it didn't explain everything, by any means. The unanswered questions were mounting up. It wasn't only Magda who was now uneasy about the circumstances of my grandfather's death.

*   *   *

Why Yorkshire indeed? I wondered again next morning, as I looked out on a dark and miserable day, the bright sky of yesterday veiled by moisture. There was a whisper of rain on the roof tiles, and through the windows the view was grey and desolate. Leaning my forehead against the glass, I gazed across the empty miles of sombre moorland on this side of the house, patch-worked with the low, dry-stone walls that were a relic of sheep-farming days, with outcroppings of dark gritstone jutting from the surface of the thin soil. In winter, when the wind could blow the snow into nine-foot drifts, they might be the only landmarks in miles, a grim prospect. But in childhood summers, beneath the high clouds, when the grass and heather smelt hot and dry, and you lay down under the sun and felt the earth spin on its axis, it had felt like nowhere else in the world. Today, although the out-look was grey with rain, I could still think without regret of that other view from my once-treasured garden flat in Muswell Hill—a sour plot of London earth, narrow and still unattractive, despite my efforts with pots and shrubs. Once full of hopeful intent, which had never materialized. But this, needing no effort on anyone's part—it was just itself. I shook myself—it was always like this: when I was here, I hated London, and when I was there, well, yes, I'd begun to hate living in London then, too. All the same, would I regret my decision to leave?

I watched a delivery lorry negotiate the difficult turning from the road into the drive, made narrower by the retaining bank of huge, craggy dark stones that flanked it, before veering to the left, towards the workshop. A car followed it, but drew up outside the house. Two men got out and hurried through the rain to the door. I recognized the one with the clipboard from our schooldays—Mike Priestley, a big, lumpy, happy-go-lucky lad, the one out of the class least likely to. And yet he now ran the town's most flourishing house agency, he'd smoothed himself out and succeeded in nabbing my very choosy friend Rebecca, who worked for him. He was keeping bad company, though, if the man he was with was who I guessed him to be—Stephen Baines, here as Cluny's solicitor, if not as her friend.

Cluny had wasted no time after making her announcement to me last night. Everyone else concerned had been told this morning that she was preparing to sell the house as soon as she could—Magda, who afterwards disappeared tight-lipped, to do some shopping. Mrs Sugden, who wondered what was going to happen to her job. And Daniel. I hadn't spoken to him yet, but after last night, I already knew what his reaction would be.

'Hi, Zoe!' Mike said. 'Long time no see.' Always one for an original phrase, Mike Priestley, but I smiled and forgave him. I'd always liked him.

While he and Cluny disappeared for an inspection tour of the house, I was left alone with Baines over the coffee. 'Another biscuit, Mr Baines?'

'Oh, Stephen, please! No thanks, Zoe.'

The salukis had run to him when he first appeared, silky tails waving, obviously familiar with him, and he was now rather nervously patting their heads while trying to keep them at arm's length. He twitched a golden hair or two from his immaculate trouser leg.

He wasn't at all as I'd imagined, he was well-dressed, his mousy hair was sharply cut, and he wore glasses with tinted, yellowish lenses and the sort of fancy frames that look as though they're on upside-down, and a gold signet ring on the little finger of his manicured right hand. Definitely the sort who fancied himself, though why, it was difficult to see.

Despite the accessories, he came across as dull and quite ordinary and, apart from the assessing looks he cast around from time to time, not at all shifty, or like one with evil intentions. But then, he would, wouldn't he? What had I expected? A pair of horns and a forked tail? I soon discovered he wasn't much of a conversationalist though, which made him

230

a very unusual lawyer indeed to my mind. All the same, I tried. 'How do you like living up here, er, Stephen?'

'Oh, very much, thank you.'

'And where did you practise before you came here?'

'London.'

I was about to launch in and ask him if that was where he'd met Cluny when I saw a shuttered look come over his face, which told me he was the sort to clam up where personal issues were concerned. I longed to probe further, but I knew it wouldn't get me anywhere. Perhaps he was more of a lawyer than I'd thought he was. After that, we talked mostly about the weather.

When Mike and Cluny returned, Mike was enthusiastic about the house, talking about period pieces, and rather less about the drawback of there being a business situated on the premises. 'But if potential buyers aren't happy with that, I'm sure I can find somewhere suitable for old Daniel,' he said to me in a confidential aside as I showed them out. 'Er— Rebecca tells me you're coming back here to live.' As if the two thoughts were connected. It must have been Rebecca who'd given him the idea they might be. She'd never given up on the idea of Daniel and me.

I sighed as I watched him making the awkward reverse turn necessary to go back down the drive. This was the downside of living around here, where your private life was never your own—but it was what I'd wanted, wasn't it? To be part, once more, of a community where everybody knew you, where you had friends who cared? Unlike Muswell Hill, where nobody knew you, and couldn't care less.

*   *   *

'I'll bet she can't wait to get away' said Mrs Sugden, settled in with her coffee as I took the cups back into the kitchen. She reached for a Hobnob and took a large bite. 'Like the first Mrs Brereton. That would be your gran—' The rest of it was drowned in a spasm of coughing, as she realized what she'd said and the dry biscuit crumbs went the wrong way. Minutes later, her streaming eyes patted dry and the crumbs washed down by half a mug of coffee, she said, 'I'm sorry, I spoke out of turn.'

'It's OK. I'd love to hear about my grandmother, Mrs Sugden.' She shook her head and I said encouragingly, 'Go on, I don't mind skeletons in the cupboard.'

It hadn't even occurred to me until I spoke that I might have stumbled on the truth, that the reason there'd been no talk of the family past from William was because there might indeed be metaphorical skeletons to rattle, something shameful to hide, like Mrs Rochester hidden in the upper regions. It

232

could even be that my grandmother might still be alive, not dead, as I'd always imagined. 'The first Mrs Brereton, my grandmother—'

'Before my time,' Mrs Sugden said hastily, getting up to rinse her coffee mug. 'Gossip. Stuff I heard from my mother, who worked here before me. Hearsay, that's all.'

Clearly, she'd been warned that the subject of the first Mrs Brereton was taboo, but I didn't intend to be put off. 'What was her name—my grandmother's, I mean?' It was really weird that I didn't even know that.

'Oh, something outlandish, I forget.' Not Sophie, then, you wouldn't describe that as an outlandish name. Besides, the Sophie of the portrait was before William's generation—she was Edwardian, or perhaps a little later.

'Janetta—no, Jacquetta, that was it.' Triumphant as she was at having remembered, however, Mrs Sugden wasn't to be drawn further. 'I'd best be getting on. It's my day for the windows, and I've no time to be sitting here, chewing the fat.'

*　　　*　　　*

I should have been flat-hunting, but the dismal weather gave me the excuse I wanted to get back to the attic. It looked more desolate than ever this morning. A single, dim bulb hung from the rafters and cast shadows into the far corners.

233

I whisked down the attic stairs, and then the back stairs, and returned double-quick with a 200 watt bulb to exchange for the dim 60 watt, also picking up a duster or two and a broom while I was at it. I rubbed vigorously at the grimy panes in the window to let in a little more light, and pushed against its resistance for some ventilation, hearing a creak and a splinter of wood, then—oops! it was open. Damp as it was, the fresh air rushing in helped to disperse the musty smell and made me suddenly feel more optimistic about what I might discover.

Half an hour later, I sat back in the pink velvet chair, defeated. I could see why the contents of that box had seemed like inconsequential trivia to Cluny. I'd been hoping, if not for the rest of that draft letter, then perhaps diaries or other letters, birth certificates even, if I got very lucky. The things I found were a few mementos from William's wartime days—an RAF cap badge, a star chart and an aircraft recognition chart, one or two photographs of young men in uniform, including one of an unexpectedly dashing Grandpa. Some of his old school exercise books, revealing little except that he'd been an average pupil, with a talent for woodwork, maths and art. Plus a whole heap of old-fashioned, unidentified sepia photographs of people who meant nothing to me, though scattered among them were some of my mother, as a child and a young woman, and of me as a gap-toothed six-year-old and a lumpy teenager. And a poem I'd written when I was eleven, about spring and daffodils, that he'd kept all these years ...

There was nothing else.

Then, as I flipped open a book about the Boer War, I came across an old black and white photo tucked inside the front flap. A group photo of about twenty people, taken on the steps of some large, colonnaded white building. It looked like a group of guests at a wedding. The women were all dolled-up in small hats and dresses with fitted waists and full skirts. Handbags and white gloves. In the early 1950s, I thought it would have been. One woman's head was circled in ink. The reverse gave the name of the professional photographer who'd taken it. Alexander Temple, it said, The Orthochrome, Salisbury, Southern Rhodesia. And in faded pencil was written 'For Elisabeth'.

Elisabeth, my mother.

I sat very still. I ought to have paid more attention in school to the way the pink parts of the globe had changed. My inner map of the shrunken British Empire was sketchy, but I was fairly certain that Salisbury, once the capital of Southern Rhodesia, was now Harare, and Southern Rhodesia itself was Zimbabwe. And Zimbabwe was where Cluny had lived before coming here, and where she was now returning.

I've never had much belief in coincidences, simple or otherwise. But it was the name of the photographer that clinched it, that gave me that lurch of the insides which made me know I was on the right track, at last. Alexander Temple. Hadn't William written that Temple, Benjamin Temple, was the name of Sophie's father—and, referring to his wife in the last few lines of his letter: *she had inherited the Temple genes?*

I left the attic, still shaken by my discoveries there, and met Cluny in the hall, a couple of large books tucked under her arm. 'I thought I'd returned all these to the workshop but I've found two more,' she said.

I recognized the two leather-covered folios with the honeysuckle and bee decoration on the front, unmistakably Brereton design books.

'I'll take them back, if you like,' I offered. 'But first, have a look at this, will you?' I held out the photo I'd just discovered.

I had to admire her control. Not a flicker of surprise showed on her face as she scanned it. But I'd have put money on it she was furious with herself for having been careless enough not to have spotted it. 'Where did you find this?' she asked sharply.

'It was with all that useless stuff of Grandpa's you were going to burn.'

Two spots of giveaway colour appeared on her face. The Cluny I'd once quite liked and admired in a funny sort of way, she of the quick wit and the amusing comeback, had been nowhere in evidence since my arrival at Ingshaw. Perhaps I was seeing the real Cluny for the first time, the one who'd married William for what she could get, the one who'd cold-bloodedly helped to orchestrate that fall to his death, if she hadn't personally fixed it?

She soon recovered herself and answered carelessly, 'Well, it wouldn't have been any big deal, would it, if it had been burnt. Some old photo that matters to nobody now.'

'You don't recognize her, then? The woman with the ring drawn round her head?'

'Heavens, no! Should I?'

'It says on the back that the photo was taken in Salisbury, Southern Rhodesia. By someone named Temple. He ran a photographic studio called The Orthochrome, and seeing as how you lived there, I thought you might have remembered such an unusual name.'

'Sorry, no.'

It was possible she was telling the truth. She could only have been a small child, perhaps not even born, if I'd been right about the date of the photo. What was more, the name, Orthochrome, must have had a passé, old-fashioned ring to it even then, as if it and its proprietor had belonged to another era. But somehow I knew she was lying.

I shrugged as if it was of no consequence. 'It just seemed such a coincidence, Grandpa having this photo, and you coming from Salisbury—sorry, Harare.'

'Not really. It was Johannesburg I came from. I only went to live in Zimbabwe after I was married,' she said firmly.

Before returning the books, I took them into the study and went through them, turning the pages feverishly, and then with more care, but alas, with no result. I'd only come across that rough draft of the first page of his letter by a sheer fluke—and it was becoming more and more probable that even if William had left me a fair copy of the whole thing somewhere, the chance of finding it was remote. But there was no way I was going to throw in the towel until I'd explored every possibility.

All the same, I felt rather low about the whole business, and my spirits didn't rise much when I found Daniel in his office, looking rather grim—for him, that is. If things did ever get him down, he rarely allowed it to show. 'I'm so sorry, Daniel,' I told him. 'About the property being sold, and everything.' Though truly, Cluny selling the house wasn't the only thing I had to be sorry about . . .

'Thanks, Zoe.'

Impulsively, I squeezed his hand. It was as near as I could get to an apology for my suspicions that he'd deliberately kept that first page of the letter from me. He squeezed back. No current of electricity this time, but as a smile warmed his eyes, something sang inside me. I no longer understood myself. Here I was, having burned my boats well and truly. Given up the lease on my flat, swapped jobs for a new one not half as glamorous and a lot less well paid. Come back to somewhere all my London friends regarded as a backwater. And it felt wonderful.

'Oh, I don't know, things could be worse,' Daniel said, bringing me down to earth, his natural optimism beginning to surface once more. 'I've other plans. Survival, it's called. I need to prioritize, you know? Focus on improving the quality of operations, become a leading-edge supplier—' He pulled himself up with a short laugh. Sounding like a young Turk in red braces wasn't really his style. 'Trouble is, I'm not up for the brainy stuff. Give me a piece of wood and I'm OK, but it'll never make me a millionaire.'

'Is that what you want?' As far as I knew, money had never been a priority with Daniel. Satisfaction for him, as for William, had always come from the quality of his work, the respect it gained.

'No, but I have to eat, Zoe.' Without enthusiasm, he said, 'The answer's fairly obvious—employ more staff and make built-in kitchens, bread-and-butter stuff like that. Plenty of demand there. I know it has to happen sooner or later. Only I hadn't anticipated it being sooner.' The worry at the back of his eyes returned.

I nodded. 'You need money to start up that sort of operation.' 'How true! A commodity in rather short supply just now. But don't look so miserable, love. I'll find a way.'

I said, 'Mike Priestley's just been to give the house the once-over. He told me he'd be able to find you some more premises, if necessary.'

'Trust old Mike not to miss a trick!'

'And Baines was with him.' I gave him my view on the charmless Stephen Baines—amongst other things, boring, bloodless . . . as for murderous, well, there didn't seem much mileage in pursuing that one.

'Right, but don't underestimate him. Not a lot of bottle, but an eye to the main chance, that's for sure. And I wouldn't trust him as far as I could throw him.'

Yes, Daniel had always set great store on people being upfront and honest. I braced myself. 'Daniel, there's something I'd better get off my chest.'

'Sounds ominous. Hang on a sec.' He opened the door and shouted, 'How long's that coffee going to be, Sean?'

'Coming up when I've finished this!'

He came back and straddled a chair. 'Fire away,' he said amiably.

I twisted my legs round the stool I was perched on. 'I—er—took something from here yesterday.'

He looked amused. 'News to me that there's anything around here worth pinching!'

'It wasn't really pinching. It belongs to me
. . . but I should've asked.' I drew in a deep
breath, and told him everything. I showed him
that first roughed-out page of William's letter,
and handed him the photo, too. It was clear he
hadn't seen either before, which did a lot to
raise my spirits.

I hoped, as I watched him read, that
he could make more sense out of it than I
could. All I really had was a series of unlikely
coincidences: the photographer's name,
Temple, being the same as the Benjamin
Temple mentioned in William's letter; the
message on the back of the photograph—'For
Elisabeth; and the place where it had been
taken—Southern Rhodesia, where Cluny had
formerly lived.

'Know what I think?' Daniel said, when
he had finally finished reading. 'I reckon
the woman circled in the picture is probably
Jacquetta, your grandmother, that she—or this
Alexander Temple, the photographer—sent it
to the Old Man after she'd gone back home,
and he kept it because he couldn't bear to part
with it. Or more likely, because he was too
bitter about her to pass it on to your mother.'

'Yes,' I said thoughtfully. 'He said she went
back home. But he said he met Sophie in
London—and Jacquetta when he was in the
RAF!'

'That doesn't mean they didn't come from
Rhodesia. And you've assumed Sophie was

241

Jacquetta's mother, but it might just as well have been Alexander who was her father.'

He was right. All I knew for certain was that Sophie had been the daughter of Benjamin Temple, and my grandmother, Jacquetta, had been Benjamin's granddaughter. I had perhaps too easily wanted the enigmatic Sophie to be my great-grandmother. For why else should my grandfather have left me her portrait?

And in all this, where did Cluny come in? I couldn't believe it was mere chance that she'd landed up here all the way from Zimbabwe and had just happened to meet Jacquetta's former husband. And not only that—had persuaded him to marry her. Which was the most astonishing thing of all. William was never easily manipulated. And it was impossible to imagine him being swept off his feet, at *any* time of his life.

'We might find the answers if we had the rest of the letter -which should, logically, be with that first page,' Daniel said in that maddeningly direct way he had of going straight to the heart of things, and he remembered, without prompting, the very book he'd been consulting when I'd walked in and nosily begun to look through it. He began to leaf through it systematically, and almost immediately found a sheet of paper lying between a design for a court cupboard and one for an inlaid rosewood table. I snatched it up, but it turned out to be simply a note of the modifications required for a customer who'd wanted a similar cupboard. I was bitterly disappointed when the book revealed nothing else. But Daniel was staring at me. 'Zoe,' he said quietly, 'Zoe, where's that portrait?'

'*The portrait?* Where I left it, wrapped up in my car boot.'

Ten minutes later, we were unwrapping it from its bubblewrap and Sophie in her velvet hat was lying face upwards on the bench, looking neat, prim and as enigmatic as the Mona Lisa. Then Daniel turned it over and his strong hands began expertly using a pair of pliers to pull out the nails that held in position the splintery old backing of thin-cut wood—the original backing that William had retained when he'd made the new maplewood frame, perhaps because stuck on it was a faded old label bearing the title, handwritten in copperplate, presumably by the artist.

'Are you sure you know what you're doing?' I asked.

'Trust me.' A moment later, the backing was off, without further damage. 'What have we here?'

A long brown envelope. With my name on the front, in William's writing. 'So *that's* why he wanted you to have the portrait,' Daniel said.

Had Magda been right? Had there been a will after all? But hidden behind a picture—how corny could he get? 'I might never have found this!'

243

'I think the Old Man would've thought of some way of making sure you did—though don't ask me how. Maybe you'll find out if you open it.'

I realized I'd been clutching the envelope for all of three minutes, and tore it open. And no, it wasn't a will inside. It was the fair copy of the whole of that letter William had written to me. I skimmed through the first, now so familiar, lines and saw there'd been no substantial changes to the first page. *I should have tried to understand her more, but . . .* that page had ended. And now the next page went on:

. . . perhaps Jacquetta was wiser than I was when she decided to call it a day, packed her bags and went back to Rhodesia, though I didn't see it like that at the time, left alone with an eighteen-month-old baby to raise. If Magda hadn't arrived on the scene like a guardian angel, I doubt whether I could have managed. My little Elisabeth became my lifeline as well as my responsibility. I worshipped her, spoiled her a bit, I admit. Maybe that's why I was so angry when she announced she was going to marry your father. I knew he was wrong for her, a charmer but not in her league. For the first time, I understood how Benjamin Temple had felt about Sophie's marriage. But I wasn't about to make the same mistake he'd made—and besides, I might have been as wrong in my judgement of Tony as he had been of Sophie's husband. As it

turned out, my fears were justified, but who can be certain of these things?

I thought of Tony Kennedy, the husband who walked away. The father I'd never known, now dead, who'd only ever written to me at Christmas, or on my birthday. When he remembered, which wasn't often. I thought of Grandpa, who'd taken his place. Blinking hard, I read on:

Benjamin Temple was a typical Victorian, prosperous, self-made, father of the twins, Alexander and Sophie. He was also a regular tyrant. Alexander worked for him in the family shipping business in London, though he hated it, since his ambition was to become an artist. As you'll see from his portrait of his sister, he was extremely talented, but Benjamin knew it took more than talent to make a living from painting, and flatly refused to support him while he tried to make his mark. It was a brave young man who would defy his father in those days, and risk being cut off without a penny. Alexander stayed.

But Sophie was made of sterner stuff. She had fallen in love with someone her father regarded as a penniless colonial upstart, and when he refused his consent to the marriage, she simply eloped with her young man. This seemed to shame Alexander into standing up for himself. He walked out of his father's business and left with the newly married couple to start a new life in Rhodesia. After a few years he set up as a photographer in Salisbury, having fulfilled his father's predictions by failing to make a living as an artist. By then he was married and had a daughter, Jacquetta, who became my wife.

So it *was* Alexander Temple, artist and photographer, of The Orthochrome, Jacquetta's father, who was my great-grandfather. I wasn't directly descended from Sophie.

Sophie's marriage, though happy, was short-lived. Her husband died, and not long afterwards old Benjamin, who had fallen ill and thought he was dying (though he still had another thirteen years to go) decided he could bring himself to be reunited with his daughter, now that she was relieved of such an unsuitable husband. He begged her to return to England for a visit. She came, but Alexander was another matter. Benjamin could not forgive his son for leaving him in the lurch, as he saw it, Alexander would not apologize, and both remained adamant in their refusal to be reconciled.

To her sorrow, Sophie was never blessed with children, and she lavished all her love on her brother's only child, Jacquetta, which made their later quarrel all the more bitter. But before that they were constant companions and when Sophie visited England in 1939, Jacquetta, then seventeen, came with her. They were caught here when war broke out, and stayed to help in the war effort. That was how Jacquetta and I met, three years later, when I was in London, on leave, and she was working in an officers' leave club. When the news came that her parents had been killed in a car crash, we were already married and Jacquetta was expecting our child. So it was Sophie who returned to South Africa to sort out Alexander's affairs. He didn't leave much money, but enough to make Jacquetta independent when she decided she'd had enough of being married to me. When your mother was eighteen months old, Jacquetta left us both and went back home.

And there it was, my sad family history, in a nutshell. A legacy of family quarrels, bitterness, abandonment, old scores never forgiven. That photo my mother might never have seen—which could not, by the way, have been taken by Alexander, since he was dead by then. Perhaps his business had been continued by someone else. It didn't matter. What really mattered was whether all this might in some way have contributed to a story that ended in my grandfather's death. A story that wasn't by any means finished yet.

Sean came in at that moment with the coffee. 'My mum's sent you some of her curd tarts.' He put a plate of little cakes on the desk. Daniel was regularly supplied with pies and cakes and casseroles by local ladies, who wouldn't acknowledge that a young man living alone was capable of being as self-sufficient as Daniel patently was. He could cook with the best of them, but was too good-natured to do other than accept their offerings graciously, as

247

he did now, thanking Sean and offering me the plate.

The tarts were worth a bit of diplomatic dissembling on his part, I decided; the pastry was crisp and golden, the sweet cheesy filling stuffed with currants. 'Yummy, tell your mum,' I told Sean.

'I will,' he promised, looking pleased.

Daniel stopped him as he was going out of the door. He'd been deep in thought while I read the letter, and now he asked, 'What do you remember about the day the Old Man died, Sean?'

Sean shot a rather embarrassed glance in my direction.

'It's OK, you can talk about Grandpa, I don't mind.'

He thought for a bit. 'Well, after you set off for the Dales to deliver that sideboard, up near Ramsgill, Magda came in to tell me she was going out for the day. Mrs Brereton had taken the dogs to the vet and wouldn't be in till late afternoon, so Magda asked me to see to the Old Man's dinner about half twelve. She'd left something cooking, but bending to get things out of the oven was awkward for him, with his lumbago. But he rang from the house and said I needn't bother, that solicitor guy had been in to see him, and he'd done the necessary before he left.' He swallowed. 'A few hours later, Mrs Brereton found the Old Man on the floor and came rushing in here for help. She thought he'd had a stroke, but when the doctor came, he said he'd broken his neck.' He looked upset, remembering.

'Thanks, Sean,' Daniel said. 'Just wanted to be sure we had things clear.' His eyes met mine when Sean had gone. 'So much for Baines as a suspect.'

'OK, if there was a booby trap, it had to be fixed while Grandpa was upstairs after lunch, so Baines couldn't have rigged it up before he left. But he could have come back later.' It was a faint-hearted protest. Anyone could have been in and out of the house during the afternoon. The workshop windows only gave a view of the back door. And did I really believe Baines capable of doing that? Could I actually believe that *anyone* had deliberately plotted William's death?

'There's always Cluny,' I said weakly. 'How long does a visit to the vet take, for goodness' sake?'

'Leave it, Zoe,' Daniel said, quite gently. 'We're getting nowhere like this. He fell, and that's it. Isn't it better to believe that?'

He was probably right. But there were still a lot of questions I'd have liked the answers to.

Frustrated, I turned back to finish reading the letter. There were only a few lines, couched in such awkwardly affectionate terms that I was on the verge of tears, knowing how difficult this whole letter must have been for William to write. I was so concerned with that, it took a while for me to absorb what was written beneath his signature, and learn that I was to contact the law firm of Alderson, Jeavons & Wyngate at an address in London.

*   *   *

'And that's about it.' I poured myself another cup of Magda's bracing tea. Explaining everything that had led up to the finding of that letter tucked behind Sophie's portrait had been thirsty work.

We were sitting together in the kitchen as dusk fell, always a nostalgic hour. From the side window I caught glimpses of the lights winking on in the town directly beneath, I could still see the clock tower on the Town Hall, and the grey face of my old school on the slope opposite, the bulk of the hill behind it rising to the moors against a darkening skyline. There was now a Tesco superstore just below the school, where the old bus garage had once been, by the viaduct. A line of sodium lights snaked towards Leeds—a handy road to have nearby, when I started my new job.

'Oh, goodness, so that's what he meant about the backing! I should have told you, but I'd completely forgotten, *dorlink!*' Magda looked stricken, stress bringing out the Hungarian in her. 'He had made the picture look so nice again, with that new frame and all. Such a disgrace it was when he brought it down from the attic! So dirty, and the frame was badly damaged. Somebody—I suppose it was your grandmother—had left it at the bottom of a trunk with all sorts of junk piled on top—'

'Magda, what was it you forgot?'

'Oh yes, well, after he did that reframing, he said to tell you to have a new backing put on, though I did wonder why he hadn't done it himself while he was at it. "Tell her to make sure it's done," he said. 'I'm so sorry I forgot.'

'That's all right.' But if Magda had told me this when she gave me the picture, I would have found out immediately that he'd wanted me to replace the old splintery backing so that I would discover the letter concealed behind. As it turned out, I was going to take the train for London tomorrow, to keep the appointment I'd arranged with that firm of solicitors.

'And then,' said Magda, with satisfaction, 'maybe some people will get their come-uppance at last.'

* * *

Henry Alderson's telephone voice was that of a tired old man. I'd been lucky to find him in the office, since he only came in once a week, nowadays. The name of William Brereton eventually emerged from somewhere in the dusty recesses of his mind as that of a client,

251

and he expressed himself shocked that he hadn't been informed when he'd died, though not entirely surprised to hear that was because no one had known of William's connection with his firm. Ah yes, it *had* been a somewhat singular arrangement, he admitted cautiously, which he would explain when we met.

The offices of Alderson, Jeavons & Wyngate, established in 1888, were in Clerkenwell, and at first glance, Henry Alderson looked as though he might have been the original of that name, so old did he seem. A small, tortoise-like man with pale eyes, his white hair was almost non-existent, and even the effort of half-rising from behind his desk to offer his hand made him breathe alarmingly hard. I feared for him, remembering the stairs I'd just climbed. But as we began to speak, I realized he must be younger than his appearance indicated, quite a lot younger, simply the sort who'd been born elderly. Time could only have made him even more lethargic.

The last time he'd actually met my grandfather, he said, had been eight years ago, just at the point when he himself was beginning to leave matters to more junior members of the firm before taking a back seat, as he put it. I translated this as marking time until he could retire and take up stamp-collecting, or if that was too energetic, maybe a little gentle *petit point.*

'We met,' he went on in his whispery voice, 'through the will of one of the firm's oldest clients, the late Mrs Sophie Venables, who lived in what is now Zimbabwe. We had previously acted for her father, Mr Benjamin Temple. She herself lived to a great age, well into her nineties, and when making her will, she came back to us, conditions in Zimbabwe being what they were—plus the fact that the beneficiary, your grandfather, was British.'

'Sophie? She left my grandfather her money?'

His light eyes were sharper than the rest of him, not missing the fact that Sophie's name was known to me. 'Most of it, yes. She left small amounts to certain people, and one or two charities, over there, but the bulk of it—a very tidy sum—went to him.'

'Surely she must have had relatives ...'

But I was rapidly working out how it might have been. Sophie had had no children, her brother Alexander had died in 1943, when she had returned from England to sort out his affairs. And according to William, she'd quarrelled bitterly with her niece, Jacquetta, my grandmother—who in any case, might very well have been dead herself before Sophie made her will. Who were Jacquetta's descendants, other than me? I didn't even know whether she and my grandfather had ever divorced, and she'd remarried.

'Distant relatives only,' Alderson said,

brushing the matter aside when I asked. 'There were—attempts—to challenge Benjamin Temple's will, but there were absolutely no grounds, I assure you. He willed everything to his daughter. Who she subsequently left it to was entirely her own business, no one else has any legal claim at all. When the money came to your grandfather, he immediately made a will of his own. Everything he possessed when he died, apart from a bequest to his housekeeper, Miss Lutz, is now yours, I'm happy to tell you.'

At least one of us was happy, then. Me, I was too staggered to be sure how I felt. 'Didn't he make a later will, leaving something to his wife? He remarried two years ago.'

If he was surprised at that, he didn't show it. 'Not with us.'

'His solicitors in Yorkshire were Brownrigg and Shaw, but he didn't leave one with them, either. We thought he'd died intestate.'

'Just so,' he said stiffly, making no secret of his disapproval that William had chosen to use one firm for his business affairs and another for his will. 'It would have been simpler had he dealt with either one of us, but for some reason he chose not to.'

Tittle-tattle, William would have said. *What nobody knows, nobody can talk about!* And he did have a point. Somehow, the fact that William Brereton suddenly had all that money to leave would have leaked out in his home town. And that was something he'd have done a lot to avoid.

'However, in the light of what you've just told me, you may have been very fortunate. Your grandfather rang me at my home about six months ago, to make an appointment to review his will and make some changes. I couldn't do that from home, so I asked him to ring me again when I was back in the office, the following week. I never did hear from him, so I supposed he'd changed his mind.'

Fortunate for me, yes, perhaps—but if only Alderson had bestirred himself to follow up William's call, the will would have been changed. And then maybe he wouldn't have died . . .

'I still don't understand why Sophie chose to leave her money to my grandfather.'

'Her actual words were that she'd found him to be an honourable man who faced up to his responsibilities, and she could trust him to use the money to see that her niece's child—your mother—was compensated. Unfortunately,' he added drily, 'it came too late.'

*   *   *

'So that was Sophie.' Cluny stared at the portrait, which I'd hung on the wall to replace a stormy looking Victorian depiction of Malham Tarn. 'She's nothing like I imagined.'

We were in the sitting-room at Ingshaw: me; Cluny, on the sofa facing the portrait;

Daniel propped against the window sill, arms folded; Magda, sitting stiffly on an upright chair and keeping a tight rein on herself for my sake, I was sure. And Stephen Baines. I'd rung him to ask him to come up to the house, feeling that Cluny would need professional, if not moral, support when she was told the news. I didn't say why and he didn't ask; no problem, he'd replied colourlessly, he'd drive up immediately.

'You never actually knew her, then?' I asked Cluny, handing round the glasses of William's Glenfiddich that Daniel had suggested as a means of helping the situation along.

'No, but I heard plenty about her from Jacquetta, Stuart's mother. Stuart Temple was my husband,' she said flatly. 'I thought it better to use van Doelen, my maiden name, when I came over here. Like Jacquetta used hers, after she returned from England, though she and your grandfather were never divorced. She called herself Temple until she died. She was never married to Stuart's father, so his name was Temple, too.'

Did that make Cluny some distant relation of mine—a kind of step-aunt by marriage? Whatever, I wasn't about to relish informing her that I'd inherited, through William, everything that had been Sophie's, though why I should feel bothered about this, when I suspected her of being involved in his death, I couldn't think. But in the end, when she finally understood, and saw that she was no longer legally entitled to benefit from the sale of Ingshaw, that William hadn't left her a penny, I had the strangest impression she was, in an odd sort of way, relieved.

'It was worth a shot.' A bitter, defeated smile played round her mouth.

'We shall claim,' Baines intervened suddenly, very cold. 'You were his wife, you're entitled to a share.'

He had a point. I was having difficulty myself in coming to terms with William having done something so petty and out of character. On the other hand, he'd valued integrity above all else and he didn't give anyone a second chance. It made me wonder just what Cluny had done to cause him to act in such a way.

It was Daniel who said, 'Zoe's told you how she came to find out about the will, Cluny. Isn't it time she heard your side of all this?'

Baines shot her a warning glance. 'You've explained too much already.' He spoke slowly and carefully, and I thought how oddly he was sitting, rigidly, as if he had a rod down his back. He'd already downed the first whisky. I poured him another.

But Cluny ignored his warning. 'Fair enough,' she answered Daniel, an unaccustomed air of sad resignation about her. 'We're talking a long way back . . . As I said, Jacquetta was my mother-in-law. Not an easy woman, always complaining she'd had a raw deal from life, particularly through the injustice of old Benjamin's will. She believed she was entitled to what should have been her father's share, had he lived, but Sophie had refused even to consider dividing the inheritance. They already had a long-standing quarrel, but this refusal soured their relationship for ever. After that, they barely spoke to each other again.'

I recalled what William had written about them coming to England together, staying to help with the war effort. 'I thought they were the best of friends once.'

'So they were—until Jacquetta walked out and left her husband and her baby, which was something Sophie couldn't condone. She'd always regarded Jacquetta almost as her own child, taught her to know right from wrong, Well—you know how it can be when there's a major row, both of you saying and doing things so awful there comes a point when it's too late to go back.'

She wrapped her arms tight around herself. Without a fire in the grate, the sitting-room felt cold and unfriendly, despite the soft, buttery lamplight that lay in pools on the carpet, but served only to emphasize the growing darkness outside and to cast shadows on the taut planes of her face. I felt cold, too, thinking of all those needless miseries which had had such repercussions.

'Sophie had always been straight-laced

and unforgiving,' she went on, 'according to Jacquetta, anyway.' She paused. 'That may have been true, though you couldn't always believe everything Jacquetta said. She craved excitement, and she'd make it up if it wasn't there. She'd led a bit of a wild life after she came back from England—until she met John Nash, that is, and Stuart was born. John was a farmer, different from the usual men she associated with. He was a good man, but in the end he proved far too dull for her and she ditched him, though it suited her to let Stuart live with him most of the time. John was a prosperous farmer and when he died, he left everything to Stuart. We both loved the farm and worked hard to keep it going, until . . . until he was killed, and I was left with literally nothing.'

She pushed her fingers through her thick, tawny hair and lifted her chin. That hard, driven look I'd seen before was back on her face. 'But when the first shocks were over, I decided I wouldn't give in. I'd start again, somehow, though I was desperate for cash. I remembered Jacquetta's insistence that she'd been cheated, that William Brereton had obtained Sophie's money under false pretences.'

'That's not true!' I protested. 'She—'

But Baines cut me short. 'Isn't it? How do you think your grandfather was able to set his business up here in the first place, in a house this size?' He spoke fast, as if making up for his taciturnity the last time we'd met. 'When he came from a working-class family, down in the valley, without a penny to bless themselves? Because he borrowed the money from Sophie, of course!'

'What? How do you know that?' He'd managed to find out more about my grandfather than I ever had.

'It's common knowledge round here. Some people still remember how he was able to set up, through that rich aunt of his wife's who thought so much of him. A crazy old woman,' he added contemptuously, 'who left her fortune to a man just because he was canny enough to pay back a loan that could have meant very little to her!'

'I don't think that's so crazy,' said Daniel. 'A lot of people wouldn't have bothered. Repaying the loan, I mean.'

Baines laughed shortly. 'No, they wouldn't, would they? But he did. Nice one, that, William!'

I was furious. 'Sophie's money,' I said, 'was left for Jacquetta's daughter—my mother. Sophie couldn't have known she was already dead. That's why Grandpa kept it for me.'

I was thinking at the same time—how could Baines have known why Sophie had left William Brereton her money? Yet who better than a lawyer to find out about the wills people left behind? 'So,' I said to Cluny, 'what did you think to gain by coming over here?'

'It wasn't like that, or not quite. After—after Stuart was killed, I decided I'd nothing to lose, so—' She swallowed. 'So I came over to England to put a business proposition to William Brereton, to remind him that at least some of the money should rightly have come to Stuart, and to ask him to invest money with me in a new venture. But when I met him, and saw the sort of straight down-the-middle man he was, I knew that sort of pressure would cut no ice. Maybe I *was* Stuart's widow, but I really had no valid claim.'

Daniel said, 'If you'd been honest with him, he'd have been fair with you. Better than getting him to marry you as a roundabout way of getting your hands on the money.'

'I married him when he asked me,' she flashed, with a return of her habitual sharpness, 'because I'd become fond of him. No matter what anybody thought, we had a good relationship. I gave him companionship, and he—he was someone I could lean on in a world gone mad. He knew my first husband had been killed, but he respected my need for silence about the details. I think he gave me back my sanity.'

No one had anything to say to that. 'So what went wrong?' I asked eventually.

'I'm afraid he might have—suspected something. Stephen and I first met during the business handover to you, Daniel, and we

261

began to see each other. But our meetings were purely business, never mind what William thought. No, Stephen, I mean to go on.'

Baines spread his hands, abrogating responsibility. If she was determined to talk, the gesture said, he couldn't stop her. But he was clearly on edge.

'Somewhere, there was a lot of money from Sophie's legacy. We made a bargain—Stephen would try to trace it in return for a share of whatever I might get. It was inconceivable William had spent it, money never meant much to him, did it? But we knew there was no will deposited at Brownrigg's. He was constantly urged to make one, but he kept putting it off. We suspected he'd drawn one up himself . . . perfectly legal, as long as it's properly witnessed . . . but though I searched the house from top to bottom, I found nothing. When he died and one still didn't turn up, I decided he'd already passed the actual money over to you, Zoe. He'd have known that if he died intestate, everything else he had—the house and so on—would automatically come to me. I suppose he thought that was fair enough.'

She must also have thought that was why I'd made no fuss when it looked to everyone else as though William had all but disowned me.

Her wedding ring had become very loose, and she twisted it round and round on her finger as she said, 'Our relationship became strained in the last few months. I think he'd begun to suspect something. All the same, he was very upset when I told him, the night before he died, that I'd decided to go back to Zimbabwe. I never dreamed it would distress him so much. He'—her voice faltered—'he said if I left him, his life wouldn't be worth living.'

Baines drained the second whisky 'If that's how he felt, it seems that fall of his down the stairs was—well, to put it kindly, a merciful accident.'

'How dare you say that? Such a thing—to suggest he took his own life!' cried Magda, in a passion. 'And it was surely no accident!'

'What rubbish is this?' Cluny had that distant look she always had when addressing Magda, the one that infuriated her.

'You call a booby trap rubbish, do you?' Magda said. Cluny stared at her, still not connecting. 'The trip-wire, which had been stretched across the staircase and fastened with tacks or drawing-pins. The holes are still there to prove it.'

Baines looked as astounded as Cluny, and for a moment they had me convinced. I had to remind myself that Cluny was a good actress— she had fooled William, not an easy man to be taken in. Maybe she'd fooled Baines, too. Or maybe he was as good as she was at acting. Or . . .

All my doubts came back. Had we in fact

been manufacturing some plot out of nothing? I myself had pooh-poohed Magda's suspicions when I'd first seen those tiny holes in the skirting board. It was only gradually that I'd come to think that, randomly placed though they might appear, they were probably too conveniently placed to be there by accident.

'Perhaps, Miss Lutz,' said Baines, coldly polite, 'you'd explain how you come to have worked this out?'

No one ever called her anything but Magda, and she took it as an insult. 'Why don't you ask her?' She jerked her head in Cluny's direction. 'She came home before she was expected— no one knows how long before. She rigged up that trip-wire, or cotton, or whatever it was, and waited for him to come downstairs and fall over it. Then she raised the alarm, pretending she'd just come home.'

'Trip-wires? Booby traps? Oh, come on! Has everybody in this house gone mad?'

'Think about it,' put in Daniel. 'It *could* have happened like that. Or, just for the sake of argument, what about this? You for one were here on the day he died, when everyone else was out. You came up to see William around lunchtime. You knew he always took a nap for an hour between one and two, so— let's say you came back while he was asleep and rigged up a booby trap. And then came back again and removed it after he'd fallen. How does that sound?'

264

'Ridiculous.' I hadn't realized quite how good a disguise were those spectacles that made him look such a dork. He had taken them off and was polishing them with a spotless white handkerchief. I saw his eyes, very pale and very cold. I also recognized that glassy look—as anyone immediately would who has worked among media people: he was, if not drunk, rather the worse for wear. That whisky of William's, into which he'd made such inroads certainly hadn't been the start of his drinking that evening. 'I'll tell you one thing,' he added, replacing the specs. 'If I *had* killed him, I'd have damn sure chosen a less chancy way of doing it.'

'A trip-wire as a murder weapon does leave something to be desired.'

'Precisely. But let me say again: I came up to the house once that day. Once only'.

'All right, Stephen,' said Cluny suddenly. 'I'll tell you all what happened, but it wasn't anything like that. The fact is, I did come home before I was expected—'

Baines opened his mouth to speak, but she waved him down. 'William was at the top of the stairs, bending over to pick up his stick, which he seemed to have dropped. He was swaying slightly, and I thought he was going to fall, so I rushed up to him and tried to steady him, but he gave me such a look, and—and pulled away. I tried to grab him, but I was too late.' She looked down at her hands, fingers

265

twisted together in her lap. 'He fell, rather than take help from me.'

For the first time, Magda looked uncertain, but she stuck to her guns. 'First you say you found him at the bottom of the stairs, now you say he fell!'

'It seemed easier than trying to explain all that about being with him at the top of the stairs . . . I was afraid—I was afraid it might be thought I'd pushed him.'

Well—had she? Even more bizarrely, had she rigged up that trap? Or had it really been the work of Baines, and his assertion just now that he would have been more careful, nothing but a double bluff? Or even . . . there suddenly occurred to me a nasty, unwelcome thought: could it have been neither of them? Stairs are notoriously difficult to negotiate, using a walking-stick. Was the true explanation what it appeared to be—a simple fall? *With those holes, in fact, put there after the event by a spiteful woman simply wanting to stir up trouble for the bereaved wife?*

Magda was not a subtle woman, and had made no secret of her antipathy towards Cluny—and William had been the very centre of her life. I had known her for ever, she was so open, so on the surface. But was it possible there were depths to her we'd none of us been allowed to see? She had never spoken of her life before she fled to England, or of the family she had been forced to leave behind, what

266

terrors of war she'd encountered which had left her alone, dispossessed, and what mark they'd made upon her. I knew how persistent she could be, once she'd got an idea into her head, but—was she capable of such malice?

I was suddenly fed up. This wasn't an abstract problem we were discussing, but my grandfather, William Brereton. I said loudly, 'I don't actually care very much which of you did it, what nasty little plots you made up. As far as I'm concerned, it was an accident, and how it happened is best forgotten.' *Leave it,* Daniel had said to me, and I knew now he was right. If anyone was responsible for it, they would have to live with it for the rest of their lives.

Suddenly, Baines stood up and walked out of the room without another word. No one tried to stop him, whether we thought his departure was an admission of guilt, or not. None of us wanted further confrontation over something we knew could be proved only with difficulty—if ever. I watched him through the window as he reached his car, wrenched open the door and flung himself into the driver's seat. The engine roared into life and he screeched the car into a reverse turn.

The headlights lit up the salukis, who had heard the sound of the engine and raced round the side of the house, expecting to be able to jump into Cluny's car as usual. For a second it looked as though Baines wasn't going to be able to avoid them, but they skeetered away to one side, almost falling over one another, their silky ears laid back, eyes rolling in fright, uttering shrill yelps of fear. The manoeuvre had made Baines lose control of the steering-wheel, and the car was careering at an odd angle down the drive towards the busy main road. But he would never negotiate the curve through those narrow gates anyway at that speed, and the drive was too short to allow him to straighten up in time.

The car hit the stone slabs of the retaining wall along the drive with a teeth-grinding shriek.

For several moments, there was that deathly silence that comes after shock. Then there came the sound of a car noisily manoeuvring, and driving off. Everyone sagged with relief.

In the aftermath, I felt incapable of movement. I stared at Sophie's portrait. She had left me with a problem, she and William between them. I'd known from the first what I would do with the house, of course. But the money? I heard my grandfather's voice. *She'll know the right thing to do,* he'd said to Magda. And suddenly, I did.

I was sure Magda wouldn't approve. I didn't think Sophie would have, either. Well, you started all this, I told her silently, as she stared primly and accusingly out of her frame, from under the brim of her velvet hat.

The salukis were barking at the door. I smiled at Cluny as she rose to let them in.

THE EGYPTIAN GARDEN

'But what has happened to the garden?' asked Mrs Palmer.

'There doesn't appear to be one, I'm afraid, dear,' replied Moira Ledgerwood, who felt obliged to take the old lady under her wing, as she'd frequently let it be known over the last two weeks. 'Just a big courtyard.'

'Well. I can see that!'

'No garden in Cairo *housses,*' the guide, Hassan, asserted sibilantly, with the fine disregard for truth which had characterized all his explanations so far.

'But there used to be one here. With a fountain in the middle.'

Hassan shrugged. The other twenty members of the cultural tour smiled tolerantly. They were accustomed to Mrs Palmer by now, after ten days together in Upper Egypt. You had to admire her spirit, and the way she kept up with the best of them, despite her age. A widow, refusing to let the fact that she was alone limit her choice of holiday to Eastbourne, or perhaps a Mediterranean cruise. Intrepid old girl, eighty if she was a day. They were always the toughest, that sort. But her younger travelling companions sensed that this trip had turned out to be something of a disappointment. Egypt was not apparently

269

living up to expectations, it wasn't as it had been when she'd lived here, though that would have been asking a lot, since it had been in the Dark Ages, before the war.

'Taking a trip down Memory Lane then, are you, Ursula, is that why you've come?' Moira had asked kindly, when Mrs Palmer had let slip this fact on the first day, utterly dismayed at the tarmac road that now ran towards the once remote, silent and awesome Valley of the Kings, at the noisome phalanxes of waiting coaches with their engines kept running for the air-conditioning, the throngs of people from the cruise ships queuing up for tickets to visit the tombs of the Pharaohs, which were lit by electric light. Before the war, when her husband had taken her to view the antiquities, they had sailed across the Nile in a felucca from Luxor, and traversed the rocky descent and on to the Valley of the Queens and the Temple of Hatshepsut by donkey, accompanied only by a dragoman. The silence had been complete. Now, they might just as well be visiting a theme park, she said tartly.

'They're a poor people. The tourist industry's important to them, Ursula,' Moira reminded her gently.

Mrs Palmer had so far managed to bear Moira's goodness with admirable fortitude, but she was beginning to be afraid it might not last.

Strangers ten days ago, the tour group

270

members were on Christian-name terms within a few hours, something it had taken Mrs Palmer a little time to get used to. But nothing fazed her for long, not even the touts who pestered with their tatty souvenirs, and craftily pressed worthless little scarabs into your palm, or even slipped them into your pocket, and then held out their own palms for payment. Moira had asked her advice on what to say to get rid of them, but when she repeated what Mrs Palmer had told her: *'Imshi! Mefish filouse!'*, the touts had doubled up with laughter and Moira was afraid that Ursula had been rather unkind and led her to say something indelicate. Ursula, however, said no, it was only the prospect of a middle-aged English lady using Arabic, telling them to go away because she had no money, that amused them, when they knew that all such ladies were rich, and only addressed the natives loudly, in English. But then, they were easily amused—childlike, kindly people, who were nevertheless rogues to a man.

The group advanced through the courtyard and made an orderly queue at the door of the tall old Mameluke house near the bazaar, now a small privately owned museum with a café for light refreshments on the ground floor, buying their tickets from the doorkeeper, an enormously fat, grizzled old man who wore a sparkling white *galabeya* and smiled charmingly at them with perfect teeth. He kept his eye on Mrs Palmer, gradually losing his smile as she lagged behind. He noticed her casting quick glances over her shoulder at the benches set in the raised alcove of perforated stonework, at the many doors opening off the large dusty inner courtyard, which itself held nothing but a couple of dilapidated pots haphazardly filled with a few dispirited, unEnglish-looking flowers. But after a while she turned and resolutely followed the rest of the party.

Inside the house, little had changed, except that it had been recently restored, and consequently looked a little too good to be true. Wide panelled wooden doors, wrought iron, and coloured-glass hanging lamps depending from ceilings elaborately carved with geometric designs; inlaid furniture and wide couches in balconies that jutted out over the once poverty-stricken squalor of the narrow street below. Mrs Palmer was so overcome she was obliged to rest on one of these couches to try and catch a breath of air through the carved trellis screening, leaving the rest of the group to be shown around the house. She had no need to go with them, she knew every corner and every item in it, intimately. She had lived here once, she had been the mistress of this house.

And there had been a garden here. She had made it.

Impossible to count the number of times she'd sat here behind the *mushrabiyeh* lattice-work, a device originally intended to screen women of the seraglio from passers-by. Listening to the traffic that never stopped, the blaring horns, police whistles, the muezzins' calls to prayer, the shouts and sounds from the bazaar, to Cairo's never-ceasing noise, noise, noise! Longing for the soft, earthy smell of an English spring, to hear a blackbird or the call of the cuckoo, and the whisper of rain on the roof.

'Rain? What rain?' her husband had repeated when he had brought her here from England as a bride, dewy-fresh, hopeful and twenty years old. 'It never rains.' She had assumed he was exaggerating, but she quickly realized it was almost the literal truth. He rarely spoke anything else.

In the short time since her wedding, she had already begun to wonder, too late, if her marriage had perhaps not been overhasty. Such a good catch, James Palmer had seemed; courteous, well-connected—and well-off, something that Ursula had been taught was of paramount importance in a husband. She knew now that he was essentially cold and reserved, and humourless, too. He was tall and thin, handsome enough, and his only disadvantage, it had seemed to Ursula, was an Adam's apple that seemed to have a life of its own. She had decided she could learn to ignore that disconcerting lump of cartilage, and also the fact that he was twenty years older than she. His lack of warmth and humour, his pomposity, however, were things she didn't think she would ever get used to.

As time went on, longing for the smiles and laughter that had hitherto been a natural part of her life until then, she began to throw herself into the pursuit of amusement, easy enough to find in the cosmopolitan Cairo of those days. It was 1938. Somewhere, beyond Egypt, the world was preparing for war, but here expatriate European society carried on as though it would go away if they ignored the possibility. Her time was filled with countless dinner parties, afternoon tea at Shepheard's, gossip, charity functions, tennis parties if the weather was supportable. When James was away, there was always someone to escort her, to take her dancing and dining every night.

But fun of this sort turned out to be an ephemeral gratification. For a while, she had believed such frenetic activity could obliterate the loneliness and dissatisfaction with her married state, but it very soon palled. Increasingly, when James was away and she was left entirely to herself, a pensive melancholy fell upon her. As an oriental export merchant, eldest son of his family business, he travelled all over the Middle East in search of carpets, carved wooden furniture, alabaster and metalwork to ship to England, and it had pleased him to furnish this old house he had bought with the best of what he had found, so that one had to accustom oneself to reclining on couches and eating off low tables, as if one were a woman in a harem. Indeed, her disappointment with the life she had let herself in for made Ursula reflect ironically that James might have been better pleased if she had been such a woman.

Spending most of her time listlessly in this very room, which was open entirely to the air on one side, drinking thick Egyptian coffee or mint tea, longing for Earl Grey, which could be bought if one knew where to look, but never, for some mysterious reason, in sufficient quantities, she had gazed over the balustrade to the barren expanse of sandy earth around the edges of the courtyard, the drifts of dust obscuring the lovely colours of the tiles, wondering if this was all life had to offer. Not even a sign of a child as yet, though her mother, in her weekly letters, constantly assured her there was plenty of time.

Time, it seemed, stood still, an hour as long as a day. A huge expanse of space, and inside its infinity, she sat alone, while the friendly chatter and laughter—and noisy, if short-lived, quarrelling—sounded above the continuous wailing Arab radio music that issued from the kitchen quarters and made her feel more alone than ever. What was she to do? Nothing, it seemed, but assume a stiff upper lip and get on with accustoming herself to the inescapable facts of her new life. The food, for one thing: the tough, unidentified meat she was tempted to think might once have been a camel, the sugary cakes that set her teeth on edge, and the unleavened bread. She must get used to the heavily chlorinated water that James insisted upon, too. The flies. The beautifully ironed napkins, so fresh from the *dhobi* that they were still damp. And especially to the *khamsin* that blew from the south-west, hot and dusty, giving her a nasty, tickling cough that wouldn't go away. Oh, that eternal dust and grit that insinuated itself everywhere!

When she had first arrived, she'd been determined to emulate her mother and maintain an orderly English household, with the dust outside, where it belonged, but she was defeated. In their attempts to clean, the servants insisted on using whisks, whose only effect was to distribute the dirt from one place to another. The grit ground itself into the beautiful mosaic floor tiles and the silky carpets under your feet. The cushions gave off puffs of dust whenever you sat on them. Even simple tidiness was beyond her capacity to convey to them, and theirs to accept. Elbow grease was a substance as entirely unknown as the Mansion Polish and Brasso she ordered from Home. Gradually, despite all her natural inclinations and her mother's training, inertia overcame her and she began to think: what does it matter, why fight the inevitable? Perhaps the servants were right, perhaps it was as Allah willed, *inshallah.*

Even more did she feel that now, sixty years later, when ghosts, and her own perceptions of violent death, were everywhere.

Sometimes, for air, she used to sit in the cool of the evening on the flat roof of the house, overlooking the expanse of the lighted city, watching the achingly beautiful sunsets over the Nile, with the ineffably foreign domes and minarets of the mosques piercing the skyline, as the darkness mercifully masked the seething squalor of the ancient, dun-coloured city. There was an especially low point on one particular night, when she almost considered throwing herself off or alternatively taking to the bottle, but she was made of sterner stuff and didn't really take either proposition seriously. Instead, when it eventually became too cold for comfort, she took herself down the stairs to her usual position overlooking the courtyard, where she faced the fact that, unless she did something about it, her life would dry up as surely as the brittle leaves on the single palm that gave shade to the dusty square below, that she might as well take to the *chador* and veil. Despite the lateness of the hour, she went outside and, picking her way over the rubbish that seemed to arrive by osmosis, stared at the gritty, trampled earth and thought of her father's hollyhocks and lupins and night-scented stock.

'Of course the courtyard's dark,' James said when she later began by mentioning, tentatively, how the walls seemed to close in on her. 'That's its purpose. Oriental houses are traditionally built around the concept of high walls providing shade. The natives like nothing more than to live outdoors whenever they can, and the shade makes it bearable.'

'No one lives outdoors in this establishment,' Ursula pointed out.

'We are not natives, Ursula. And while we're on the subject, it's not a good thing to get too friendly with the servants. They'll lose all respect for you.'

It wasn't the first time she'd been tempted to laugh at his pomposity, but she knew that it would have been a mistake. She didn't laugh now, she was only half listening, anyway, absorbed by her new idea. She didn't bother to point out that the only friend she had in the house was Nawal, the one female amongst all the other servants who, as one of Yusuf the cook's extended family, had been brought in to work for her. At first sulky and unco-operative, she had gradually accepted Ursula's friendly overtures. Now she was all wide Egyptian smiles and good humour; she delighted in looking after Ursula, making her bed, taking care of her silk underclothes, and being allowed to brush her mane of thick, red-gold hair. She brought magical, if foul-tasting, syrup for Ursula's cough when it became troublesome, and had become fiercely protective of her, pitying her, so far from home and with no family around her, no one except that cold and distant husband.

The next day, Ursula obtained—with difficulty—a spade, a garden fork and a hoe, took them into the courtyard and began to dig the hard, flattened earth around the edges of the tiles, where surely there had once been plants and trees growing—and would be again, after she'd arranged for a delivery of rich alluvial soil from the banks of the Nile, in which anything grew.

James predictably disapproved strongly when he'd got over his first disbelief at this crazy notion of actually tackling the making of a garden, alone. It was unnecessary. She could occupy herself more profitably elsewhere. Why not take up sketching, or Byzantine art, his own particular passion? But Ursula's inclinations didn't lie either way; she couldn't draw for toffee, and she found Byzantine art far too stylized to be either comprehensible or interesting. For once her stubbornness overcame his disapproval. Very well, he said reluctantly, but had she considered how such eccentricity would reflect on him in the eyes of their European acquaintances? They needn't know, said Ursula. And neither was it, he could not resist reminding her yet again,

279

ignoring her interjection, something calculated to enhance her authority with the servants.

And of course, he was right about this last, as he always contrived to be. They came out in full force to see what she was doing and laughed behind their hands at the prospect of an English lady wielding a spade, even sometimes going down on her knees, getting her hands filthy, grubbing in the earth for all the world like one of the *fellaheen*. She didn't care, but was nevertheless a little discouraged. Digging in the heat was harder work than she'd anticipated; and meant she could only do it for short periods. It did not seem as though her garden would progress very fast.

On the third day, she saw the boy watching her. He watched her for a week. She didn't know who he was, why he was here, how he'd arrived. If she spoke to him, or even smiled, he melted away. He appeared to be about sixteen or seventeen, slim and tall, liquid-eyed, with curly black hair and skin as smooth as brown alabaster. A beautiful youth in a *galabeya* white as driven snow, with a profile straight off a temple wall.

'Who is he?' She asked Yusuf, at last.

'He Khaled,' Yusuf said dismissively, and Ursula, intimidated, asked no more questions. She wondered if Khaled were dumb, or perhaps not entirely in his right mind, but dismissed this last, recalling the bright intelligence in his face.

The first time he spoke to her was early one morning, when he said shyly, 'I *deegiéd* the kennel for you.' His face was anxious. Kennel?

Following his pointing finger, she saw that the first of the series of blocked irrigation channels, which led from the source of the fountain, had been cleared. He had anticipated her intention, to clear the conduits so that she could draw water for her thirsty new plants. She smiled. He smiled back, radiantly. He took up the spade and began on the next one.

Miraculously, he persuaded the fountain to work. Water began to jet into the basin again, and at once the courtyard was transformed with possibilities: colour and scent, visions of lilies and lavender, marguerites, blue delphiniums and phlox in white and pink swam about in her head. Roses, roses, roses. She saw her dream of a lush and opulent garden coming true at last, the tiles clean and swept and glowing with colour, with the reflection of light and shade dappling through the leaves on to the dark walls, under the burning blue sky, the cool, musical playing of the water into the basin.

He came most days after that to help her, unselfconsciously tucking his *galabeya* up between his legs. She discovered he had a sly wit, and they laughed together, sharing their youth as well as the work—she was not, after all, so many years older than he. He sensed quickly what she wanted done, but shook

281

his head when she showed him the plant catalogues her mother, overenthusiastically, had sent from England. Roses, yes, Khaled made her understand—his English was picturesque, but adequate as a means of communication, and he learned quickly—roses would flourish. Were not the first roses bred in Persia? But lupins, hollyhocks, phlox—no. She thought it might be worth a try, however, if she reversed the seasons, pretended the Egyptian winter was an English summer, then for the fierce summer heat planted canna lilies and bougainvillea, strelitzia, perfumed mimosa, jacaranda and jasmine, oleander . . . The names were like an aphrodisiac.

She arranged, mistakenly as it turned out, to pay Khaled for his work, and though it seemed to her pitifully little, after some hesitation he accepted gravely, while making her understand he would have done it for nothing. 'It help pay my bookses,' he said ingenuously.

Nawal, with a blush and a giggle and a lowering of her eyes whenever she spoke of Khaled, had told Ursula that he was hoping to attend the University of Al Azhar, to study architecture, in order some day to build good, clean houses for poor people, both of which ambitions his uncle, Yusuf, regarded as being impossible and above his station. Nor was Yusuf, it seemed, pleased with her arrangement to pay the boy. Shouting issued from the domestic quarters shortly after she

had made him the offer. When she asked
Nawal what was the matter, Ursula was told
that Yusuf, while able to shut his eyes to the
help Khaled gave freely, could not entertain
the idea of his accepting payment for it. The
noise of the altercation in the kitchen was so
great it brought James from the house's upper
fastness, where he immured himself whenever
he was at home. After a few incisive words
from him, an abnormal quietness was restored.
He then turned to deal with Ursula.

'When will you learn?' he shouted, marching
out into the courtyard, his face red with anger,
his Adam's apple wobbling uncontrollably,
his patience at an end. 'Don't you see that
paying him money, when he freely offered his
services, is tantamount to an insult? You will
abandon this ridiculous project at once, *do
you understand?* No wonder the servants look
down on you, working out here like a peasant!
If you want a garden so much, I can have one
made for you, dammit! There's no need to
make such an exhibition of yourself!'

'No! You've missed the point, that isn't
what I want at all!' Now that she had found
her *raison d'être,* something that gave meaning
to the enforced idleness and aridity of her life
in Egypt, Ursula was in a panic at the thought
of losing it.

Khaled had followed them outside. He had
endured Yusuf's shouting with equanimity,
but when James turned on Ursula, those liquid

eyes of his flashed, simply flashed. He plucked out the garden fork that was driven into the earth nearby and for a terrified moment she thought . . . But he merely dashed it to the ground with a dramatic gesture worthy of the wrath of God. Before anyone could say anything, after another murderous look, he was gone.

And that's the last I'll see of him, Ursula thought sadly.

She had no prescience then of the dark future, otherwise she would have left, too, taken the next available ship. Left Egypt then and there and gone back to England, as James had been urging her to do for some time, in view of the ever-increasing talk of war in Europe. But that would have been admitting failure, and a certain innate stubbornness was keeping her here, a refusal to admit defeat. A tacit awareness by now had arisen between herself and her husband that their marriage was not a success, but divorce in those days was not to be contemplated lightly. Paramount was the scandal, as far as James was concerned. As for Ursula, it would have felt as though she were being sent home in disgrace, like a child, for not being good, which she knew was unfair. She had been too young for what she'd had to face, and her marriage had been a foolish leap in the dark, but no one had attempted to warn her. And for another, although James simply would not, or could not, understand, Ursula was not going to abandon her project at this stage. He could not *make* her give it up.

The garden had become an obsession. Ignoring his disapproval, she worked every day, until the perspiration poured off her and her thick hair became lank as wet string, until the sun or the *khamsin* drove her indoors. Sometimes she was so hot she took off her hat in defiance of the sun and her fair skin got burnt. Her English rose looks faded and she was in danger of becoming permanently desiccated and dried, as English women tend to be under the sun. It was obvious that James was beginning to find her less than attractive. But her garden was starting to take shape.

She had been wrong about Khaled. Eventually, without explanation, he returned. Nothing was said, he simply took up where he had left off. Ursula bought him books and gave them to him as presents, so that honour was satisfied. James, surprisingly, said nothing. Perhaps he hoped the garden would be completed all the more quickly and Ursula would regain her sanity. Then, one day, he announced, 'I've found a live-in companion for you.'

'What?' She was so furious she could scarcely speak, in a panic, imagining a stringy old lady who would torment her with demands to play two-handed patience, and prevent her from gardening. How could he do this to her?

But the stringy old lady turned out to be a

bouncy and athletic young woman not much older than Ursula, called Bunty Cashmore. Three months out of England, with short, dark, curly hair, hockey player's legs and a healthily tanned complexion enhanced by the fierce Egyptian sun rather than ruined by it, unlike Ursula's. And then Ursula understood the reason for James's sudden concern for her friendless state.

Rather than regarding the brisk bossiness of her new companion as a threat to his own authority he seemed amused by it, and showed not a trace of disapproval of her, or impatience with her meaningless chatter. In fact, he paid more attention to her than to Ursula, no matter that she showed enthusiasm for the garden project. But then, Bunty was enthusiastic about everything, most especially when it came to learning something of Byzantine art, about which she cheerfully admitted she was ignorant.

She knew nothing about gardening, either, but it didn't prevent her from interfering—or pitching in, as she cheerfully put it. She pulled up tiny, cherished seedlings, believing them to be weeds. Oops, sorry! Surveying the garden through its haze of dust, which was hosed off each night when the garden was watered, she informed Ursula that she needed bedding plants to provide more colour in the courtyard, that the yucca in the corner, chosen for its architectural form, was ugly and should go. She suggested that 'the boy' was no longer needed, either, now that she was here to help Ursula, now that the garden was at last almost finished, apart from the very last strip of bare earth which Ursula was reluctant to deal with, since that would leave little else to do but tend the garden while waiting for it to mature.

Khaled bent over his work at hearing what was proposed for him, hiding his thoughts and the resentment in his eyes.

And Nawal, meanwhile, noted every look that passed between Bunty and James, enraged on behalf of her mistress, fiercely jealous of the time Ursula was now forced to spend with the usurper, Bunty.

As for Ursula herself, she gritted her teeth at Bunty's insensitivity and refused to let her get on her nerves, hoping that all she had to do was wait, and the untenable situation going on in her own house would resolve itself. For England had declared war on Germany in September 1939, and Bunty was forever talking of going back Home and becoming a WAAF. Ursula, entirely sick of her, couldn't wait. Yet talk, it seemed, was all it was. Something held Bunty here, presumably in the person of James Palmer: she was by no means as naïve as she seemed, she knew very well which side her bread was buttered.

Though he was too old to fight, James was presently offered a job with an army intelligence unit, and was threatening to close the house and pack his wife off Home whether she wanted it or not. An ugly atmosphere developed at her point-blank refusal to do his bidding. Egypt was neutral, maintained Ursula, she would be safer here than in England. Depend on it, James countered, sooner or later the war would be on their doorstep, and who knew what would happen then? But it wasn't her safety that was in question, they both knew that; it was a face-saving ploy for getting rid of her.

Yet how could she have willingly left the only thing she had ever created, her garden?

*   *   *

What had it all been for, the struggle and the unhappiness? More than sixty years later, despite all the love and dedication lavished upon its creation, that garden, that bone of contention, but still the one shining star in an otherwise dark night, had disappeared as though it had never existed. The old feeling of melancholy overwhelmed Ursula as she contemplated where it had once flourished. It wasn't only, however, that the garden had gone and the courtyard had reverted to its original air of sad, dark desolation, with the fountain in the middle as dried-up as when she had first seen it, one could cope with that. It was something about the atmosphere itself that provoked such thoughts, a sort of pervasive

288

accidie. A stain on the air, left by the events that had happened here. She felt oppressed by the thought, and the weight of her years. Or perhaps it was just that the last ten days had taken it out of her.

'Mrs Palmer?'

She turned with weary resignation, but it wasn't Moira Ledgerwood, being responsible. There was still half an hour of interesting things to see on the upper floors before the group descended for glasses of tea in the café. It was the doorkeeper who stood there. He said softly, 'I'm sorry, the garden is no longer there. It grew wild. They cut it down, during the war, when the house was occupied by English officers.'

The filtered light from the windows fell on the ample figure of the doorkeeper in the white *galabeya,* and as he turned slightly, she saw his profile. He knew her name. And suddenly, she knew his. It was a shock. The dark curls were silvered now, but the smile was the same. She saw the young, slim, beautiful youth inside the grossly fat old man. And he, what did he see? A scrawny old woman in her eighties. 'Khaled? How did you know me?' she asked faintly.

'By your hair, first of all.'

Involuntarily, her hand went up to her white, serviceably short locks. 'How could you? I had it cut off years ago, and it turned white before I was forty.'

289

'I recognized the way it grows.'

There was a silence between them. A feeling of what might have been, had they been born in other times, other places. Perhaps. Or perhaps not.

'Mrs Palmer.' He came forward with both hands outstretched and she saw he wore a heavy gold ring with an impressive diamond on his little finger. He clasped both her hands, something he would never have done in the old days, and she allowed him to. 'It is so good to see you.' Something had radically changed, apart from the fact that his command of English was now excellent. He didn't look like a *boab,* a doorkeeper, a man who sat at a table and took money. He looked like the sort of man who made it.

'But next year would have been a better time to come,' he went on. 'Then, there will be another garden. The men come next week to begin. I needed to have the house restored first.'

She stared at him. 'Khaled, are you telling me—?'

'Yes, the house belongs to me now, Mrs Palmer. After the war, after the officers left, that is . . .' He paused. 'It stayed empty, as you must know, until seven years ago, when I bought it, through your lawyers. The condition, the neglect!' He threw up both hands. 'But I was too busy to do anything about it until now. A retirement project, you might say, hmm?'

290

He smiled.

She digested, the information that he was rich enough to do all this. 'You did go to university, then? You became an architect?' The guilt that she had carried around for more than half a lifetime began to shift a little.

'Alas, no, that was not possible, in the circumstances.'

There was a long pause. 'And did you marry Nawal?'

His soft, dark eyes grew inscrutable. 'No, I never married anyone at all.' He shrugged. *'Malish.'* That unquestioning submission to fate. *Malish*—never mind—it doesn't matter. Then he laughed. 'I became successful instead. I sell souvenirs to tourists. I have co-operatives to make them, and also shops now in New York, Paris, London. Many times I have thought of you when I am in England.'

The hopeful young man with his lofty ambitions, now an entrepreneur, a curio-seller, in effect—albeit a rich one. To such do our hopes and aspirations come.

'Why did you run away, Khaled?'

He looked at his feet. 'It was necessary. Who would have believed me?'

'There were no questions asked, you should have stayed.'

'I heard that, but I was far away by then.' He smiled again.

Death due to extreme sickness and diarrhoea in this land wasn't so unusual as to

291

cause many enquiries to be made, especially when it was known that the victim was not Egyptian and had been suffering from stomach upsets for ten days or more before dying. It had been put down to one of the many ills European flesh was heir to, and for that matter Egyptian flesh, too, in this land, where clean water was unknown and a mosquito bite could kill.

*   *   *

She and Khaled had been pruning the shrubs. The jasmine had already grown into a tangle, and the pink, white and red oleanders, though pretty, needed to be kept in check. Bunty, decidedly under the weather, was sitting in the shade of the stone alcove, too unwell to do anything but watch. Ursula threw her a long, speculative glance and pensively snipped off an oleander twig, careful not to let the milky sap get on to her hands. 'That's a nasty cough you have there, Bunty,' she said eventually. 'Why don't you ask Nawal for some of her cough syrup?'

'It's this wretched dusty wind,' said Bunty, coughing again, her eyes red and sore. 'This *khamsin*. I'm going indoors.'

'Go and lie down, and I'll bring you the medicine. It's very good.'

'We-ell, all right. Do you think she might have something for my gippy tummy at the same time?'

'I go bring,' said Khaled, and departed with unusual alacrity.

The dry, rasping cough came again and another griping pain almost doubled Bunty up. It wasn't only cholera and malaria, or worse, that one had to fear, here in Egypt. Stomach upsets, and quite often being slightly off-colour for unspecified reasons, were unavoidable hazards, facts of life. Bunty looked wretched, but Ursula had little sympathy for her predicament. She had a passion for sticky native sweetmeats, and one didn't care to think about the flies. Ursula had actually seen her carelessiy drinking water from the earthenware *chatty* by the kitchen door because it was always cool, and because the water which Ursula and James forced themselves to drink tasted so nastily of chemicals and didn't, as Bunty pointed out, necessarily make them immune; James himself hadn't quite recovered yet from the same sort of malaise that Bunty was suffering from now, and was still extremely queasy, even with the care he took. As for Bunty, it was hardly surprising that her usual rude health sometimes deserted her.

Death, though! No one could have foreseen that. These things took unexpected turns, however, madame, they said at the hospital, shrugging, affected different people in very different ways. A constitution already weakened by bouts of sickness and diarrhoea

293

... *inshallah*. There were few formalities.

Afterwards, the desire to shake the dust of Egypt from their feet had been mutual. Home was all there was now, wartime England. It had been Ursula, after all, who joined the WAAF, taking a rehabilitation course in horticulture when she was demobbed.

'I made another garden, Khaled, in England, in Surrey. It became a commercial success. Hollyhocks and lupins, as well as roses.' They smiled, remembering. 'But no oleander. The climate is too cold there for oleander.'

'Ah.' The smiles faded as their glances met.

That day, after she'd administered Nawal's medicine, which Khaled had brought, Ursula had come downstairs again and sat on the carved wood bench where Bunty had sat, to wait. The garden was tidy, and so still, apart from the splash of the fountain. The oleander twigs which had lain scattered on the brightly patterned tiles had already been swept away and cleared, she noticed.

Nerium oleander. All parts of which, including the nectar, are deadly, even the smoke from the burning plant, and especially its milky sap. Causing vomiting if ingested, sweating, bloody diarrhoea, unconsciousness, respiratory paralysis and, finally, death.

The memory of that day was etched into her brain for ever: the sultry heat, the metallic smell of dust, the perfume of the roses. The silence in her head, as though the habitual din of life beyond the high walls had been stopped to let the world listen to what she was thinking. Even the Arab music from the kitchen was stilled. The waiting.

Within half an hour, the sickness had begun, and twenty-four hours later, it was all over.

*　　　*　　　*

Khaled was looking at her earnestly. 'And you, Mrs Palmer? Have you had a happy life, Mrs Palmer?' he questioned acutely.

A happy life! How could that have been possible? Living with the tedium of Bunty's bright inanities, year in, year out. But there were many ways of expiating guilt. In the end, she'd become quite fond of her. A delicious irony indeed.

'I have—had no regrets.'

'Meesees Palmer!' Hassan's voice, rounding up his flock, echoed down the staircase.

'Ursula!' Moira Ledgervvood was coming in, looking for her protegée, finding her. 'Oh, the things you've missed! What a pity you didn't come with us.' She looked curiously from the old lady to the old doorkeeper.

Ursula held out her hand. 'Goodbye, Khaled. Good luck with your project.'

She turned to go and then turned back, as he said softly, for her ears only, 'Your husband should not have died. Nawal's medicine was

295

good.'

She smiled. 'It must have been intended, Khaled. *Inshallah,* hmm? He must have been too ill for it to make any difference. Who knows?'

Khaled watched her go. And perhaps Bunty Cashmore would have died, too, if she hadn't been so violently sick again, immediately after swallowing her own dose.

'Who knows, Mrs Palmer?' he said into the empty room.